EXPOSING A KILLER

"If you were going to kill yourself, wouldn't you leave the note sitting out where someone could find it?" I asked.

"Well, Ms. Travis, I don't like to speculate about something like that. However, I will tell you that in this case the possibility of suicide seems remote."

"Why is that?"

"According to the medical examiner's report, Mrs. Maguire died of circulatory failure brought on by chronic arsenic poisoning."

Petronelli paused as though that should mean something to me. It didn't.

"Traces of arsenic were found not only in the victim's digestive tract, but also the hair, fingernails, liver, and kidney," he explained.

"So she died of arsenic poisoning."

"Chronic arsenic poisoning."

"What's the difference?"

"Acute poisoning would mean that she ingested a large quantity of arsenic and died as a result. In the case of Mrs. Maguire, however, traces of the element were found in her organs. It was the opinion of the medical examiner that the poisoning had happened slowly over a period of time."

"Slowly, over a period of time," I said, frowning. "So she was definitely murdered."

"Right now, it looks that way. . . ."

Books by Laurien Berenson

A PEDIGREE TO DIE FOR
UNDERDOG
DOG EAT DOG
HAIR OF THE DOG
WATCHDOG
HUSH PUPPY
UNLEASHED
ONCE BITTEN
HOT DOG

Published by Kensington Books

Underdog

A MELANIE TRAVIS MYSTERY

by

Laurien Berenson

Kensington Books
Kensington Publishing Corp.
http://www.kensingtonbooks.com

For Bruce and Chase

❧❋ *One* ❋❧

Bringing a new puppy into the family is not unlike having a new baby. Both cry at night when you wish they were sleeping. Both benefit from being kept on a regular schedule; and both immediately set about demonstrating how little you really know about the job of parenting.

My son Davey just turned five, so he's had plenty of time to acquaint me with the things he thinks I should know. Our new Standard Poodle puppy, Faith, is six months old. One theory has it that the first year of a dog's life is equal to fourteen human years. Each year thereafter is worth seven. That makes Faith and Davey approximately the same age so I wasn't surprised when they immediately became best friends.

At six months, puppies are both hopelessly endearing and full of mischief. In the case of Standard Poodle puppies, they're also smart as a whip. Davey's already got Faith carrying his backpack, sleeping on his bed, and eating the broccoli he slips her under the table.

I should protest, but my son has wanted a pet for a long

time. I don't imagine a little over-indulgence will harm either of them and I'm a single parent, so it's my call. We had a frog briefly last summer but Davey took it outside to play and lost it in the grass. We're trying hard to take better care of the puppy.

If we don't, we'll have my Aunt Peg to answer to and Margaret Turnbull is not a woman to be trifled with. She's nearing sixty, but she could probably outwrestle a person half her age. I know she could outtalk one. She wears her gray hair scraped back off her face and has sharp, dark brown eyes that notice everything. She was married to my Uncle Max for more than thirty years until his death last spring. She is also Faith's breeder, and in the dog show world that counts for a lot.

Aunt Peg can be blunt to the point of pain, which is why she'd be the first person to tell you that her Cedar Crest Standard Poodles are among the finest in the country. Rank has its prerogatives and Aunt Peg doesn't sell her puppies to just anybody. Rather, a prospective buyer must deserve the privilege of owning a Cedar Crest dog.

Or, as happened in my case, you can earn it.

Of course, nothing is ever as simple as it seems and Faith came with strings, as do most of Aunt Peg's projects. She'd had a litter of puppies in the spring—all black, the only color Cedar Crest Poodles come in—and had run on the three best bitches. That means she kept three girls until they grew up enough so that she could be certain of their potential for the show ring. When the puppies were five months old she did another evaluation and made her decisions. Hope she kept for herself. Charity went off to a show home in Colorado. And Faith came to live with Davey and me.

Aunt Peg showed up one Saturday morning in early October with the Poodle puppy sitting beside her on the front seat of her station wagon. She and I had spent a good deal of the previous summer together and I'd learned enough about showing dogs to realize what a Saturday visit meant: there weren't any good judges at the area shows, otherwise Aunt Peg would surely have been off exhibiting. Instead she sat down at the kitchen table, drank a cup of strong tea, and introduced me to the joys of dog ownership.

I've seen Aunt Peg lose her car in a parking lot because she thinks all station wagons look alike, but when it comes to her puppies, she's very thorough. She plunked a ten-page booklet down on the table—mine to keep, for easy reference—and worked her way from "b" for bathing all the way to "w" for periodic worming.

By the time she got to the part about how she fully expected Faith to finish her championship in the show ring, then spent an additional half hour outlining the extra time and effort that endeavor would involve, Davey had long since fallen in love. Aunt Peg and I sat in the kitchen and watched child and puppy scamper through the autumn leaves in my small backyard. We both knew it was already too late to say no.

Aunt Peg likes wringing unexpected commitments out of me and she seemed to take great delight in the way she'd managed this one. Even so, she doesn't make things easy. Before she left she pressed the number of a fence builder into my hands. Clearly there was to be no roaming about the neighborhood for any Cedar Crest Poodle.

On my teacher's salary it seemed much more likely that I'd be putting up econo-mesh myself than having someone else install post and rail, but I took the card and figured I'd think about it later. For the first few weeks I solved the problem by walking Faith on a leash. It was not a perfect solution.

Poodles are shown with a mane coat of long thick hair. In order to grow the coat required for competition, the hair must be protected at all times. Show Poodles are never supposed to wear collars except for training or when they are actually in the ring. Then again, I've had a lot of practice with making do in my life and I thought I was managing okay.

Peg apparently disagreed because one day in mid-October, Davey and I returned home from school to find our backyard fully enclosed.

"Wow!" cried Davey. "When did you do that?"

Like a deer entranced by oncoming headlights, I stared at four feet of post and rail *and* wire mesh that hadn't been there in the morning when we'd left. "I didn't."

"Cool!" Davey still believes in Santa Claus and the tooth fairy. No doubt the image of a fence fairy was taking shape in his mind.

As we climbed out of the car, he grabbed the key from my hand and ran ahead to let himself into the house. With his light hair and dancing brown eyes, my son is the image of my ex-husband. They also share approximately the same level of maturity. Then again I may not be the best judge of that as I haven't seen Bob in four years.

He and I had bought this house together, back when we were newly married and filled with dreams, before he'd decided he was far too young to be tied down by the demands of something as mundane as fatherhood. Putting all the money we could scrape together into a down payment had seemed like a great leap of faith at the time.

But then again, so had marrying just out of college. Frankly, the house had turned out to be a better deal.

It's a really cute little cape in a subdivision in Stamford, Connecticut, that was built in the fifties. In step with those times, we got solid construction, an extra half bath and sidewalks on most of the streets. What we didn't get was land, or for that matter, privacy. There isn't much that goes on in Flower Estates that the neighbors don't have an opinion on. I was sure I'd be hearing from mine in due time.

I took one last look, then went inside to call Aunt Peg. The machine was on, taking messages. No doubt she'd guessed I was going to be steamed over her high-handed tactics and made herself scarce. It's hard to work up a good head of anger on a recording and I didn't even bother to try.

She couldn't hide forever, though, because two days later we had breed-handling class together. Among the new things I'd discovered since Faith became part of the family is that there are all sorts of classes dog owners can take their pets to: everything from puppy kindergarten, to agility, to advanced obedience training. The purpose of our class is to teach a dog and its owner how to present themselves correctly in the conformation ring.

Class is held at the Round Hill Community House in back country Greenwich. Despite its auspicious address, the white clapboard building is durable rather than pretentious. Things in New England are built to last and the community center has been around for more than a century, serving as a gathering place for several generations of Fairfield County residents. On Thursday nights, it goes to the dogs.

The class is run by a husband and wife team named

Rick and Jenny Maguire. Both are professional handlers. Their specialty is sporting dogs and according to Aunt Peg, they maintain a large and successful string serving a variety of clients. Luckily for me, they also like to teach beginners.

Judging by the cars in the parking lot, I'd gotten there before Aunt Peg. Davey was home with a sitter, so that was one less distraction to worry about. I parked just beyond the door, slipped on Faith's leash and collar, then exercised her on the grass for a few minutes before going in.

I had more practical things in mind, but the puppy sniffed, and scampered, and danced playfully at the end of her lead. All Poodles are clowns at heart and Faith was no exception. Of the three sizes of Poodles—Toy, Miniature, and Standard—Standards are the biggest. Faith wasn't going to be large for a bitch, but already her head was level with my hip.

Her ancestors had been bred to retrieve and I could see how that capability had been preserved through the generations. Her beautiful head had a long muzzle, strong underjaw and even white teeth. Faith's dark brown eyes were meltingly expressive, and her compact body was covered with a plush coat of dense, coal black hair.

Poodles are certainly among the most intelligent breeds; but what really sets them apart as companion dogs is their innate desire to please and an almost intuitive connection to their owners' needs. When I glanced at my watch, Faith knew it was time to head inside. Don't ask me how. I'm new to this dog-owning business. I gathered the leash in my hand and followed along behind.

Before class starts, Rick gets the room ready by laying

down the mats the dogs need for traction, while Jenny takes attendance and collects fees in the lobby. A long line had already formed and Faith and I took our place at the end.

I hadn't known Jenny Maguire long, but already I liked her a lot. She was bright, and funny, and had a wonderful hand on a dog. I was also intrigued by her viewpoint on the sport of dogs since I'm a real neophyte and she's been around forever. I'm not tall, but Jenny is truly petite. She has shiny, seal-brown hair and an engaging, dimpled smile. She's the kind of girl I'd spent my high school years envying: the one born to be a cheerleader and have all the boys think she was cute.

She and Rick make a great pair. Even after seven years of marriage, his eyes still follow her around the room. His sturdy build complements her slender frame and they often teach the class standing side by side, with one of his arms draped protectively over her shoulder. I should be so lucky.

Slowly the line inched forward. Faith was busy touching noses with the Pointer in front of us and eyeing the male Beagle to the rear. She's a natural-born flirt and the more I thought about that, the more I realized that maybe I shouldn't be so upset about the fence.

When we'd almost made it up to the doorway, I started looking around for Jenny's dog, Ziggy. Despite her background in setters and spaniels, her pet is a black Miniature Poodle. That's probably one of the reasons why we hit it off so quickly. Jenny was delighted to find two Poodles signed up for her class along with the usual assortment of Cocker Spaniels and Bichon Frises. I told myself that that was why she'd singled me out for extra attention, and not because I'd looked as though I'd needed it so badly. She's also been generous with lots of Poodle specific advice about top-knots and coat care and feeding.

While things are getting organized, Ziggy's usually racing around the room. His favorite game involves tossing his stuffed rat high in the air and catching it on the fly. Even though he's seven—middle age for a dog—he hasn't lost a step. Once the class gets down to business, Jenny settles Ziggy on the stage, where he lies down to oversee the proceedings.

But when Faith and I finally reached the front of the line and I got a look at Jenny, I knew immediately that something was wrong. Her hair was pulled back into a careless ponytail; her eyes were red-rimmed and downcast. When I held out a ten-dollar bill, she made change without even looking up.

"Jenny?" I said. "Are you all right?"

Wordless, she shook her head.

"What's wrong?"

"Ziggy."

The word was so soft, I could hardly hear it. I looked around the room but didn't see the little black Mini anywhere. "Where is he?"

"He's gone."

"Gone where?"

"He's dead."

"*Dead?*" As if repeating the terrible news would help. "What happened?"

"It was all my fault." She bit down hard on her lower lip. "He's always so good. You've seen him. He would never run away."

"Of course not." I tangled my fingers in Faith's top-knot, looking for comfort, or maybe just the reassurance that she was all right. Sensing I was unhappy, the puppy pressed against my legs. She tipped her muzzle upward and licked the inside of my wrist with her tongue.

"I was out in the kennel and he was back at the house. I guess the front door wasn't latched securely because it must have blown open. Ziggy got out and he was run over on the road out front."

"Oh Jenny, I'm so sorry." The words were hopelessly inadequate, but I couldn't think what else to say. "Is there anything I can do?"

"No. I'm dealing with it."

I stepped out of line and the Beagle man took my place. He paid for the class and moved on. Two other students followed, then we were alone.

"Where are you and Rick showing this weekend?" I asked.

"Northern New Jersey. Why?"

Good, that meant the shows would be day trips. "Come to my house for dinner tomorrow night. I make a great lasagna. We can drink a little wine . . ."

Jenny smiled wanly. "And forget all about our troubles?"

"Something like that."

She thought about it for a minute. "Sure. Why not? I'd like that."

I scribbled directions down on the back of the sign-up sheet and we decided six o'clock would work for both of us.

"Come on, people!" Rick clapped his hands loudly. "Let's get ourselves into some kind of order or we'll be here all night. Everybody line up along the side. Big dogs in front, please."

I was moving to comply when the front door opened and slammed shut in the outer hallway. "I'm here! I'm here!" called Aunt Peg. She and Hope came barreling into the room and she was shedding her coat as she ran. "Don't start without me!"

Rick grinned and shook his head. Even Jenny managed a small chuckle. Good old Aunt Peg. Never let it be said she didn't like to make an entrance. She stopped grandly in the middle of the mats.

"Where do you want me?"

I'd taken a place about halfway down the line. Aunt Peg purposely avoided looking my way.

"How about right up front?" said Rick.

Some things never change.

⊂⊃❋ *Two* ❋⊂⊃

We started by gaiting around the room in a circle, just as a class would begin in the dog show ring. More than a dozen dogs were present and once we all got moving, the old wooden floors shook. When we were back where we started, Rick and Jenny began the individual examinations: Rick up front with the big dogs that were to be gone over on the ground, and Jenny in the back with the smaller dogs on the table.

That gave those of us in the middle a chance to relax, play with our dogs, and talk to our neighbors. People come to breed-handling classes for one of two reasons. Either they know what they're doing and they're trying to train a new puppy; or they haven't a clue what the dog show business is all about and they're hoping to learn. Our group was pretty much evenly divided along those lines, which was good because it meant I wasn't the only beginner.

I watched Aunt Peg go through her routine with Hope. As usual her handling was both graceful and effective.

Even though the Standard Poodle puppy was obviously inexperienced, they still made an impressive team. One thing I've learned so far is that handling a dog correctly is much like rubbing your stomach while patting yourself on the head. There are moments when it seems as though your hands—and your attention—must be everywhere at once.

And I've only tried it in practice. I hated to think how I might perform in the actual show ring with the added pressure of nerves and competition thrown in.

When Rick was finished with Aunt Peg, she and Hope came back to join those of us waiting our turn on the sidelines. But now that I finally had a chance to yell at her for the sneaky way she'd outmaneuvered me, the news about Ziggy had pretty much taken the wind out of my sails.

I went over anyway. Hope and Faith immediately touched noses, wagged their tails in happy recognition, then leapt up to air-box with their front paws.

"Go ahead," said Aunt Peg, juggling her lead from hand to hand so the puppies wouldn't get tangled. "Spit it out and get it over with. But bear in mind that the job needed doing and I didn't see you getting anywhere with it. You know perfectly well I don't sell my puppies to people without fenced yards. Just because you're family doesn't mean I was going to make an exception."

I was pleased to see she was on the defensive. That probably meant she was feeling guilty. "I wish you hadn't done it, but I *am* grateful. I'm also going to pay you back."

A brow lifted. No doubt she'd expected me to make more of a fuss. I would have, too, if I hadn't just heard about what could happen to dogs whose yards weren't fenced.

"Finish Faith to her championship. That's all the payment I require."

Not exactly a small order, but one I was already pretty much resigned to. "Have you heard about Ziggy?"

Automatically her gaze went to the stage. "No. Where is he?"

"He was run over."

"Killed?"

I nodded, and she harrumphed under her breath. There's nothing Aunt Peg hates more than people who are careless with their dogs.

"So that's how I got off the hook."

Was I that transparent? I guessed so.

"Jenny must be devastated. She adored that dog."

We both looked toward the other end of the room where the handler had a Dachshund up on the table. She was running her hands down its long sides and chatting happily with the little hound's owner.

"She's covering it up," I said, thinking of the near-tears I'd seen earlier.

"Poor girl. I guess she's had a lot of practice."

"What do you mean?"

"I gather she didn't have the happiest of childhoods. Her parents were handlers, too. Did you know that?"

"She told me when I signed up."

"Roger and Lavinia Peterson. They've retired now and gone on to judging, but that pair was one of the strongest handling teams in the country for several decades. As children, Jenny and her sister, Angie, were always at the shows with them. Everyone just assumed that someday the girls would take over the family business.

"But the moment Jenny turned eighteen, she moved out and started up on her own. That wouldn't have been so odd, there's no rule that says parents and children have to agree all the time. But what made people wonder was that a few months later, Angie joined her. The girl was barely sixteen at the time."

I glanced once more toward the back of the line. Jenny was repositioning a Cocker and talking about cow hocks. She seemed to have forgotten about Ziggy, at least for the time being. That was probably just as well.

"Do you know what the problem was?"

"No. They weren't Poodle people," she said, as if that explained why she'd missed being privy to the best gossip. "But there definitely was some sort of estrangement there. I don't think they talk to this day."

A throat cleared loudly in front of me and I turned to find that while Aunt Peg and I had been chatting, the line had moved on. Faith's turn was next and while Rick was moving the dog ahead of me, I was supposed to be getting ready and setting up. I led Faith up to the front of the mat. Taking control firmly but gently, as I'd been taught, I stacked the puppy, which means I set her up in the four square position that best showed off her conformation and balance.

When I was done, she looked terrific. Unfortunately, the effect only lasted about ten seconds. That was how much time Faith gave me before deciding she'd held the pose long enough and demonstrating her feelings by leaping straight up in the air. She landed just as Rick turned our way. Perfect timing.

"Ah, the flying puppy. I believe I saw your sister earlier."

"Yes," I said, mortified. "But *she* behaved."

"Wouldn't you with Margaret Turnbull on the end of your lead?" Rick slipped me a wink, and I immediately felt much better. But when I started to reset Faith's legs, he reached out and stopped me. "Rather than fussing with her again right here, walk her in a small circle and start over. We want her to learn how to do this right from the beginning."

I followed his advice and, of course, it helped. Faith stood for his examination and we performed our triangle—trotting down one side of the mats, around the end, then back across the middle—smoothly and steadily. Faith even stood and baited for a piece of liver at the end.

"She's learning," Aunt Peg said when I'd rejoined the line. "And so are you." Coming from her, that was high praise.

Satisfied with what we'd accomplished, I watched the last of the big dogs take its turn. The sleek gray Weimaraner was being handled by Jenny's sister, Angie. Since she worked as Rick and Jenny's assistant, that probably meant he was a client's dog that was being tuned up for the shows.

Angie Peterson was a taller, paler version of her sister. Her medium brown hair fell to below shoulder length, but I'd never seen it hanging free. Tonight, as usual, it was fastened back with a clip. Her eyes were nearly the same shade of brown as Jenny's—soft cocoa with amber highlights. A spray of freckles stood out against her fair skin.

She wasn't plain so much as unremarkable, and the same held true of her handling. She presented the Weimaraner well, but it was easy to see why Jenny headed the operation and Angie was the assistant. Though technically proficient, Angie's handling skills lacked the intuitive magic of her sister's. Although to be fair, so did most everybody else's.

Even my untrained eye could see that Jenny was one of those rare people who could pick up a leash and have the dog at the other end suddenly appear two hundred percent better than it had only moments before. It was as though an electrical current passed between them, and magic was the only way I'd figured out to explain it. I'd seen her take class dogs in hand to illustrate a point and within seconds, the animals were transformed from everyday hounds into show stoppers.

It was a gift, Aunt Peg had told me. Unfortunately it was one I didn't share.

Faith, being a puppy and having a Standard Poodle's sense of humor, felt honor-bound to demonstrate that to me repeatedly over the course of the next half hour. I prayed for patience and wished for invisibility. Class clown was not a role I intended to assume willingly.

"Don't worry," Aunt Peg said, when Rick finally called a halt to the proceedings and I celebrated by sinking in an exhausted puddle into one of the chairs that lined the walls. "It will get much easier as it goes along. The problem now is that you and Faith are both trying to learn together."

"No, the problem is that she's faster than I am and has more energy."

"You're raising a child. Puppies are easier than that."

"Only because when you really get worn out, you can put them in a crate and take a break."

"I've seen children I thought deserved the same." Never a mother, Aunt Peg had wasted no time mourning the loss. She tolerated children politely, but I'd never yet seen her clasp one to her bosom.

"Not Davey, I hope."

"Not usually."

Well that was comforting. "Jenny's coming to dinner tomorrow night. Why don't you come too?"

"Tomorrow?" Peg thought for a moment, then shook her head. "I can't."

"Got a date?"

"I should be so fortunate." Her look was stern. "And now that you mention it, so should you."

Aunt Peg heartily disapproved of the fact that since my divorce, my relationships with men had been sporadic and largely unsuccessful. Not that that was my fault. I was hardly the first thirty-year-old woman to discover that all the good men were already spoken for. And adding a young child into the mix didn't improve my chances.

Then last spring, I'd met Sam Driver. Even though I'd suspected he might be involved in the theft of one of Aunt Peg's Poodles, I'd still been intrigued. Luckily my suspicions had been wrong, and things had progressed from there. Neither one of us was sure where the relationship was headed, and we were enjoying taking our time about finding out.

Try explaining that to Aunt Peg, however, whose two speeds in life were full throttle and fast forward. She had a soft spot for Sam because he was a fellow Standard Poodle enthusiast and she'd taken an interest in the relationship from the beginning. Which is another way of saying that she'd pushed us together repeatedly without finesse or subtlety, neither of which was her strong suit.

I knew what she was asking and it was easier just to give it to her. Persistence must run in the family because I'd seen Davey use the same method to get Popsicles before dinner.

"Sam's traveling," I said.

"Business, I hope."

"Either that, or he's meeting his new girlfriend in L.A."

"You needn't be so flip, Melanie. I'm only trying to look out for your best interests."

That was precisely the problem. When it came to my love life, I wasn't sure my interests needed quite so much attention.

"Did you say Jenny was coming over?" asked Aunt Peg. "Just Jenny? What about Rick?"

"He can come along too if he wants. I asked her on the spur of the moment. Jenny seemed so down over Ziggy, I was looking for a way to cheer her up."

"She seems fine now."

I turned in the direction Aunt Peg was looking. Jenny was talking and laughing with a young man who handled a Smooth Fox Terrier in class. As they chatted, the terrier was busy wrapping his leash around their legs, binding them together.

Angie and Rick were on the other side of the room, rolling up the mats. Rick must have looked up about the same time I did because he got up and went over to help Jenny. Taking the leash, he disentangled dog and people then hooked an arm over his wife's shoulder and drew her to his side. The terrier man stayed on only a moment longer. When he left, Rick and Jenny headed our way.

"What's this I hear about my wife coming to your house for dinner?"

"Girls' night out," I said, teasing him.

Was it my imagination, or did Jenny stiffen slightly? There was no mistaking Rick's frown.

Too late, I began to back-pedal. "Just kidding. Of course you're welcome too. I'd love to have you come."

"The night before a show weekend? I don't think so. There's too much to get done at home."

If I put my foot in my mouth one more time it would be a wonder if I could still talk. "I guess I wasn't thinking," I said to Jenny. "I'm pretty new at all this. It doesn't have to be tomorrow. If you'd rather make it another night . . ."

"No," she said quickly. "Tomorrow's good. Really. I'll see you then."

"Angel?" called Rick, turning away. "How are you coming with those mats?"

"Almost there." She looked up at him and smiled. "Why don't you bring the van around and you can help me load."

"You got it."

The room was nearly empty by now. I got up and Aunt Peg and I headed for the door. "He didn't look happy, did he?" she mused.

I'd noticed the same thing, but I wasn't about to give her the satisfaction. One thing about Aunt Peg—hand her the ball and she'd surely run with it.

"Clearly you need a man of your own," I said pointedly.

"I might take yours. You don't seem to be getting much use out of him."

She led the way out the door and there was nothing I could do but follow. This business about always getting the last word was just like handling. It was a gift. It had to be.

⌐❊ *Three* ❊⌐

Five days a week from nine until three, I work as a special education teacher in Stamford's public school system. I still think of myself that way because back when I got out of graduate school, that's what we were called. Since then, in an ongoing effort to make everything as needlessly complicated as possible, my title has been modernized. I am now known as a Learning Disabilities Resource Room Teacher.

Same job, same pay; bigger sign on the door.

I'm lucky in that most days I really like my work, especially when I'm with the kids. I could do without some of the administrators and most of the politics, but I've been at Hunting Ridge Elementary long enough so that I don't have to deal with either too much if I don't want to.

Davey started kindergarten in September. After five years of juggling daycare, pre-school, car pools, and baby sitters, not to mention sick days, snow days, and holidays, we are finally both on the same schedule. What a relief. Not only that, but if he sits on his lunch somewhere along the way, I can usually slip him part of mine in the cafeteria. My stomach may growl a bit, but my thighs appreciate the sacrifice.

On Friday, Davey and I went straight to the supermarket after school. I envy women who make dinners ahead and freeze them. At my house, I'm lucky to have the ingredients for a meal on hand, much less the finished product. Impromptu guests get nachos and salsa if they're lucky; Pop-Tarts if they're not. Aunt Peg has been known to solve this problem by bringing her own pastries. Either she has to find a low-fat bakery, or I'm going to have to develop some self-control.

Jenny arrived promptly at six. I was back in the kitchen, but my early warning system spoke up loud and clear. First Faith began to bark, then Davey ran to the front hall, jumping up and down and yelling, "She's here! She's here!" From the way these two were carrying on, you'd think we never had company.

With that much notice, I had time to get the door open before she could even ring the bell. Jenny stood on the top step with her hands full.

"The wine's a gift," she said, handing me a bottle of cabernet sauvignon on her way in. "The book's a loan. It belongs to Rick and he'd kill me if I gave it away. But there are a lot of good tips in here, and I think you might enjoy reading it."

The book was called *An Owner's Guide to Successful Dog Showing*. I tucked it under my arm. "Thanks. I'll give it back to you next week."

"No hurry."

"Hi," said Davey, thrusting himself forward. There's nothing he hates more than to be left out of a conversation. "I'm Davey. I'm five."

Jenny grinned down at him. "Five? Really? You must be big for your age."

"I am." Davey's small chest swelled with pride. "This is my Poodle. Her name is Faith."

Even without the introduction, the puppy would have been hard to miss. As soon as I'd opened the door, Faith had launched herself at our guest. Luckily Jenny was used to dealing with exuberant puppies and the initial onslaught had barely fazed her. Now that her hands were free she had one scratching behind Faith's ears and the other rubbing under her chin.

"Faith is a Standard Poodle," Davey informed her. "That means she's going to be big."

As if she wasn't already.

"Did you know that Poodles come in three sizes?"

"I'm sure she does, Davey," I broke in. Once my son started showing off how much he knew, he could go on for quite a while. "Let's give Jenny a chance to get in the door before you monopolize her. You can talk to her some more later."

"Okay. Can I have a snack?"

"No. Dinner's in half an hour."

"But I'm hungry now."

"Good, then you'll still be hungry in half an hour. Why don't you take Faith to the back door and see if she wants to go out?"

The two of them headed off down the hall and Jenny's gaze followed their departure. "They're so cute at that age."

"Puppies or kids?"

"Both." Her tone held the wistful sound of someone who's never lived with a five-year-old twenty-four hours a day, seven days a week. "I can't wait."

Jenny couldn't have been more than a year or two younger than me. I wondered what she was waiting for. "How does Rick feel?"

"Ambivalent. He thinks we ought to be better established, have a larger base of clients. But the problem with handling is that except for a few regulars that you work with all the time, it's not a steady thing. Dogs come and go. We have a champion Cocker now that's been doing a lot of winning, but he's retiring at the end of the year. After that, who knows? There's an English Setter coming along that might take his place, but we won't know that until we try. Sometimes I think that if you want something badly enough, you just have to jump in and do it."

As she talked, we'd been walking back to the kitchen. I could see Davey through the window over the sink. He was running around the backyard with a jacket on over his pajamas. Faith was chasing him. I set the wine down on the counter, found a corkscrew, and poured us each a glass.

"Davey's father thought we were too young too. And actually, we probably were. But I got pregnant and neither one of us liked the idea of abortion, so there we were."

"Was he angry?"

"More resigned, I think. He spent the nine months I was pregnant in denial. Like if he didn't think about it, or talk about it, it wouldn't really happen." I sampled my wine, decided it tasted good and followed the first sip with another.

Jenny's gaze strayed out the window. "How long did it take him to get used to being a father?"

"I don't think he ever did. As far as he was concerned,

Davey was just this unexpected interloper who kept waking us up all night long. He moved out when Davey was ten months old."

That was the polite version. In reality, he'd skipped in the middle of the day, taking the car and the stereo system with him. He'd left behind a three-line note in which he'd spoken about his unmet needs. I'd read it twice—incredulous the first time, furious the second—then burned it.

"It must be hard being a single parent."

A comment like that called for more wine. I topped off both our glasses. "Harder on Davey than me, unfortunately. I'm coping. He's just beginning to figure out that most of the other kids have two parents and he only has one."

The screen door banged as it swung open against the wall of the house. Davey and Faith came barreling inside. He looked at the two of us standing there. "Isn't dinner ready *yet?*"

"Soon." I reached out and tousled my son's hair. Grimacing, he squirmed out from beneath my hand. "Everything's about done. I just have to finish the salad. Why don't you set the table?"

"Can't we eat in the kitchen?"

"Davey, we have company."

"I'm not company," Jenny said with a grin. "I'm a friend."

So we ate in the kitchen. When I pulled the small butcher block table away from the wall, there was just enough room for the three of us to sit around it. Jenny poured on the dressing and tossed the salad, while I got the bread and lasagna out of the oven and onto plates.

Faith, who knew a good opportunity when she saw one, managed to wedge herself underneath the table, ready for handouts. With Davey in attendance, she didn't have long to wait.

"I saw that," I said as Davey took a piece of tomato-covered noodle from his plate and slipped it beneath the table.

"But Faith's hungry. And she likes lasagna."

"She likes anything she thinks she's not supposed to have. And she wouldn't be so hungry if she'd eat her own food."

"She doesn't like her food. It tastes gross."

"How would you know?"

"I ate some." Davey stuck out his tongue and grimaced. Nothing like having the weight of empirical evidence to support the hypothesis.

On the other side of the table, Jenny looked as though she was enjoying herself. "What do you feed?" she asked.

I named the brand of high-quality kibble that Aunt Peg had recommended. "I mix that with some cottage cheese and a little bit of canned food. Aunt Peg says her Poodles love the stuff. But Faith is fussy. She barely picks at her food."

"Does she get a lot of table scraps?"

"Not *that* many." I shot my son a glare.

"Let's see. Come here, girl." Jenny enticed the puppy out from under the table and ran an experienced pair of hands down her sides. "She *is* thin. You don't want a puppy to be fat, but she should be carrying more weight than this."

"Aunt Peg's told me the same thing. She says that conditioning's one of the most important aspects of getting a dog ready for the show ring."

"She's right. Especially in a breed like Poodles. Once they're a year old and you shave off that hindquarter there's no hiding a thing. If a dog has no muscle or is underweight, it's just about the first thing the judge sees. Lots of Poodles are finicky about what they eat, and that makes it tough. I had a terrible time keeping Ziggy in weight when I was showing him."

I was glad to see she could mention the Mini's name without becoming visibly upset. Maybe our company was cheering her up. Or maybe it was the numbing effect of the wine.

"What did you feed him?"

"In the beginning I tried just about everything which is terrible for a dog. They thrive on routine. But then I met Crystal Mars. Do you know who she is?"

I shook my head.

"She owns a small boarding kennel in Stratford. It's about half an hour from here. She's an interesting woman, a big believer in holistic care and homeopathic medicine. Everything at her place is pure and natural. You know the type?"

I did.

"Apparently she'd been doing the same thing I was, switching from one brand to another, looking for the perfect dog food. Running the boarding kennel she had plenty of dogs who were upset about being away from home, and that meant plenty of bad eaters. After a while she simply started making her own food, mixing everything together in big bowls and baking the kibble in the oven."

"What's in it?"

"It's a rice and chicken base, with lots of garlic and corn meal, and God knows what all. The dogs love it. Ziggy, too. It's expensive, but it's worth it."

"You mean she sells it?"

Jenny nodded. "I was just up there last week and business is booming. Lots of her customers were pleased with the way their dogs came home and asked what she was feeding. Pretty soon she was selling as much kibble as she could make. She calls it Crystal's All Natural Dog Munchies. You might want to give it a try."

The name was a little overly cute, but then again so were lots of things people did to dogs, like putting Dachshunds in raincoats and tying bows on Poodle's ears. If Faith would eat it, I could manage to deal with the label.

"Thanks," I said. "I'll look into it."

"When's dessert?" asked Davey.

His plate was suspiciously clean. I wondered how many mouthfuls of lasagna Faith had enjoyed while my attention had been elsewhere. At least that might put a little weight on her.

"Dessert's when everybody's finished," I informed him. "Grown-ups like to eat more slowly. Why don't you go and play for a little while and I'll call you when we're ready?"

"Okay." He hopped off his chair and left the room. Faith went with him. She's only been around a month, but clearly the puppy knows which side her bread is buttered on. Davey turned on the TV in the living room and found *Roseanne* in syndication. He liked to root for D.J. and was trying to develop a big belly laugh like Roseanne's. There are worse goals.

"I hope you didn't send him away on my account," said Jenny. In contrast to Davey's plate, hers was still nearly full. She pushed the lasagna around with her fork, but didn't pick any up. "I think he's great."

"He is great. But like every five-year-old, he has no patience. He knows full well there's cake for dessert, and we'll be lucky to get a moment's peace from now until he gets his."

"I can sympathize." Jenny laughed. "I have a sweet tooth, too."

I looked, but the lasagna on her plate still didn't seem to be going anywhere. Maybe that was her way of telling me she was finished. "Right," I said. "On to the cake."

I'm not a good enough cook to get offended when people don't eat something I've made. But the chocolate mousse cake I had for dessert came from the St. Moritz bakery in Greenwich, which means it was probably about the best in the world. But when I'd piled the dinner dishes in the sink, brewed some coffee, given Davey his dessert in the living room, then served our cake, Jenny started pushing that around her plate, too.

Well, that made me wonder. It's probably possible that there are people in the world who don't like lasagna or who don't like chocolate. But both? I doubt it. Jenny didn't look thin enough to be anorexic, and though I'd invited her over to cheer her up over Ziggy's death, she didn't seem terribly depressed.

I've never been one for finesse when bluntness will work just as well. It's a family trait.

"Not hungry?" I asked.

"Hmm?" Jenny looked up. She finally had a piece of

cake in her mouth and was chewing slowly. She seemed to be enjoying it.

"You've hardly eaten a thing. I know I'm not the greatest cook . . ."

"No, the food's wonderful. You must have really worked hard. I'm sorry I haven't done it more justice. It's just that I haven't been feeling all that well lately. I guess I caught some sort of bug, but it's been hanging on for a while and I can't seem to shake it."

"Like the flu?"

"Something like that. It comes and goes, headaches, nausea, cramps."

I'd heard all those symptoms before. Lately everyone on Fairfield County seemed to be coming down with them. "You should have a Lyme test. Even if you haven't seen a tick or a rash. You'd be amazed how many of the people I work with have come down with Lyme Disease this year. Especially working with dogs like you do, there's probably a pretty good chance you've been exposed."

"I know. I've been thinking the same thing. I'm going to get it checked out. Just as soon as I have some spare time."

"Spare time? What's that?"

We laughed together, and I was pleased to see her finish the rest of her cake. Later, she even let me wrap up an extra large piece to take home. I knew that Rick was waiting for her, so we made it an early evening. Davey fell asleep on the couch in front of the TV around eight-thirty and she and I took him up and tucked him in. Jenny left a few minutes later.

The book she'd brought was still sitting on the table in the front hall. "Thanks again," I said, picking it up.

"No problem." Jenny lingered on the step. "Take care of yourself, okay?"

"Sure, you too. I'll see you at class on Thursday, right?"

"Not this week, I'll be away. But don't worry, Angie will be filling in for me and I'm sure she'll do fine. Thanks for dinner. It was great."

"Anytime," I said, and meant it. Next time I'd know better than to ask her for a Friday night though; and to make sure there weren't any ruffled feathers, I'd invite Rick along, and maybe even Angie, too.

Davey and I spent most of the next week going to school and raking leaves. The yard isn't that big and the job wouldn't have taken so long except that every time I got a decent-sized pile together, Davey and Faith dove in. They were so cute together that I had to go into the house and get the camera. Now I'd have to be sure that Aunt Peg never saw the pictures of her show puppy with leaves intertwined through that all important coat of hair.

Wednesday afternoon, we finally bagged the last of what was on the ground. While Davey was taking a bath, I brushed through Faith's coat with a pin brush, then took down her top-knot which is the hair on the top of her head. If a Poodle is going to be shown, that hair is never cut. Eventually it will grow nearly a foot long. To keep it out of the dog's face, the hair is gathered into a series of small ponytails which are held in place with tiny colored rubber bands. I cut loose the old bands, brushed through the hair, then reset it with new ones. I was just finishing when the phone rang.

It was Aunt Peg. "This is so awful," she said.

"What is?"

"I was just talking to Rick Maguire."

As I waited for her to continue, I slipped Faith a piece of cheese as a reward for being good, then hopped her down off the portable grooming table I'd set up in the kitchen.

"What?" I asked again when a moment passed and she still hadn't said a word.

"I just can't believe it." Peg's voice was oddly flat. "Rick was so upset I could barely understand what he was saying. Melanie, Jenny Maguire is dead."

❧ *Four* ❧

She couldn't be dead, I thought. I just saw her. She was much too young, much too vibrant, to be dead.

"Melanie, are you there?"

"I'm here." All at once I felt drained. I leaned back against the counter and let it support my weight.

Years earlier, when I'd heard the news about my parents' deaths, how their car had run off a lonely stretch of road and plunged over an embankment, I'd wanted to scream out loud as if noise alone could negate the awful truth. But this time grief had a different effect on me. I could barely summon the energy to make a sound.

"What happened?" I asked.

"I'm not sure. Rick was hardly coherent. He said Jenny collapsed last night right after dinner. He and Angie thought she'd fainted. They lifted her up on the couch, then Rick realized she wasn't breathing. They called for an ambulance but by the time they got her to the hospital, it was too late."

I exhaled slowly, feeling pain as the air left my body.

There was a constriction in my chest I couldn't seem to breathe around. "She told me last week that she hadn't been feeling well. I thought maybe she had Lyme Disease."

Aunt Peg snorted softly. "People sometimes die from Lyme Disease, but not suddenly like that. It had to have been something else. What did she say was the matter with her?"

I thought back, trying to remember. "Something like the flu, except it wouldn't go away. She wasn't eating much, that's how it came up, and she said she'd been having cramps."

"They'll do an autopsy. They'll have to. People can't just up and die for no reason. That girl was a child."

Not quite, but I knew what she meant. "Rick must be devastated. The two of them seemed so close."

"They were always together," said Aunt Peg. "Even at the shows where things get hectic and the handlers with big strings have to be everywhere at once, you almost never saw one of them without the other."

"I wonder what he'll do now."

"Carry on, I'd imagine. What choice does he have?"

Davey called from the bathtub, and I went to dry him off and bundle him into his pajamas. He was warm and clean and filled with excitement about the field trip his class was taking the next day to the fire station. I hugged him close and let him chatter on.

He didn't notice how quiet I was, so I didn't have to explain. And that was good. I couldn't break the news to Davey just then. I couldn't even understand it myself.

The next morning when I had a break, I stopped by the office and called Rick and Jenny's kennel. A kennel girl picked up, and I was able to find out that a wake would be held on Friday evening in Ridgefield. I called Aunt Peg and gave her the news and we made arrangements to go together.

That's when it began to sink in that Jenny was really gone. I wished I'd had the chance to get to know her better. Even so, her death left me feeling all hollow inside. She'd been so young. She should have had so many things still ahead of her. How could she have already run out of time?

On my way to my next class, I stopped by Davey's kindergarten classroom. There was a glass panel in the door and I was able to look in without disturbing anyone. Davey was at the block station, constructing a skyscraper and laughing with two of his friends.

I went back to work feeling a little better.

My only sibling is a brother named Frank, who lives in Cos Cob. He's four years younger than me and there are times when the age difference seems enormous. Most little girls grow out of the idea that their brother is one of the most annoying people they've ever met, but I never have. Frank can be irresponsible, opportunistic, and thoroughly charming; often all at the same time.

One thing I will say for Frank though, is that he loves his nephew dearly. Over the years, he has stepped in to provide Davey with a stable male influence in his life, and for that I will always be grateful. He also spoils Davey shamelessly. I'm less appreciative of that, but I figure it comes with the territory. Frank has always been a bit of a hedonist.

One Saturday a month, he comes and collects Davey

for what the two of them have come to call "boys' day out." Their adventures have included everything from roller blading in Binney Park to a trip to the Maritime Center in Norwalk. So far he's always brought Davey back in one piece and since they both seem to enjoy having secrets that I'm not privy to, I try not to ask too many questions.

Frank had called early in the week, hinting around about tickets to a Yale football game for that Saturday. Needless to say, I was not invited. After talking to Aunt Peg, I checked with Frank. His love life must not be much more exciting than mine because he said he'd be happy to have Davey sleep over on Friday night. All that remained after that was to call the funeral home and get directions.

Most of the towns in lower Fairfield County serve as bedroom communities for New York City commuters and they look it. There's an urban sophistication to the downtown areas which owes much to the rapid growth of the eighties and the advent of the ubiquitous chain store. A dozen miles north, the town of Ridgefield has resisted such changes. With its quaint shops and clapboard buildings, it still maintains much of the character and flavor of a small New England village.

The Falconi Brothers Funeral Home was a white brick, two-story edifice on the outskirts of town. It was early evening when we arrived but the sun had already set. Aunt Peg was driving, which meant that I spent much of the trip holding my breath. Her station wagon is new this year, but already it's showing signs of strain. Going sixty miles an hour on curving back country roads will do that to a car.

We were met at the door to the funeral home by a somber-looking man in a black suit, one of the Falconi brothers, no doubt. He directed us to the proper room whose door was the only one leading off from the wide center hall that was open.

The room was large and already crowded, but the first thing I saw when I entered was the casket. It was closed, for which I was grateful. I've never had any desire to look at dead people and I've never figured out why anyone would. I wanted to remember Jenny as she'd been, not lying pale and still in a satin-lined box.

Rick was standing near the front of the room. Angie was at his side. They were talking to two men who looked familiar in a vague sort of way.

"Sean Summers and his partner, Doug Henry," Aunt Peg whispered. "They handle terriers. You've probably seen them in the group ring."

Now that she mentioned it I realized that nearly all the faces in the assembled group were those I had seen at dog shows. Some were exhibitors; others handlers. A few were judges.

"I heard that the funeral tomorrow is private," Aunt Peg continued in a low tone. "It's just as well. The rest of the weekend nearly everybody here will be at work."

"There's certainly a crowd tonight."

"There would be. Rick and Jenny are popular, but Roger and Lavinia Peterson lived in the area back when they were handling. Lots of old friends would come to pay their respects."

I looked around the room, scanning some of the older faces. "Speaking of Jenny's parents, which ones are they?"

"I don't see them. They live down in Louisiana now. Maybe they're on their way."

Jenny had died Tuesday night, I thought. How long did it take to get on a plane and fly up?

Slowly we worked our way to the front of the room. Of course we had to pay our condolences, but I was dreading the moment we'd get there. I'm terrible in situations like this; I never know what to say. One look at Aunt Peg and I knew she wasn't going to be much help. When we reached Rick and Angie, she was staring off in another direction entirely.

Rick held out his hand and I took it in both of mine. There were shadows beneath his eyes and his Adam's apple bobbed prominently in his throat, but he seemed to be holding up pretty well. It was Angie, beside him, who looked like she was on the verge of breaking down. Her make-up was smeared as if she'd been crying and she held a wad of crumpled tissue in one hand.

"Thank you for coming," said Rick, and Angie nodded silently.

I wanted to kick Aunt Peg to get her attention. What could she possibly have been looking at? "I was so sorry to hear about Jenny. She was a really wonderful person."

Angie sagged against Rick's side and he reached out as I'd seen him do so often with Jenny and placed a comforting arm over her shoulder. I'd been holding my emotions in check pretty well, but that simple gesture was enough to bring me to the verge of tears.

"Angel?" he whispered. "Are you all right?"

Her lower lip trembled. Wordlessly, she shook her head.

"Do you want to sit down?" I asked. There were chairs all around, although none up here near the casket.

Ignoring my question, Angie looked up at Rick. "I want to get out of here," she said. Her voice was low and choked with emotion.

"I know this is hard, Angel, but we can't leave—"

"I won't stay here. You can't make me."

She sounded like a child and I realized I'd always thought of her that way. She was only a few years younger than her sister but while Jenny had always seemed mature for her age, Angie had retained the youthful demeanor of a teenager. Right now there was enough of the lost waif about her to bring out my maternal instincts.

"Come with me to the ladies' room," I said. "You can splash some water on your face and sit down for a few minutes. It'll make you feel better."

The vague look Angie gave me made me wonder whether she even knew who I was, but obediently she disengaged herself from Rick and prepared to follow me from the room. Rick gave me a grateful glance and turned to the next person waiting for his attention—Aunt Peg, who'd finally managed to get her mind back on the business at hand.

People parted for us as we made our way out. Angie walked slowly like an invalid. I took her hand in mine and she didn't protest. Her fingers were cool and limp.

One of the doors in the hall was marked "Rest Rooms" and I guided Angie there. There was a small sitting area as well as a bathroom. She sank down on an ornate brocade love seat and covered her face with her hands. Over by the counter I found a stack of paper cups and poured her some cold water. She drank only a sip, then put the cup aside.

The couch was hard and scratchy when I sat down beside her. Clearly it hadn't been designed for lingering.

Though the room was warm, she felt cold, and I found myself rubbing her back.

"It isn't fair," Angie sniffled.

There was a full box of tissues on the counter. I got up and brought it over. "No, it isn't."

"I don't want to be here. I don't want to think about her lying there in that box. I knew she was unhappy but . . ."

I stopped where I stood. "But what?"

"I don't know . . ." Angie shook her head forlornly and her ponytail swung from side to side. "I just never thought she'd go this far."

My legs felt heavy, like lead. I sank down on the couch. "Angie, what are you talking about?"

She looked up as though the question surprised her. Instead of answering, she took a tissue from the box and blew her nose loudly. When it became clear she wasn't going to answer my first question, I tried something a little easier.

"What was Jenny unhappy about?"

The girl's slender shoulders rose and fell. "Just stuff, you know . . ."

No, I didn't know, and stuff could mean anything. Or nothing at all. "You mean like what happened to Ziggy?"

"Yeah, that too. My sister really loved that dog."

"Angie," I said softly. "How did Jenny die?"

She turned to look in my direction, but rather than focusing her eyes seemed to stare right through me. "She just stood up and fell over. And then she was dead."

"But—"

Abruptly Angie stood. "I've got to get back, or Rick will come looking for me. He looks after everybody, you know?"

She tossed the wad of tissue in the wastebasket and

walked out. The door had swung shut behind her before I even thought to move. What *had* Jenny died of? Aunt Peg had mentioned she'd thought there'd be an autopsy, but I'd forgotten to follow up. Obviously a cause of death had been established, otherwise they couldn't bury the body. But what was it?

I found Aunt Peg back in the room where I'd left her. Angie had returned and was once again standing at Rick's side. She looked somewhat better although still not strong enough for the task at hand. Aunt Peg was over to one side, talking to Crawford Langley, a long-time Poodle handler who lived in Bedford.

Crawford was one of the first people I'd met in Poodles after Aunt Peg. According to what she'd told me he'd been the top Poodle handler on the East Coast for many years. He'd had the best clients, the best dogs, the best buzz. In his fifties now, he was gradually being nudged aside by a new generation of up and comers, but fighting every inch of the way to maintain his advantage.

"Hi, Crawford," I said, joining them.

"Melanie." He nodded.

"We were just discussing Jenny's parents," said Aunt Peg. "Crawford's an old friend of theirs."

"Not that old," Crawford corrected, his gray eyes glinting. "But we did all get started around the same time."

"Why aren't they here?" I asked.

"They've been in Australia, judging. I haven't spoken to them, but I understand that they're flying in tonight."

Aunt Peg's connections were legion, but Crawford Langley's were no less impressive. "Do you know what Jenny died from?" I asked.

Aunt Peg frowned. "Now that you mention it, we never did find that out, did we?"

"Rick told me yesterday when I called to find out about the arrangements," said Crawford. "Somehow Jenny ingested a fatal dose of arsenic."

"You mean she was poisoned?" Aunt Peg's voice rose and I jabbed an elbow into her ribs.

"Apparently so."

I thought about what Angie had said earlier. "How did it happen?"

"I don't know," Crawford admitted. "But it must have been an accident. Rick didn't want to talk about it and I certainly wasn't about to push him. Gossip being what it is in this sport, I'm sure we'll all get the details soon enough. Now if you'll excuse me, I'd like to have a few words with Sean and Doug."

"I don't believe it," I said as the handler walked away.

"I don't blame you," said Aunt Peg, looking no happier than I felt.

I was standing too close to a large arrangement of orchids. Their heavy scent seemed to permeate everything. I took Aunt Peg's elbow and guided us both a few steps away. "Angie just told me that Jenny was unhappy. Were you aware of that?"

"Not in a general sense, no." She thought for a moment. "I mean everybody has days where everything seems to go wrong. And with Rick and Jenny working *and* living together, it can't have been easy. Handling's a high-stress job. The pressure's always on to produce results. They're out there week after week, especially with the top dogs. And if they don't win, well . . . you'd better believe everyone else is keeping score."

"But Rick and Jenny were winning, weren't they? She told me something about a top Cocker . . . ?"

"That would be Charlie. Champion Shadowland's

Super Charged. He *is* good. I think he even has a shot at the Quaker Oats Award this year. Of course, now with Jenny out of the picture, that may change."

Aunt Peg had been coaching me on how dog shows worked for nearly half a year now. Little by little I was getting so I could understand most of the shorthand. All of the different breeds recognized by the American Kennel Club are divided into seven groups, according to form or function: Sporting, Hound, Working, Terrier, Toy, Non-Sporting, and Herding. The Quaker Oats Award is an extremely prestigious prize given out just before Westminster to the dog in each group that had won the most group firsts during the preceding year. Jenny's Cocker Spaniel would have been competing in the Sporting Group.

"Rick will continue to show the dog, won't he?"

"I imagine he will. Of course that will be up to Mrs. Byrd, Charlie's owner, but this close to the end of the year, they'd be foolish not to go for it. Charlie was Jenny's dog, though. I'm sure the judges thought of them as a team. With Rick, it just won't be the same."

Aunt Peg turned and looked across the room. "I imagine Harry Flynn will be pleased about that. I wonder if that's why he's here."

A thin stoop-shouldered man was standing off by himself next to a spray of lilies. His wiry hair had receded back to the middle of his head and was graying slightly at the temples. His suit, a drab shade of brown, had been paired with a loud multi-colored tie whose tails hung down below his belt. Despite the two "No Smoking" signs posted at either door, he'd cupped his hand around a lit cigarette he held down at his side.

"Is that who you were staring at before?"

"Staring?" Aunt Peg mused. "Was I really? I just hadn't expected to see him here, that's all."

"Why? Who is he?"

"Another sporting dog handler. He's got a Cocker and a Springer of his own and they've both been bumping up against Charlie all year. After he'd lost one too many times, I gather he lodged a complaint accusing one of Jenny's dogs of being dyed."

"Dyed? Is that possible?"

"It's more than possible, it happens all the time in Poodles and in some of the other breeds as well. The Cocker in question was black, and Harry alleged that the dog had a rather large white spot on his chest that was being covered up. If that was true, the dog would have been disqualified and the AKC would have taken punitive action against Jenny as his handler."

"And what happened?"

"As things turned out, not much. At the moment, the American Kennel Club doesn't have a testing procedure in place for proving or disproving an allegation like that. And to disqualify an entry simply on the basis of hearsay? I can't think of anything that would expose them to a lawsuit faster.

"In the end, there was nothing they could do. The black Cocker quietly finished his championship and went home, while Jenny continued to win everything in sight with Charlie. Of course, there's been bad blood between Harry and the Maguires ever since."

"It does seem surprising he'd come here then, doesn't it?"

"After all the years I've been showing Poodles, nothing

surprises me anymore. I think we've stayed long enough. How about you?"

I nodded and we headed for the door. Aunt Peg has always been pretty crafty and I wondered later whether her sudden desire to leave was prompted by the fact that Harry Flynn was also making a move in that direction. Whether by accident or design, we met at the door.

"Mrs. Turnbull," said Flynn, nodding briefly.

It was clear he intended to keep on walking, but Aunt Peg thrust me forward. "Harry, I don't believe you've met my niece, Melanie. She's new to showing dogs."

He stopped then and looked me up and down. "Nice to meet you. Since you're new, I'll offer you a bit of advice. Find another hobby."

I didn't know what to say to that, so for a moment I said nothing at all. That gave Aunt Peg the opening she needed. "I didn't expect to see you here today, Harry."

"Why not? Just because we weren't friends doesn't mean I wouldn't show up for something like this. Hey, for me this is good times. Besides, I wanted to make sure the bitch was really dead."

Well, that turned a few heads. Including mine. Thank goodness Rick and Angie weren't close enough to hear.

Aunt Peg drew herself up to her full height which was a good several inches higher than the handler. "If you weren't leaving, I'd throw you out myself."

"I'll save you the pleasure, Mrs. Turnbull. Maybe some other time." He was whistling under his breath as he left.

ᴏ❖ *Five* ❖ᴏ

Sam Driver returned from L.A. late Friday night. I found that out when he called Saturday morning to see what I was up to. Davey was still off with Frank, Aunt Peg had driven to Camden for a show, and I wasn't up to anything. Our relationship was new enough however, that I wouldn't have dreamed of telling him that.

He probably figured it out anyway when he suggested we take the dogs and go hiking in the woods near his house, and I jumped at the chance. There's an art to being coy which, unfortunately, I have yet to master. I told him I'd meet him at his house in an hour.

Late October in Connecticut is my idea of perfect weather: brisk, but not yet cold. In accordance with the plans, I didn't dress up. Blue jeans, a flannel shirt, and a pair of sturdy running shoes completed the outfit. I have hazel eyes and brown hair that hangs straight down to my shoulders and I didn't do much with them either. Before I had Davey, I worried about things like that. Back then, I had time. Now my style is pretty much come as you are.

Sam lives in Redding. In lower Fairfield County we consider this a northern outpost. Compared to the coastal communities, it is sparsely populated and open land abounds. Sam's house is a contemporary made of glass and shingles. It's perched on a hillside and surrounded by woods. My ancient Volvo handled the country roads fine, but balked at the steep, unpaved driveway. By the time I'd coaxed it to the top, Sam had heard us coming and was outside waiting.

When I opened the door, Faith leapt out of the car first. That was partly because she's younger and faster than me and partly because I took a moment to compose myself. Sam and I have known each other a few months but I still feel a nerve-tingling rush every time I see him. If I were a dog, I'd probably be sitting up and begging. Of course that's enough to make me want to slow things down right there. Sam doesn't feel like a fling to me. In some ways, I'd be a whole lot more comfortable if he did. For Davey's sake, I'm trying to keep my mistakes with men to a minimum. And for the time being, Sam isn't pushing. So far, so good.

By the time I got myself out of the car, Faith had already jumped all over Sam and was chasing one of his Standard Poodles around the yard. Though he has half a dozen, only one Poodle was outside. Charm is the matriarch of the line and Sam's undisguised favorite. She was black in her youth, but now most of her coat has gone gray. She still had enough energy however, to give my puppy a good trouncing whenever she ventured near. I left them to their play and turned my attention to Sam.

He looked good. Sam always looks good. He stands an inch or two over six feet, has slate blue eyes and blond hair that usually looks as though he's just raked through it with his fingers. He was wearing jeans too, with a down vest over a soft brown corduroy shirt. He held out his arms and I walked straight into them.

That man can kiss. I tipped back my head, closed my eyes, and held on for the ride. When we broke apart, I was feeling a little tipsy. That gave me a good excuse to hang onto his arm as he whistled for the dogs, picked up a backpack, and pointed toward a path leading off from the side of his yard.

"The foliage is incredible this time of year and the view from the top of this hill is spectacular. It takes about half an hour to hike up. Is that okay with you?"

"Fine. What's in the backpack?"

"Lunch, cold beer, all the necessities."

I've tasted Sam's cooking. It's several notches up from mine. I kicked back, relaxed, and went with the flow.

The sun was warm on our backs as we crossed the yard. In the woods it was slightly cooler, but still comfortable. The path was wide enough that we could walk side by side. Leaves crunched beneath our feet. The Poodles circled around us, running in and out of the trees, chasing squirrels and checking for deer.

"How was L.A.?" I asked.

"Warm, sunny, same as always."

"I don't think I could live there. I'd miss the seasons too much."

"Me too. There's nothing in all of southern California that looks quite like this." We'd come to a small clearing from which we could see down over the surrounding hills. Vivid splashes of red, gold, and orange formed a mosaic of color over the countryside below us. We enjoyed the view for a few minutes, then moved on.

"What have you been up to while I was gone?" Sam asked.

He knew I'd been taking Faith to handling class, but having recently moved to the East Coast, he didn't know Rick and Jenny Maguire personally. Still, he was shocked when I told him what had happened.

"How did she die?"

"Arsenic poisoning, apparently." I plucked a bright gold leaf off a tree beside the path and twirled it between my fingers. "Aunt Peg and I went to the wake last night and Crawford Langley told us that much. He said it must have been an accident."

Both of us stopped as there was a sudden crashing in the underbrush. With two graceful bounds, a doe leapt across the path and disappeared into the trees on the other side. I grabbed for my puppy and missed. Immediately both Poodles took off in pursuit. Luckily Charm was too old to give much of a chase and when she circled back, Faith came with her.

Having recaptured the dogs, we decided it was time for lunch. I was just as glad the subject had been changed. The summer before Sam had done a great job of comforting me after I'd stumbled across a dead body. I didn't want him to think of me as some sort of damsel who was perennially in distress.

Sam had packed ham-and-cheese sandwiches and tucked a pair of beers into a small thermal pouch. The dogs begged shamelessly and probably ended up with more than their share as we talked about Sam's trip, Aunt Peg's new puppies, and the judges for the upcoming winter shows. The scenery was breathtaking, the company delightful, and the afternoon passed a whole lot faster than I wanted it to.

Frank usually dropped Davey off around five. When we got back down the hill to Sam's house, I knew I would have to hurry if I was going to make it. His arm was around my waist, his fingers skimming lightly just above my waistband.

"Want to come in?" he asked.

"Yes . . ." I smiled an apology. "And no. I have to get back. My brother will be bringing Davey home."

Sam was great with kids, and he and Davey were friends. I knew he wouldn't press; Sam understood that I had responsibilities. But that didn't make it any easier to leave. I tried for a compromise. "Five minutes . . . ?"

"Doesn't begin to cover what I had in mind." Sam chuckled softly. His arm fell away, and my skin felt cool where it had been. "Go get Davey."

Not on that note, thank you very much. Bracing my hands on his shoulders, I reached up and kissed Sam on the lips, hard. For a moment he let me lead, then his arms came up, one high, one low, both pulling me close along the warm, hard length of his body.

By the time I came up for air, my resolve was completely gone.

Sam didn't look much better; but fortunately for my child, he seemed to have kept some wits about him. "Davey?" he said.

I nodded dumbly.

I got in the Volvo and drove down the hill and turned back into a pumpkin. Or a mother, as the case may be. Sometimes it all feels the same.

On Tuesday after school, Davey had a play date. He was going to Joey Brickman's house and I didn't have to pick him up until dinner time. My last class ended at two-thirty. I drove home and let Faith out in the yard where we played ball for a few minutes. Handling class had been canceled again for that week, and I still needed to return the book Jenny had lent me. Reading it had been a mixed experience. I'd learned a lot, but I'd also been reminded of her on nearly every page.

I hopped the Poodle puppy into the car and headed north. Faith sat upright on the front seat beside me, staring out through the windows and woofing gently when she saw something she liked. Children on bicycles were a special favorite. She'd jump up, tail wagging, alternately pressing her nose against the window and nudging it against my arm to get my attention. I finally realized she thought they were all Davey, being left behind by the side of the road.

Thanks to Faith's antics, the drive went quickly. I'd never been to the Maguires' kennel before, but I knew that it was located just off Route 7, on the Ridgefield-Danbury border. As I drew near, the large green sign was hard to miss. *Shamrock Kennels*, it said. *Dogs Boarded and Professionally Shown.*

I pulled in the gravel driveway and parked in a shady spot in the small lot out front. To the left was Rick and Jenny's house. It was a raised ranch, roomy and comfortable looking, covered with light gray aluminum siding. Cream-colored shutters matched the door, and low, well-tended holly bushes lined the flagstone walk. The kennel building was on the other side of the driveway, and sported the same color scheme as the house. Its roof line extended outward in the back and although I assumed I was looking at covered runs, stockade fencing shielded the dogs from my view.

Clearly a lot of thought and effort had gone into the

layout. The yard was well kept up, the gravel in the driveway neatly raked. Every effort had been made to make an excellent first impression on potential clients.

I cracked the windows all the way around for Faith and left her sitting on the front seat with a rawhide bone. The house looked quiet, so I headed over to the kennel. The first door I came to opened into a small office. Rick was sitting behind a wide metal desk, his chair tipped back at a precarious angle as he talked on the phone. Seeing me, he smiled and held up a finger to indicate he'd be off in a minute.

I closed the door behind me, walked a few steps into the room and had a look around while I waited. Like nearly all the kennels I'd been to, the walls were covered with pictures, the majority of them "win photos" from all the top dog shows. Dozens of framed shots attested to the success Jenny and Rick had been having with their clients' dogs.

There were a number of pictures of a buff colored Cocker Spaniel that I figured must have been Charlie, but there were also Setters, Springers, even a pair of Pointers. Some of the dogs were with Jenny; some, with Rick. All were majestically displayed.

"Melanie, hi." Rick hung up the phone and stood. "I hope you didn't come all this way to find out about class. It's canceled again this week, I'm afraid."

"No, I knew that. Aunt Peg told me. Actually, I came to return this." I held out his book. "Jenny lent it to me when she came to my house for dinner."

"Oh?" Rick took the book and put it down on his desk. "I didn't even notice it was gone."

Why would he? I thought. He'd had plenty of other

things to worry about. "I wanted to tell you again how sorry I am. She was really a nice person."

"She was great," Rick said softly. He glanced over at a photograph that was prominently displayed opposite the door: Jenny and Charlie winning Best in Show at Bucks County, dog and handler both aglow with pride at their achievement. Briefly I wondered how he could bear to be surrounded by so many reminders of happier times. As if reading my thoughts, he shifted his gaze away. "Jenny was everything to me. She was my whole life. I'll never find anyone like her again."

I wished there was something comforting I could say; something that wouldn't sound trite or shallow. But the truth was, I agreed with him. Jenny would be a hard person to replace.

"Crawford said you found out what happened . . . ?" I let the question dangle. He didn't have to answer it if he didn't want to, but I was hoping he would.

"Arsenic poisoning." Rick sank back down in his chair. "That's what the autopsy said."

"Do you know how?"

"God, no. I wish I did." He raised his face and I saw that his expression was anguished. "The police have asked me about this a dozen times and none of it makes any sense. They wanted to know if we had any arsenic here. Of course we do, we're a kennel for Pete's sakes. Where there's this much kibble, there are rats. We keep the dog food in big metal bins, but they still hang around. You've got to control them somehow and it's not like we were going to get cats. . . ."

"You think Jenny was poisoned with rat poison?"

"What else can I think? That's the only place we had

arsenic. She handled it, I handled it. She must have slipped up somehow."

A pretty big slip-up, I thought. It couldn't be easy, or pleasant for that matter, to ingest enough rat poison to kill a human being. I couldn't imagine it happening by accident.

"What do the police say?"

"They keep asking questions, but so far they haven't come up with any answers. Did Jenny have any enemies? Had she been depressed about anything lately? Things like that."

"And had she been?"

"Hell no," Rick snapped, with the vehemence of someone who's answered the same query one time too many. "Jenny was fine, the same as ever. Things were going good for us, real good."

"What about what happened to Ziggy?"

"Sure that upset her. A thing like that would upset anybody. But Jenny'd been in this business a long time. She grew up in it. You know when you get dogs that you're going to outlive them. It's a fact of life and you either figure out how to deal with it or you don't last very long."

Angie had thought Jenny was unhappy. Rick didn't. Angie was her sister; Rick, her husband. Which one of them had known her better? And what had Angie meant when she'd said, I never thought she'd go that far?

"So you don't think Jenny could have poisoned herself?"

Rick started to reply, then stopped. His shoulders rose and fell in a weary shrug. "I don't know what to think anymore. My wife is dead. That should be the worst of it, but it's only the beginning. Half the clients are sympathetic, but the other half are in an uproar. The business is going crazy. Jenny fired our only kennel help ten days ago and I haven't had a chance to replace her yet. I had the Petersons to deal with over the weekend, and the police are stopping by every other minute to ask questions. My whole life's shot to hell anyway. What does it matter what I think?"

The door in the far wall pushed open and Angie stuck her head in. She was holding a fluffy white Bichon Frise under one arm. "Rick? Sylvie Dumas called earlier and said she wants to pick Buttons up at five. I think you ought to call her back and try to change her mind, but I gave him a bath anyway so he's ready to go if she comes."

"Got it, Angel," said Rick. "Thanks."

Angie withdrew and the door shut quietly behind her.

"See what I mean?" Rick muttered. "Dog people are cold, don't ever let anyone tell you they're not. Jenny hasn't even been buried a week and there's another client wanting to come and get her dog. Thank God for Angie. With Jackie gone, I don't know how I'd be managing right now without her."

"Jackie was the kennel girl?"

Rick nodded.

"I think I spoke with her last week."

"Yeah, she was probably in picking up her things. Jenny was really furious at her. Told her to leave and never come back. I don't think she'd have dared to show her face except . . ."

He didn't finish, but we both knew what he meant. Except that by then, Jenny was gone. He didn't want to talk about it and neither did I. Instead, I went back to something he'd mentioned earlier. "I've seen you at the shows, Rick. You're a good handler. Why can't you show Buttons?"

"He hates men, always has. In time I'm sure I could bring him around, but when Jenny was here to show him, there was no need. Now he only needs three singles to finish and Sylvie figures another woman handler will get the job done faster. That's the name of the game in the dog show world. Win now and win big." He slumped back and covered his face with his hands. "God, I sound cynical, don't I?"

"You sound like a man who's just gone through the worst week of his life."

"You can say that again." He rubbed his eyes roughly and left them red and puffy. "Well, I guess I'd better call Sylvie and see what I can do."

"Good luck."

"Thanks. Listen, about class . . ."

I stopped on my way to the door.

"We'll probably be able to get it going again next week. Angie can take Jenny's place. She's pretty good. She's just about saved my life around here the last few days."

"Don't rush back to class on my account. And I'm sure everyone else feels the same way. Come back when you're ready. We'll be waiting for you."

"Thanks, I appreciate that."

I kept my eyes down on the way out. I couldn't bear to look at the pictures either.

ᴄ⃝✳ *Six* ✳ᴄ⃝

Davey has been best friends with Joey Brickman since the two of them were less than a year old. At that age the two biggest factors in determining a child's friends are proximity and how well the two mothers get along. The Brickmans live right down the street from us in Flower Estates; and from that first shared cup of coffee, Alice and I had known we were on the same wavelength.

Aside from Joey, Alice has a daughter, Carly, who's sixteen months old. Her husband works long hours as a lawyer in town and he wasn't home yet when I arrived to pick up Davey. I would have rung the doorbell, but the front door was standing ajar. I opened the storm door and let myself in.

"Hello?" I said.

"In here," Alice called from the back of the house. Joey and Davey were in the living room, totally engrossed in a game of Nintendo. They didn't even turn around as I walked by.

In the kitchen, Alice had Carly in a high chair and was

spoonfeeding her dinner. Mother and daughter shared strawberry-blond hair, pale, freckled skin, and pleasingly plump bodies. Alice was still struggling with the last ten pounds from her pregnancy the year before.

"I closed your front door."

"Thanks. The boys must have left it open. They've been outside most of the afternoon, but once it starts to get dark . . ." She reached for a napkin as pureed banana oozed out of Carly's mouth and down her chin.

"I know. You give up and let them turn on the TV. How come nobody told us ahead of time that motherhood involved so much guilt about all the things you think your children should be doing, but either you can't find the time or else they're totally disinterested?"

"Like chess lessons?"

"Roddy Wade," Alice and I said in unison and grinned.

"If that child's a prodigy," I said, "I'm Cindy Crawford."

"You know his mother has him up to three lessons a week now?"

"It's crazy. It's this area, the whole fast-track, make-it-big, New York metropolitan mentality. The older teachers say that twenty years ago in an average incoming kindergarten class, one or two of the kids would be reading already. Now most are. Either their parents have taught them, or Big Bird has, or the newest wrinkle in all of this—they've been tutored in reading readiness programs. Some of these four- and five-year-olds are even doing math."

"And to think," said Alice, "I feel like I'm doing well when Joey brushes his teeth after I've only reminded him twice."

"Hey Mom, we want something to eat!" Joey came tearing into the kitchen with Davey close behind him.

"Dinner's coming soon," said Alice. "I don't want you to spoil your appetite."

Davey slid to a halt beside me. "What are you doing here?"

"Nice to see you, too." I reached down to give him a hug.

He glanced at Joey and pulled away. "Is it time to go already?"

"Yup. Faith's outside in the car. Where are your shoes?" Winter or summer, it made no difference to Davey. His goal in life was to be barefoot. I'd tried everything from zip-up boots to slip-on sneakers, but nothing stayed on his feet for long.

"I think they're in the living room. I beat Joey at Nintendo."

"Did not!"

"Did too!"

I ignored the squabble and pointed at his feet. "Go look, okay?"

Davey and Joey left the room the same way they'd arrived—at a dead run. Carly watched them go, then reached out, grabbed a handful of her mother's hair and gave it a good yank.

"Ow!" Alice disentangled the strands from her daughter's chubby fingers. "You left that puppy in the car? Is that a good idea? She's probably eaten your steering wheel by now."

"She's fine," I said, hoping it was true. "But I probably shouldn't leave her too long, or she'll start to bark." I picked up Davey's backpack from the kitchen table. His jacket was slung over a chair. When he reappeared—

sneakers on, but untied—I dropped it over his shoulders.

"What do you say?" I asked him.

"What's for dinner?"

"Not to me. To Mrs. Brickman."

"Thanks for having me," Davey mumbled.

"You're very welcome," said Alice, eons more gracious than her guest.

Joey walked us to the door. If I hadn't pulled it closed behind us, he probably would have left it open again. In the car, Faith was bouncing up and down with excitement at our reappearance. As soon as Davey got in, she jumped over the back of the seat and landed on his lap. He was giggling as the two of them rolled down on the floor.

"Did you have fun this afternoon?" I asked when he'd stuck his head up for air.

"No."

"Why not?"

"Joey cheated at Nintendo."

"Really? I thought you said you beat him."

Davey was silent for a moment, considering the ramifications of trying to have it both ways. I could read his thought processes as clearly as my own. He was wondering which he was more in the mood for—sympathy or gloating. Finally he opted out all together.

"I'm hungry," he said as we turned in the driveway and coasted to a stop in front of the garage.

"You're always hungry."

The look he gave me was one of pure exasperation. No doubt about it, kindergarten had matured this kid. I reached out and ruffled his hair.

"Don't grow up too fast, okay?"

"Aw, Mom." Davey opened the car door and unfastened his seatbelt. Faith was sitting on his lap. He lifted the flap of her ear and whispered, "Last one to the house is a rotten egg!"

No surprise who that turned out to be. "You lose!" Davey cried gleefully. Faith spun in a circle and barked.

Some day I'd beat that team, but I doubted it was going to happen any time soon.

The next day after school, Davey and I drove over to Aunt Peg's. She lives in a rambling old farmhouse in back-country Greenwich which probably has about six times as much living space as she needs. The land surrounding it is beautiful though, and there's enough room so that the fact that she has more than a dozen Standard Poodles usually doesn't bother the neighbors.

Roughly half her Poodles are finished champions that have retired from showing. Most of those live in the house with her. The long, profuse coats that are required for competition have been trimmed back, which means that these Poodles look pretty much like normal dogs. At any given time however, Peg usually has a handful of Poodles that are either currently being shown or else growing hair in anticipation of an upcoming career. Those are housed in the small kennel building out back.

There was no answer at the front door when Davey rang the bell, but Peg's station wagon was in the driveway so Davey, Faith, and I walked around back to the kennel. Aunt Peg was there in her grooming room. She'd just finished bathing an older puppy named Lulu and was using a big, free-standing hair dryer to blow her dry.

Lying on the floor in a shaft of the late afternoon sun

was Beau, her top-winning Poodle and beloved pet. He'd been missing for nearly three months over the summer. Now, when Peg was home, he rarely let her out of his sight. As I opened the door, he leapt up and barked sharply.

"It's only us," I said as Faith bounded into the room. With a puppy's typical lack of caution, she charged over and jumped on Beau who suffered her attentions with dignity and a gently wagging tail. "You know you really ought to hook up your doorbell so that it rings out here."

"It does."

"Well?"

"Well what?" Aunt Peg gave me a mild look. "That way I know if someone's come. It doesn't mean I have to drop what I'm doing and go traipsing up to greet them. Anyone who knows me well enough, knows to come and look out here. Anyone who doesn't, I'm probably not interested in seeing anyway." She turned her attention to Davey. "How's my boy today?"

"Fine."

She lifted him up and sat him on the edge of the grooming table. "And how are you enjoying your new puppy?"

"She's neat."

"Better than a frog?" Aunt Peg shot me a disapproving look over my son's head.

"Much better," Davey said happily.

"I should hope so."

Urged on by Faith, Beau had decided to play. As the two of them began to chase each other around the room, Lulu stood up on the table and barked. The area wasn't that big. I pressed back against a wall of shelves and narrowly avoided being run over by the onrush of activity.

"Hey!" Aunt Peg said sternly as Beau grabbed one of Faith's ears in his mouth. "You know better." Then she grabbed the big black dog and gave him a hug, totally negating the effect of her words. "If you're going to be wild, you can take it outside."

"Me too," said Davey, hopping down off the table as Aunt Peg opened the door.

"The house isn't locked," she told him. "If you're hungry, I'll bet you can find yourself a snack in the kitchen."

"Doughnuts?" Davey's eyes lit up.

"Maybe. Go see."

Doughnuts. You could tell these two were related.

The door slammed shut behind him. Aunt Peg got Lulu resettled on the table and continued her blow drying. I pulled over a stool and sat down to watch. The nozzle on the dryer was as long as my arm and twice as thick. The stream of hot air emanating from it was strong enough to ruffle the curtains across the room.

"I saw Rick Maguire yesterday," I said.

Her fingers moved nimbly through the hair, parting and drying it section by section. "Where?"

"At his kennel. I drove up there."

"All the way to Ridgefield? Whatever for?"

"Jenny lent me a book. I wanted to return it."

Aunt Peg stopped and looked up. "And you used the excuse to find out what happened to Jenny."

"I tried. I didn't learn much. She did die of arsenic poisoning. Crawford was right."

"That doesn't surprise me. Crawford's rarely wrong. How did it happen?"

"Rick said he didn't know. He said they kept rat poison on hand, that for a kennel that wasn't unusual."

Aunt Peg nodded.

"But he had no idea how Jenny might have gotten herself poisoned with it. He said she must have slipped up somehow."

"Slipped up?" Aunt Peg said incredulously. "Slipping up involves spilling a little on the ground, not ingesting enough to poison yourself. What have the police had to say about all this?"

"According to Rick, they're still asking questions."

"I guess that's something. They didn't even do that much when Beau was stolen."

"Beau's a dog. Jenny's a person. A woman who was relatively young, healthy, and happy only a week ago. Somebody's got to ask questions about that."

Aunt Peg gave me a long look. "Like you, maybe?"

I pulled in a long breath and let it out slowly, trying to make sense of how I felt. Jenny and I had shared a rapport and the promise of a friendship in the making. Our affinity had been based, at least in part, on our similarities and what we had in common. And that's what was making me so uncomfortable now.

I wanted to know why Jenny was dead while I was alive. What had been the difference between us? What choices had she made that had led to this unexpected ending, and in similar straits would I have done the same? Or did the blame lie somewhere else entirely and it was all only a matter of luck and destiny?

I looked up and saw that Aunt Peg was waiting. I sighed softly, frustrated by all the things I didn't know. "I want to understand what went wrong. Believing that Jenny's death was an accident is too easy. Thinking of it as murder or suicide seems truly bizarre."

"Suicide?" Her brow lifted. "When did that become a possibility?"

"It was something Angie said at the wake. She was really upset and she mumbled something about knowing Jenny was unhappy but never thinking she'd go that far."

"Angie? What would she know about anything? The girl's a child."

"Not really." I reached out and patted Lulu's long muzzle as she lay patiently on the table. "She's probably only a couple of years younger than Jenny. And she certainly knew her sister better than anyone."

Aunt Peg thought for a minute. "Jenny wanting to commit suicide? I just don't see it."

"Neither do I. When I asked Rick about it, he said that he and Jenny were doing great, that she had no reason to be depressed."

Aunt Peg shook her head slightly. "That's Rick's version."

"Do you like Angie's better?"

"To tell you the truth, I don't like either of them. But I also don't like the fact that Rick feels so comfortable speaking for his wife. He did that when she was alive too."

"What do you mean?"

"Just that he's the kind of man who likes to be in charge. You saw a little bit of what I'm talking about when you invited Jenny to dinner."

"You're right," I said, thinking back. "At the time, it seemed pretty funny."

"Then maybe, but not always. Come on, turn over." Peg patted Lulu's rear and the puppy stood up and turned over so that the other side could be dried. In a million years, Faith would never be that well trained. "I used to see them together all the time at the shows. Rick could be obsessive about controlling things right down to the smallest detail. Let's just say that when he said jump, Jenny usually did."

"You just told me you didn't think Jenny would have committed suicide. Now you're agreeing with Angie that she was unhappy."

"Don't put words in my mouth. I said nothing of the sort. What I said was that Rick was definitely the one of the two of them who was in charge. Who knows? Maybe she wanted it that way."

"Maybe," I mused, although her version of events didn't jibe with my recollection of the woman I'd thought I was coming to know. Another inconsistency to file away for future consideration.

"How much do you know about arsenic?" I asked.

"Slightly more than the average layman, I suppose." Aunt Peg finished going through the puppy's neck hair and switched her pin brush for a slicker. "Amazing as it seems, in the old days some of the more unscrupulous handlers used to give arsenic to their dogs in small, hopefully controlled doses. It made them grow huge coats that looked great in the ring."

"That's terrible!"

"It certainly is. Especially for the owners whose dogs overdosed on a drug they had no idea they were being given."

"They don't do that anymore, do they?"

"No, although unfortunately it's not because ethics have improved any. Now the drug of choice is steroids. It produces heavy coats *and* muscles. At the moment there's no drug-testing program in place to ferret out an abuse like that. Luckily it's too risky to be widespread. Why do you want to know?"

"I was wondering about the rat poison in the Maguires' kennel. Rick said that all of them handled it. Is arsenic something that could be absorbed through the skin if you weren't careful?"

Aunt Peg shook her head. "That's not the way it works. If Jenny died from arsenic poisoning, she had to have ingested it somehow. Like maybe in the food she ate for dinner that night."

"Rick and Angie were right there. Presumably they ate dinner with her."

"I didn't say that it was a sensible solution, only that it was a possibility."

I had plenty of possibilities. The problem was, there wasn't a single sensible solution in sight.

"Mommy, Aunt Peg, come find me! I'm hiding!"

Davey's shout from outside was followed by a high-pitched yip from Faith. My son loves to play hide and seek. He started when he was two by covering his face with his hands. Since then his skill at concealing himself has improved enormously. Having recently dug him out from beneath a steward's table at a dog show and behind the bagel bin at the supermarket, it was a game I was hoping he'd soon outgrow.

"Do you want to get him or shall I?" asked Peg.

"I'll go." I slipped down off the stool and zipped my jacket. "You keep drying."

I pushed open the kennel door and found Beau outside, waiting to come in. At least that's what I thought he was doing. He was whining urgently and dancing in place with impatience. But when I opened the door wide, he didn't slip past me. Instead he turned and trotted off in the other direction.

"Here, Beau," I said, calling him back. "Go on in. Peg's in here."

He stopped and turned around to look at me. I'm not one of those people who ascribes human characteristics to dogs. At best you might call me a recent convert to the joys of dog ownership. But I could swear Beau was trying to tell me something. Not only that, but he seemed to be baffled by my apparent stupidity in not understanding.

I looked around, scanning the large yard. Davey and Faith were nowhere to be seen.

"Do you know where they are?" I asked.

Beau wagged his tail.

So it had come to this. I was not only talking to dogs, but also expecting them to answer. Thank God Aunt Peg wasn't outside to see it.

"Okay," I said. "Let's go."

Beau trotted across the lawn and around the side of the house. A wide veranda started in front and wrapped around both sides. In summer, Aunt Peg had filled up some of the space with a grouping of white wicker tables and chairs. Now, with the leaves already coming down from the trees and winter not far behind, she'd pushed the chairs to one side, piled them in a heap and covered them with a tarp for storage.

Barking triumphantly, Beau scrambled up the steps. As he jumped up and placed his front paws against the pile of furniture, there was an answering bark from within.

"Shhh," whispered Davey, his voice clearly audible. "They'll find us."

"They already have," I said, drawing back the tarp. Faith and Davey were snuggled together in the seat of an upturned chair. "Beau led me straight to you."

"No fair!" cried Davey.

"Says who? If you can have a Poodle on your team, so can I."

By the time I'd gotten both child and puppy extracted, Aunt Peg was finished in the kennel. She joined us on the porch and we went inside to be greeted noisily by the herd of house Poodles. Aunt Peg offered hugs and biscuits all around, then shooed them affectionately out of the way.

The dogs draped themselves around the kitchen, Beau sitting in the place of honor beside her chair as she put the kettle on the stove to make tea. I loathe tea, not that that's ever mattered to Aunt Peg. She serves refreshments the same way she does everything else, with the belief that anyone who thinks they have a better idea can make their own. I'd spent enough time in Aunt Peg's house recently to have stashed a jar of instant coffee in the freezer. We got down two mugs and went to work.

Davey boosted himself up on the counter, munching his way happily through what was doubtless not his first doughnut. He broke off a piece and fed it to Faith. I pretended not to notice. Aunt Peg, who is apparently a stricter parent to her Poodles than I am to my child, interceded immediately.

"Don't do that," she told Davey. "The sugar's bad for her teeth. Besides, you'll spoil her appetite."

Bad for her teeth? Spoil her appetite? This from a woman who'd been feeding my son doughnuts all afternoon?

"What about Davey's teeth?" I asked mildly.

Aunt Peg gave me a look. "I assume *he* brushes."

"I do," Davey chimed in.

"Well, there you are. Are you brushing Faith's teeth?"

I smiled, thinking she was joking. Slowly the smile faded. I was almost afraid to ask. "Should I be?"

Aunt Peg lifted the puppy's lips and had a look. "They're in good shape now, but it wouldn't hurt. Especially as she gets older."

Yeah, I thought. Right.

But Aunt Peg was already moving on. She laid critical hands around Faith's ribcage. "She's still thin. Not that you ever want puppies to be fat, mind you, but a little more heft than this wouldn't hurt."

"I was going to try a new food . . . ," I said, then stopped. Right until that moment, I'd forgotten all about it. "Something Jenny told me about."

"Really? What?"

"There's a woman named Crystal Mars in Stratford. She bakes her own all-natural kibble. Jenny said Ziggy was pretty picky and he used to love it."

"You know you want to make any switch in diet like that gradually."

I nodded.

"And you'll have to check and make sure that the protein content isn't too high—"

"Aunt Peg!"

She stopped mid-lecture. "What?"

"I'm not two years old."

"No, you're not." Aunt Peg shook her head firmly. "You got Faith in September. It is now October. By my calendar you are less than one month old, which means that a little advice won't kill you."

That shut me up, as I guess she'd known it would. I let her lecture on and didn't bring up the subject of Jenny's death again until later when we were ready to leave.

"None of the choices make any sense to me," I said. "Could someone have wanted to harm Jenny? Is it possible that she wanted to harm herself?"

"Don't look at me," said Aunt Peg. "I don't have any answers."

That was definitely a first. Too bad the timing wasn't better.

❧❋ *Seven* ❋❧

Hunting Ridge Elementary School is a one-story brick building situated just above the Merrit Parkway in north Stamford. The second wave of the baby boom—the original boomers having children of their own—caught our administration by surprise. For each of the last six years enrollment has been substantially above projections, which means that even though the facilities are up to date and well maintained, we suffer from overcrowding and understaffing. In spite of the fact that the school is bursting at the seams, each spring the town legislators vote to look the other way and hold our budget firm.

When Davey and I pulled into school at eight-thirty the next morning, we saw that a delivery truck had stalled outside the kitchen door, blocking off a full third of the teachers' parking lot. Business as usual at Hunting Ridge. I swung back around the front circle, avoided a bus making a wide turn and nabbed a spot in visitors' parking.

Like nearly everything else at the school, the parking lots are inadequate for the number of cars that have to use them. In theory our security force is out daily, checking for parking violations. In reality, the force consists of old Mr. Simms. As far as I can tell the major part of his day is spent drinking coffee and chatting with the school nurse. Habitual offenders like myself have little to fear.

I delivered Davey to the kindergarten playground and headed over to my classroom, which is really an annex to the school library. My first three years at Hunting Ridge, I'd had a room off the main hall like the rest of the teachers. Crowding had been less severe then and popular thinking had dictated that children with learning disabilities were taken from their regular classes and taught in special sessions for at least part of the day.

Now all that has changed. The new goal is to mainstream the LD kids, that is, to get them to be successful within their own classrooms. I spend most of my day going from grade to grade, taking aside those children that have been identified as needing extra help, and working with them in small groups. We do the same curriculum; we just work a little harder at it. The classroom teacher paints the broad strokes. For the kids who need it, I'm there to fill in the gaps.

The door to the annex was open and when I went inside I found out why. Betty Winslow, who teaches third grade, was perched on the edge of my desk waiting for me. Betty's forty years old and built along ample lines. Her skin is the color of dark chocolate and she has a short, neat Afro that's just beginning to turn gray. Her taste in clothes runs to bright colors and flowing fabric, and she wears her glasses on a chain around her neck. She can move amazingly fast for someone her size and even in a room filled with twenty-four eight-year-olds, she never misses a trick.

The aroma of hot, ground roast coffee hung in the air

and I sniffed appreciatively. Betty picked up one of two styrofoam cups sitting on the desk and handed it over. One sip and I was in heaven.

"This didn't come from the teachers' lounge."

"Of course not. That's stuff's undrinkable. Hay Day Market. I stopped on my way in."

The way I looked at it, I was probably being set up. That being the case, I might as well take another sip and enjoy the bribe.

"I've got a kid I want you to take a look at."

"Test, you mean?" The process for identifying children who were eligible to be part of my program could be long and needlessly complex. Among other things, it involved determining the difference between an individual's potential and achievement, then bringing the results before a meeting of a Pupil Placement Team.

"No, nothing that formal. Besides, using the usual quantitative methods, I don't think he would qualify."

I put down my briefcase, pulled out the desk chair and had a seat. "So, what's the problem?"

"His name is Timmy Doane and he's new to the school this year. He's not LD, I'm almost sure of it. But he's been slow to make friends and he has trouble concentrating on his work. We're six weeks into the school year and he's beginning to fall behind. Nothing big yet, but all the same, something I'd just as soon nip in the bud."

"What do you want me to do?"

"Take him into your group for a couple of weeks, see if the extra attention draws him out. He's a sweet kid, smart too. I'm pretty sure all he needs is a jump start to get him going."

I thought for a moment. Currently the third grade

group was one of my smallest, probably because Betty was doing such a good job. I knew who Timmy Doane was; I'd seen him when I was working in the classroom. He was small and quiet, and integrating him into my group shouldn't be any problem at all.

"Are you going to do the paperwork?" I asked her.

"Hell, no." Betty laughed heartily. "I'm just going to look the other way."

It sounded like a plan to me. Betty levered herself up and left. As I finished off my coffee, the first bell rang.

By the time Davey and I get home in the afternoon, Faith has been cooped up for a good part of the day. That's hard on a dog, especially a puppy. Luckily she's a Standard Poodle which means that she's gifted with enough patience and intelligence to cope.

I barely had the front door open before Davey shot past me and ran down the hall to the kitchen. That's where we keep Faith's crate, which is where she stays while we're gone during the day. I heard Faith whining excitedly as the locks on her crate snapped open. Then the back door opened and slammed shut and they were gone.

Thumbing through the mail, I made my way to the kitchen more slowly. Davey'd left the crate door open and although by now I should know better, I still managed to trip over it and tear a hole in my pantyhose.

"Damn," I muttered, nudging the door shut with my toe. The crate didn't exactly fit in the kitchen, which was why I was always knocking into it. Getting it had been Aunt Peg's idea. In the beginning I'd resisted like crazy. I'd thought of it as a cage, one that any self-respecting dog owner should be loathe to stuff her pet into.

But in the last month, I've become a convert. For starters, the crate made housebreaking a breeze. Then it eliminated the problem of unwanted chewing when we weren't around to oversee what Faith was up to. But what really sold me on it was Faith herself. It didn't take me long to see that she doesn't think of the crate as a cage; she sees it as her den, the place she can go to get some privacy when she wants to escape from humans for a while.

Like parenting, this dog-owning business is a continual learning process. I saw the crate as punishment. Faith thinks of it as home.

I got up and tossed the mail on the counter. No notification from the lottery. Not even an envelope from Publisher's Clearinghouse. Only a few bills and a catalogue from Victoria's Secret. Just looking at those pictures depresses me. In my next life I plan to join an aerobics class, lose ten pounds, dye my hair blond, and learn how to apply eyeshadow to smoldering effect.

In the meantime I have Davey, and now Faith, to keep me busy.

I looked out into the backyard through the window over the sink. Boy and dog were spinning in ever smaller circles around the swing set. I wondered how long it would be before one of them missed a step and knocked himself silly. In general, these are the types of questions that occupy my day.

I opened the back door and stuck my head out. "Come on in. Get a drink, grab a cookie. We've got to get going."

Without missing a beat, the two of them included me in their circle and came flying up the stairs. "Where are we going?" asked Davey.

"Out for a ride in the car."

"Can Faith come?"

"I don't see why not."

"Yippee!"

Oh, to be five again, and to live a life where things were just that simple.

Stratford is a good half-hour drive from Stamford; and north Stratford, where Crystal Mars's kennel was located, took even longer. Davey, who gets impatient on any trip that's longer than around the block, entertained us with eighteen verses of "Frère Jacques" which he'd learned that week in school. He gave the words a spin all his own: Frère Jacques became fair-o jock-o. Despite the efforts of the Stamford school system, I don't think my son will be bilingual any time soon.

Crystal's North Moon Boarding Kennel was located out in the country at the end of a long, rut-filled, dirt road. Driving in, I wondered about the name. North Moon. Did such a thing exist? And if it did, could one by implication, designate a south moon? Maybe the name had some sort of astrological significance that I was unaware of, which is entirely possible because when it comes to astrology, I'm unaware of a lot of things.

Crystal was obviously taken with the lunar motif because moons were pictured everywhere: on the sign, the gate, and the building itself. Some were full and round and had the unfortunate luck to be decorated with eyes and a mouth. Maybe Crystal had been aiming for the nursery rhyme effect but I thought they looked like an anemic version of those stupid yellow happy faces people had plastered everywhere a few years back.

Davey didn't want to come inside the kennel with me, and I saw no reason to insist. The Volvo had come perilously close to losing its axle on the road coming in, so it was a good bet nobody else would be arriving at any great speed. I slipped Faith's collar on and looped the end of her lead around Davey's wrist. Leaving them to explore, I went off in search of Crystal Mars.

From what I'd heard and seen so far, I half expected her to be an overage hippie with tie-dyed clothing and hair down to her waist. A pot of incense burning in the corner wouldn't have surprised me either. So when I walked into the reception room of the kennel and found it to look very much like all the others I had visited, I was almost disappointed.

Wind chimes did tinkle above my head as I opened the door. I guessed that was something.

"Be right there," a voice called from the next room.

"No hurry."

The room was large enough to hold a desk, two file cabinets and a tattered-looking couch. The faint odor of cigarette smoke hung in the air. Here there were no show pictures on the walls; instead the space was filled with an assortment of warm doggie sayings. *Happiness is a Cold Nose. Home is Where the Beagle Lays His Head.*

One was not so warm, but was deliciously funny. *"I got a Schnauzer for my husband,"* it said across the top. Below, *"It was a very good trade."*

I was still chuckling over that one when Crystal Mars appeared. She was certainly old enough to have enjoyed the hippie era, but nary a love bead seemed to have survived. Her gray hair was close cropped and finger combed. Her blue jeans were worn; and her turtleneck sweater, sturdy and serviceable.

Her blue eyes followed the direction of my gaze and she grinned. "Lots of women get a kick out of that one. I've had it printed on a tee shirt in case you're interested."

"Maybe," I considered. That would be one way to explain Bob's absence. "Actually I came to buy some of your kibble. I hear it's great for problem eaters."

"It is. Even more important, it's good for them. I use only the highest quality products and I buy everything fresh locally. Chicken, rice, corn meal. It's all natural, no additives, no preservatives, and no filler. Remember that ethoxyquin scare a couple years back?"

I shook my head, but it didn't matter to Crystal. She just kept going.

"All the big dog food companies went through it. That's what happens when you manufacture in huge batches that end up sitting on supermarket shelves for months. Ethoxyquin's a preservative. All of a sudden, somebody decided it was dangerous and nobody wanted any part of it. Dog breeders stampeded in eight different directions at once. Trouble was, it was in almost every manufactured kibble. Except mine, of course."

"All right, you've sold me," I said when she paused to take a breath. "I'll try twenty pounds."

"Small bite or large?"

"Small, um . . . large."

Crystal smiled. Obviously making customers' decisions for them was nothing new to her. "What kind of dog?"

"Standard Poodle puppy. Six months old and growing even as we speak. I was thinking small, because she's a puppy; large because twenty pounds should last awhile."

"We'll start you with small." Crystal disappeared into the next room and came back toting a twenty-pound sack with ease. "Next time you can move up. What's your puppy's name?"

"Faith."

"Faith," she repeated, writing up a slip. "I like that."

She would. I decided not to ruin it by telling her the puppy had sisters named Hope and Charity.

"Hey, Mom!" A slender girl of about nine or ten poked her head out of the back room. She had dark, pixie-cut hair and a gap between her two front teeth. "What's the capital of Ethiopia?"

"Look it up," said Crystal. "That's why I got you those encyclopedias."

"But they're all the way up at the house and my homework's here!"

"Life's tough." Crystal was grinning, but she held her ground.

"Hi, I'm Sarah." The girl turned to me. "Do you know the capital of Ethiopia?"

"Khartoum?" I guessed and got a disgusted look.

"That's the Sudan."

"The encyclopedias are in your room," Crystal repeated.

Sarah slammed the door on the way out.

"My daughter," she said unnecessarily.

"My son's outside."

"How old?"

"Five."

"Nice age. Can I get you anything else?" Crystal glanced meaningfully toward the sayings on the wall.

"Not today." The temperature was a brisk forty-five. It

would be months before I'd think of wearing tee-shirts again.

"I've got a special running on rawhide bones, just today. They're pure and unbleached. Puppies have a natural instinct to chew, you know, and the bones are great for their teeth. . . ."

By the time I got out the door I was juggling twenty pounds of kibble, two rawhide bones, a sampler box of treats, and a brochure about the boarding kennel she'd tucked in my hand, just in case. "You never know when you might want to get away," she said.

Luckily it was just that phrase that got me moving. If I didn't get away from Crystal soon, I was going to have to trade her the Volvo to pay for the supplies.

For once Davey was more or less where I'd left him. I threw everything I'd bought in the back of the Volvo and went to see what he and Faith were looking at. Crystal's kennel didn't have runs. Instead there were two large pens, one opening out on either side of the building. The one on the left held a sable Collie with a gray muzzle who'd offered up a few halfhearted yips when we came in, then gone back to sleep in the sun. Davey and Faith were standing beside the pen on the right.

"Hey champ," I said, coming up behind them. "What's up?"

Davey turned and grinned. "We found a Poodle, just like Faith. Look Mommy, they want to be friends."

I stepped in closer and was able to see through the chain link behind him. The pen held only one occupant, a black Mini who was touching his nose with Faith's through the fence and wagging his tail like mad.

There was something about him. . . .

I looked again quickly, expecting my first impression to change. It didn't. I'd seen the dog in the pen before. It was Jenny's Miniature Poodle, Ziggy.

❧❅ *Eight* ❅❧

That wasn't possible; Ziggy was dead. Jenny had told me so herself. But even knowing that, I had to admit that this Poodle looked exactly like him.

I blinked slowly and took a deep breath. I reminded myself of the difficulty I'd had in positively identifying Beau the summer before, even after I'd found him. I thought about how many times I'd moaned that all black Poodles looked alike.

And they did, up to a point.

But with Aunt Peg's persistent coaching, I'd finally begun to see the subtle differences in conformation, movement, and expression that distinguished one Poodle from the next. Living with Faith, my education had continued. She and Hope were litter sisters, and similar in many traits. But now, like Aunt Peg, I could tell them apart easily. My eye was becoming that much more discerning.

And damn it, this Poodle looked enough like Ziggy to be his twin.

"Mommy, what's the matter?"

"Nothing, honey." I took Davey's hand and looped Faith's leash around my own fingers. "I was just looking at the Mini."

"He wants to come out and play with us."

"Of course he does. It's no fun being cooped up like that."

I started to walk away, pulling Faith and Davey with me. I wanted to see what the Mini would do; maybe bark at us or run away. I was sure that almost any response would push aside the image of Ziggy that had lodged itself so firmly in my mind.

For a moment the little Poodle simply stood, pressed up against the fence and whining. Faith looked back and pulled against her collar. When I kept walking, she followed reluctantly. Then the Mini turned and ran to the other side of the pen. He bent down and picked up a toy and tossed it high in the air. A stuffed rat. It tumbled end over end and when it was in range he leapt up and snatched it on the fly.

I was back at his fence in a flash. "Ziggy?" I bent down and threaded my fingers though the wire. "Come here, boy."

Of course he came. It was no fun to have nobody to play with. Hadn't I just told Davey that?

So I discounted the way he pricked his ears when I said his name and wagged his tail up over his back when I scratched the sides of his muzzle. Any Poodle would have responded to that.

But throwing the toy up and catching it, then racing it proudly around the pen? I'd seen Jenny's Mini do that every week before the start of class. That move was Ziggy, through and through.

"I thought we were going," said Davey.

"We are, in just a minute. You and Faith stay out here and play with this Poodle some more. I just have to see the lady inside about something."

"Okay." My son grinned devilishly. "Did you forget to pay?"

We'd had stern words recently about a pack of bubble gum he'd pocketed in a drugstore. Once outside, he'd produced his booty proudly as if a new and wonderful trick had been accomplished. *Look Mom, and I didn't even have to spend any of your money.*

"No, I didn't forget to pay." Don't ever let anyone tell you motherhood isn't a full-time job. Just this instilling of values business is enough to keep me up nights. "This is about something else, okay?"

The wind chimes tinkled again and once again, Crystal called that she'd be right out. This time I was too impatient to wait. I walked through the doorway into the next room which turned out to be a small, well-stocked storage area. Several papers spread out over the top of a packing crate indicated where Sarah had been doing her homework. Crystal looked like she was in the process of taking inventory. She was shifting through several bags of kibble and making notations on a clipboard. She turned around, saw me, and smiled.

"Back already? Don't tell me—you want the tee shirt, right?"

"No, I want to talk. Do you have a minute? It's important."

"Sure." She set the clipboard down. "Come on, let's go back out to the office."

"It's about the Miniature Poodle in the pen outside. Whose dog is he?"

We lost eye contact so fast it was almost dizzying. Up until that minute, Crystal's gaze had been confident and direct. Now she looked away and busied herself with clearing space for us on the couch.

"Seat?" she offered.

I sat, only because it wasn't worth arguing over. Then I got right back to the point. "Whose Mini is that, Crystal?"

Her hands fluttered briefly in her lap. "He's a boarder dog."

"Who owns him?"

"I don't understand why you want to know. What business could it possibly be of yours?"

The question was a valid one. In her place I probably would have asked the same thing. But Crystal's waffling had only served to solidify my suspicions. I was sure that Ziggy was outside and I wanted to know why.

Jenny had told me that her dog was dead. Now Jenny was dead. And I wasn't leaving until I got some answers.

"I'm asking because I've seen that Poodle before. His name is Ziggy and he belonged to Jenny Maguire."

"So?"

I'd been prepared for her to deny it. The unexpected ease with which she confirmed his identity left me feeling almost deflated. "I thought he was dead. What's he doing here?"

"Boarding," Crystal said shortly. "Just like I told you. Why on earth would you think he was dead?"

"Because that's what Jenny told me. That's what she told everybody."

"I'm sure you must have been mistaken."

"I'm not." I was shaking my head hard. Maybe I was hoping that would shake some sense into my jumbled thoughts. "Let's back up for a minute. I probably should have started by explaining a few things. Jenny Maguire was my friend. I took a handling class from her and she came to my house for dinner just before she died. The reason I came here today was because she recommended your food to me."

"Jenny did?"

"Yes. She said that Ziggy loved it and that my puppy probably would too. She was always giving me helpful hints like that—because we both had Poodles, you know? She adored Ziggy, she never went anywhere without him. And the last time I saw her at class, she told me he'd been run over by a car."

"I don't understand," said Crystal.

"Neither do I. That's why I want to know what the dog's doing here."

She thought about that for a long minute. "You were Jenny's friend?"

I nodded.

"What was her pet name for Ziggy?"

That was easy. I'd heard her call to him often enough in class. Angie would snicker, and Rick would roll his eyes. But Jenny didn't care.

"She called him Ziggy Zoo," I said with a grin. "Not only that, but he answered to it."

Crystal smiled too. "Some dogs have no pride. I once had a German Shepherd whose name was Duff. I hate to admit it but around the house he was known as Fluffy Duffy."

Faith hadn't been around long enough to acquire any silly nicknames. I wondered if I should mention that I'd been known to call my son Daveykins? Apparently it wasn't necessary. The dog talk had done enough.

"There's not much I can tell you," Crystal said. "Jenny

dropped Ziggy off about three weeks ago. She asked if she could leave him for a while and she paid two weeks' board up front. I was happy to have him around. He's a great little dog."

Stratford was a long way from Ridgefield. What reason could Jenny possibly have had for bringing Ziggy here? I tried to remember what she'd said about Crystal. There hadn't been anything to indicate whether or not they'd been friends.

"Were you and Jenny close?" I asked.

Crystal's eyes shifted. Even before she'd said a word, I knew her wariness had returned. "Close enough. She stopped by every month or so to pick up some food, but we didn't keep in touch much beyond that. I didn't find out that she'd died until after the funeral, and then only by accident.

"The first week Ziggy was here, Jenny called a couple of times to see how he was doing. When she stopped calling, I figured she was just busy. But even so, I knew she'd enjoy hearing a report so I called her. I got her sister instead."

"Angie."

"Right. She told me what had happened. Of course I felt terrible. For Ziggy's sake, too. He's happy here, but you can tell he's waiting for Jenny to come back for him."

"So why hasn't Rick picked him up?"

To my surprise, Crystal looked defiant. "The way I figure it, Ziggy's my dog now. He's happy here. He's got a good home. Why mess with that?"

I stared at her. "But he belongs to Rick."

"Legally, I guess he does. But Rick hated Ziggy. Jenny didn't exactly spell it out, but she hinted as much. Think about it. How many other reasons could there be for boarding out a dog when you've got a kennel of your own?"

Good point.

"Besides," said Crystal, "I haven't heard word one from Rick. So either he doesn't want Ziggy back, or else he doesn't know he's here. Either way, that tells me the Mini's better off with me. I'm not giving him back. I figure I owe Jenny at least that much."

Jenny had certainly inspired loyalty in the people who had known her; but in Crystal's case, I had to wonder if the woman wasn't carrying things too far. It turned out we weren't going to be discussing that, however. Crystal stood up and looked at the door pointedly. My time was up.

Outside, I gathered up Davey and Faith, said good-bye to Ziggy, got in the car, and headed home. I had thought Crystal would give me answers, but all she'd done was leave me with more questions.

Why had Jenny hidden Ziggy away and told everyone he was dead? Did Rick know where Ziggy was; and if so, why hadn't he come to get him? Why had Jenny paid for two weeks in advance? What was supposed to happen at the end of that time?

Between Davey's singing and my own tumultuous thoughts, by the time I got home my head was spinning. The more I found out, the less everything made sense. The only good news was that Davey had torn a hole in the bag of kibble and Faith was eating it out of his hand.

At least I seemed to have found a new dog food.

I couldn't wait to call Aunt Peg and tell her about Ziggy but as soon as we walked in the house, Davey made sure I knew that death by starvation loomed imminently in his future. So I fed Faith—three quarters old kibble, one quarter new—then made a delicious and nutritious dinner for Davey and me. Hamburgers and french fries. When they're five, ketchup counts as a vegetable.

By the time I got Peg on the phone, she had one foot out the door. A champion male Poodle she'd sold two years earlier was supposed to be breeding his first bitch up near Hartford. The trouble was, the dog had taken one look at the bitch and turned his back; and the novice owner was too inexperienced to know how to encourage him along. Aunt Peg was rushing to the rescue. I wondered what she was going to do to get the stud dog interested in the job at hand, but decided I didn't dare ask.

"When will you be back?" was a much safer question.

"Late. And unless Waldo catches on pretty quickly, I may end up devoting the rest of the week to this. God save me from first-time owners."

There was a comment just begging to be made there. Something about first-time owners who hadn't had a choice. As usual, Aunt Peg went on without me.

"But I'll see you this weekend, right?"

"This weekend?"

"Melanie, you haven't forgotten! The Queensboro show. I did your entries three weeks ago with mine."

"Of course not," I stammered. Faith's first dog show. Aunt Peg and I had discussed it a month ago, but since then I'd tried to put it out of my mind. Even though it was only for experience, I was still feeling a twinge of nerves.

The show was on Long Island, only an hour's drive away. But Faith would need to be clipped, bathed, and blown dry between now and then. I didn't have the expertise yet to trim her. Aunt Peg would do that for me at the show. Still, I was looking at five or six hours worth of work over the next two days.

"Right," I said, none too pleased at the prospect. "I'll see you there."

After I hung up with Peg, I tried calling Sam. I knew from experience that he made a pretty good sounding board. Not only that, but he's great at figuring out puzzles. His machine picked up.

I listened to the message and even composed one of my own, but in the end I hung up without saying a word. I'm a firm supporter of women's lib, but sometimes my conservative streak wins out. Besides, the last time I'd made the first move I'd found a blonde in a tight mini-dress cooking pesto in his kitchen.

I'd like to think our relationship has progressed since then, but we're still in the process of discovering what works and what doesn't. Since that's more my fault than his, I don't have much right to complain.

It didn't stop me from feeling grumpy though.

❧ ❊ *Nine* ❊ ❧

With the exception of Christmas, dog shows are held every weekend of the year. What started as a sport among gentlemen has grown over time to embrace the masses. There's a reason for that. For anyone who loves dogs, there's no better way to spend a day.

Showing dogs can be enjoyed on any number of levels. Class competition is a comparison of potential breeding stock within each individual breed. Dogs and bitches are judged separately and entries may be made into any of six classes: Puppy, Young Adult, Novice, Bred-By-Exhibitor, American Bred, and Open. The class winners are then judged against each other for the title of Winners Dog and Winners Bitch. These two alone receive points toward their championships, the number of dogs defeated on the day determining the number of points awarded. It takes fifteen points to make a champion and somewhere within those fifteen, a dog must win two "majors," that is, he must defeat enough dogs in a single event to be awarded at least three points.

After the class competition comes Best of Breed where the Winners Dog and Bitch compete against the champions. Each dog winning his breed is eligible to compete in the group. The seven group winners then go head to head for the title of Best in Show.

In the beginning the class competition was what dog shows were all about. But as the sport grew bigger and more intensely competitive, a number of different rating systems began keeping score of the top winning dogs. Now there are year-end awards for all sorts of achievements. While there are still plenty of exhibitors like Aunt Peg who are content with simply finishing championships, there are also others who dedicate their lives to chasing the glory of the big wins. The very top dogs often spend half their lives on an airplane, accompanying their handlers in a never-ending search for the biggest shows and the most accommodating judges.

To me, all that running around doesn't make a lot of sense, but then neither do televangelists and look at the following they have. On the other hand, what Aunt Peg did looked like fun. I'd entered Faith in the Puppy class, which is where most novices get their start. With Peg's guidance—not to mention her determined hand at my back—I was hoping our debut would go smoothly.

Queensboro is the last show held outdoors in my area each year. By the end of October, the chances of getting good dog showing weather on Long Island—not too cold, no rain, no strong winds—are about fifty-fifty. This year, we got lucky and southerly winds ushered in a warming trend. I zipped Davey into a warm jacket as a precaution, but at least it looked like we wouldn't spend the whole day shivering.

Showing Standard Poodles is not only a hobby, it's a dedication requiring a great deal of work, both ahead of time and on the day of the show. According to the judging schedule our class went in the ring at noon, but when Davey, Faith, and I reached the showground just before ten o'clock, Aunt Peg was already there. From the summer's experience, I knew to head to the handlers' tent, a covered expanse filled with crates and grooming tables where exhibitors gathered to put the finishing touches on their dogs before they went into the ring.

What those finishing touches might be, varied from breed to breed. For Poodles, the preparations were elaborate. First Faith needed to be thoroughly brushed, then the hair on her head would be gathered up into a topknot. Her trim would be scissored to set the lines and effect a smooth finish, then hair spray would be liberally applied to lacquer everything into place.

Amazingly enough, the Poodles didn't seem to mind any of this. Indeed, they loved the extra attention. The first time I'd seen these things going on, I'd given serious thought to the sanity of the participants. Now I accepted them as routine. What that augured for the state of my own mental health was an issue I didn't care to pursue too closely.

I pulled the Volvo up beside the grooming tent and saw that Aunt Peg had staked out enough space so that I could set up my table and crate next to hers. Since she didn't need the practice like I did, Peg had left her puppy at home. Instead she was showing an older bitch who already had half the points she needed to finish her championship. When Davey hopped out of the car and raced over to Aunt Peg's set-up, arms wide for a hug, the Poodle reclining on the grooming table opened one eye but didn't stir. Ah, training.

"Good morning," Aunt Peg crowed, sounding impossibly cheery. Dog shows have that effect on her.

I hauled my table out of the back of the Volvo and headed her way. "Do you know how many messages I've left on your answering machine in the last two days?"

"More than a dozen, I should think." Aunt Peg was rummaging around in her carry-all. To no one's surprise, she came up with a honey bun for Davey. "You ran the tape through almost all the way to the end."

Not that it had made her return any of my calls.

"I'm glad you noticed," I said huffily.

"I was busy. I told you I would be. Waldo never did catch on. In the end, we had to AI the bitch. I only hope it takes."

AI, artificially inseminate. There was no end to the new things I was learning. But surely Waldo's reproductive problems paled beside the news that Ziggy was still alive. Or they would have if I'd had a chance to deliver it.

"Listen," I said urgently. "We have to talk—"

"Of course we will. There'll be plenty of time. Now finish unloading and go park your car. Davey can stay here with me."

I did as I was told. I'm not usually so obedient, but I figured that way I would be able to tell her the whole amazing story straight through from start to finish with no interruptions. But when I got back to the grooming tent I saw that judging must have just ended in one of the sporting rings. There was a flurry of activity in the set-up next to ours as Rick Maguire dropped off one dog and picked up another. Angie, who'd come running back from the rings with him, pulled a black Cocker out of its crate and put it up on a grooming table.

"What are they doing here?" I hissed under my breath as Angie spritzed the Cocker heavily with water and began fluffing through its hair with a brush and a hand-held dryer.

Aunt Peg lifted a brow at my tone. "Making a living, I would imagine, just like all the other handlers. Lucky for us they had some extra room and I was able to squeeze in. These tents seem to grow smaller all the time."

Small enough so that our tables and Shamrock's were virtually on top of each other. There was no way I was going to be able to tell Aunt Peg anything with any degree of privacy. And although I dearly wanted to sound Rick out on the subject of Ziggy, I hadn't yet decided what I was going to say. Until I had more information, I certainly wasn't about to blurt out the news that the Mini was alive and well and living in Stratford.

I hopped Faith up onto her table, laid her on her side, and went to work. Maybe this proximity could be made to work to my advantage. "Hi, Angie," I said.

She looked up from the Cocker and squinted in my direction.

"Melanie Travis," I prompted. "I'm in your handling class."

"Of course. Nice to see you. Is this your puppy's first show?"

I nodded.

"Well don't worry about a thing. She's very pretty. I'm sure you'll do fine."

"Thanks. How have you been doing?"

"Great." Angie smiled broadly. "Couldn't be better."

Handlers are natural-born salesmen. They have to be, especially at dog shows where, when they're not selling their dogs to the judges, nearly everyone they talk to is a potential client. So for a moment I wondered if Angie was simply telling me what she thought I wanted to hear.

But as she turned her attention back to the Cocker, I realized she'd meant what she'd said. Aside from that brief moment at the kennel, I hadn't seen Angie since the wake. But the woman standing here, juggling the needs of a professional's string with calm efficiency was worlds away from the pale, fragile girl I'd escorted to the ladies' room. Everyone dealt with grief in his own way. Angie had obviously thrown herself into her work.

She also looked strong enough to handle a few questions.

"I'm going for a cup of tea," said Peg. "And I've promised Davey we'll hunt down some hot chocolate. Do you want anything?"

"No thanks." Despite Angie's words of encouragement, butterflies were already fluttering in my stomach. I didn't dare drink anything for fear of spending the rest of the morning waiting in line for the port-o-johns.

"Keep an eye on Peaches for me?"

"Sure." That was easy. All Aunt Peg's Poodles were table-trained. Even though they weren't tied, they wouldn't jump off unless invited.

I watched as they walked away, Aunt Peg dignified and sedate; my five-year-old son holding her hand and skipping merrily at her side. When they were gone, I turned back to Angie. She was working on the other side of the Cocker now which meant that she was facing in my direction.

"I've been thinking about something you said at Jenny's wake," I ventured.

"Really?" She nudged a wad of gum from one cheek to the other. "What?"

"When we were in the ladies' room together, you mentioned that Jenny had been unhappy. . . ."

"Yeah? So?"

I'd hoped that gentle prompting might get her started talking, but obviously Angie required more. Maybe flattery would loosen her up. "You were Jenny's sister. I bet you knew her better than anybody."

"I did. Jenny wasn't just my sister, she was my friend." Angie applied the brush methodically, her hand lifting the hair and letting it fall into the stream of hot air. "I looked up to her, you know? She took care of me."

"She probably confided in you, too."

"Sometimes. And sometimes she didn't tell anyone what was on her mind. That was just the way she was."

"But you thought she was unhappy. What did she have to be unhappy about?"

Angie's brushing hand slowed. "What happened to Ziggy was the biggest thing, I guess. That really busted her up. Jenny wasn't thinking straight. I mean, she couldn't have been, right? Who could get that attached to a pet that they couldn't go on living without it?"

Especially a pet that wasn't dead at all.

"What makes you think Jenny died because of Ziggy?"

"Because that's what the note said."

I'd been running a comb through Faith's neck hair. Abruptly I stopped and looked up. "What note?"

"Jenny wrote a suicide note. I found it a couple of days after she died. She said she was unhappy and she had nothing to live for, that losing Ziggy was the last straw."

So much for my feeling that Jenny couldn't have killed herself. The presence of a suicide note changed everything. Or did it?

"Angie, where did you find that note?"

"It was in Jenny's desk."

"On top? Like she'd left it out for you?"

"No, it was under a whole bunch of stuff. I was going through her things when I found it. I mean, somebody had to sort things out."

That made me think of when my parents had died. Several months had passed before Frank and I could bring ourselves to go through their things and close the house. We hadn't found anything unexpected though. I hadn't learned of my father's drinking problem until a good deal later. By then it was almost too late for me to readjust the rosy image of my parents' marriage that I'd carried for so long in my mind. I shook my head slightly and came back to the present.

"When you were going through Jenny's things, did you find anything else unusual?"

Angie snapped her gum loudly. "What was unusual was what I didn't find."

"What was that?"

"I was looking for some jewelry. Two rings and a pin. They used to belong to our grandmother and since Jenny was the oldest, Gram left them to her when she died. Now they should have been mine. But I couldn't find them anywhere."

"Was the jewelry valuable?"

"I guess so. One of the rings was platinum and diamonds. The other had an emerald. Jenny always kept them in a special little box. But they're gone now."

"Maybe Rick knows where they are."

"He doesn't. I asked him."

"Did you show him the note?"

"Yeah. First thing, right after I found it."

Yet later when I'd spoken to Rick, he'd ruled out the possibility of suicide.

"Do the police know about the note?"

"I gave it to Rick and he said he'd take care of it, so I guess he did. It hasn't stopped them from asking questions, though."

"Really?" I kept my voice casual. "What kinds of questions?"

"Like if Jenny had any enemies, or if she might have had a fight with anyone recently."

"And did she?"

"Sure. Anyone who wins as much as Jenny does, has enemies." Angie affected a look of world-weary blasé. "It's the nature of the game."

I remembered the handler I'd met at the funeral. "Like Harry Flynn?"

"He'd be one."

"There are more?"

"Sure." Angie's Cocker shook its head violently. She lifted up one long ear and took a careful look inside. "Take Jackie, the girl we had who was helping around the kennel."

"The one Jenny fired."

"Right. Now, she was pissed."

"Why did Jenny let her go?"

"There were a couple of things. Jenny suspected she'd been pilfering stuff around the kennel. Nothing big, nothing you had to take a stand about. But just enough to make you crazy, you know? Then one day Jenny caught her being rough with one of the dogs. She just about hit the roof over that."

"Were you there?"

"I sure was." Angie grinned. "Jenny was great, screaming and yelling and chasing Jackie around the place with a broom. Smacked her with it once or twice and said, 'There, how do you like it?' That was Jenny all over. She wasn't about to stand for anyone beating up on one of her dogs."

I smiled at the image and thought about how much we'd lost. "Where's Jackie now?"

Angie rolled her eyes. "Like I would really know. Rick said a pet grooming salon in New Canaan called and asked for references, so maybe she ended up there."

"Angie!" Rick was standing just outside the tent, waving a hand frantically. "Isn't that dog ready yet? You were supposed to meet me at ringside."

"Oops." Angie snatched up a leash and slipped the looped end over the Cocker's head. "Gotta go."

"Sure. Sorry if I held you up."

I watched Angie hurry out of the grooming area, the Cocker tucked securely under her arm. When she reached Rick, the two of them took off toward the rings. The apology was just for show. I wasn't sorry one bit.

❧✳ *Ten* ✳❧

Aunt Peg and Davey returned right after Angie left. Peaches jumped up and danced on her table, wagging her tail in greeting. That meant Faith had to get up too. Of course once she was on her feet she couldn't figure out what all the excitement was about, since her person had been there all along.

Using both hands, I laid her back down, left side up. The left side of the dog is also known as the show side. It's the one that faces that judge during competition and is always brushed last for maximum effect.

Aunt Peg boosted Davey up onto the top of her large metal crate. He was munching on a candy bar and looking very pleased with himself. At nine-thirty in the morning, no less.

"Davey, where did you get that?"

"Aunt Peg bought it for me."

"Aunt Peg?"

"Hmm?" Her face was buried in her tack box, no doubt because she could guess what I was going to say.

"I thought you were going to get Davey some hot chocolate."

"I was, but they didn't have any. So we did the next best thing."

The next best thing? "A candy bar? At this hour of the morning?"

"He asked for it," Aunt Peg said innocently. "He told me he was allowed."

"Of course he did. He's five years old. You're a grown-up. You should know better."

"Oh pish. I'm an aunt, not a mother. Mothers have to worry about things like that, aunts don't. That's the beauty of the whole thing."

Indeed.

I might have harped on the topic a little, not that it would have done any good, but just then Angie came hurrying back to the set-up next door.

"Did you make it to the ring in time?"

"Just barely." Her cheeks were flushed becomingly and she reached up and tucked a stray strand of hair back behind her ear. "Rick's sent me back to finish getting Charlie ready. The schedule didn't look like it was going to be too bad but now ring eight is running late, which means we're going to have a conflict."

"With who?" I asked and Aunt Peg chuckled.

"A timing conflict," she explained. "Two dogs in two different breeds that have to be in two separate rings at the same time. It happens to handlers all the time."

Angie fished Charlie out of a crate and plopped him up on the table. "Ascob Cockers go in right after blacks. Pointers should have been done half an hour ago, but the judge is slow as molasses."

Ascob Cockers was Charlie's class. The word was actually a string of initials, a.s.c.o.b., which stood for "Any solid color other than black." Like Poodles, Cocker Spaniels have three varieties within the breed. Poodles are divided by size; Cockers, by color. Their varieties are black, ascob, and parti-color. Since he was a buff, Charlie was shown in the ascob class.

Rick came running across the field to the tent. He dodged around crates and tables to reach his set-up. The black Cocker was beneath his arm, and there was a red and white Best Of Opposite Sex rosette clutched between his teeth.

"Congratulations," I said, and Aunt Peg poked me, hard.

"Never congratulate the loser," she said under her breath.

"But he won Best Op," I whispered back.

Best of Breed was obviously the optimum award, but what Rick had won wasn't too shabby either. Best of Opposite Sex was exactly what it sounded like. If a dog won Best of Breed, the best bitch became Best Opposite. If a Bitch won the top award, then BOS went to a dog. Only the Best of Breed winner went on to compete in the group.

Rick's ears were better than I thought. "Harry Flynn won," he said. "All we were was second best."

"But you still beat all the others—"

I hadn't lifted my voice at all, but Aunt Peg poked me again. By the time I got home my ribs were going to be black and blue. I decided to keep quiet for a while. That turned out to be just as well because there was enough commotion going on next door.

Rick had whipped open a crate door and pulled out a large lemon and white Pointer. "Take Charlie up to ringside as soon as he's ready," he said to Angie. "You're going to have to start him for me. Go to the back of the line and I'll get there as soon as I can."

"Got it."

Rick didn't even wait for Angie's reply. Pointer in tow, he was already racing off toward ring eight. Angie quickly finished some last minute grooming, then she, too, took off. If I shifted my position several feet to the right, I could just about see the Cocker ring. I watched Angie pick up her numbered armband from the steward.

"Charlie's the specials dog," I commented. Finished champions that were being campaigned for additional wins were referred to as specials. For professional handlers, class dogs were bread and butter; specials dogs were a chance for glory. "Why would Rick choose to show the Pointer? Isn't winning with Charlie more important?"

"It certainly is," Aunt Peg agreed. "But Rick's planning to juggle things so that he can show them both."

I gazed over toward the Cocker ring. Angie was filing into the ring with the rest of the exhibitors, which meant that the Best of Variety class had been called.

"How's he going to do that? Angie's already taking Charlie in the ring."

"She's starting the dog, just like Rick told her to. Conflicts like this aren't unusual. The successful handlers bring big strings to each show and they can't be everywhere at once. What they do is have an assistant take the dog into the ring so it won't be marked absent from its class. Then the dog goes to the back of the line, so it's last to be judged. As long as the dog hasn't yet had its individual examination by the judge, a change of handlers is allowed. You'll see. Rick will get done in Pointers and come and take over."

"Maybe," I said dubiously. "But Angie and Charlie are at the front of the line, not the back."

"Let me see." Aunt Peg moved over and had a look. "You're right. What is that girl thinking now?"

The judge sent the group of Cocker champions around the ring. Ears and legs flying, Charlie led the way. Angie stopped beside the table and lifted the little spaniel up to be examined.

"It's too late now," Aunt Peg mused aloud as the judge put his hands on the dog. "Even if Rick gets there, they won't let him make the switch."

Watching this drama unfold was a good deal more entertaining than the brushing I was supposed to be doing. Aunt Peg must have felt the same way because we were both still staring a few minutes later when Rick came dashing up to the gate. The class was still in progress. Obviously assuming Angie had followed his instructions, he argued with the steward for a moment before being turned away. Even from across the field, I could tell by the set of his shoulders that he was angry.

"Why would Angie do something like that?" I asked. "Especially after she told him she understood what he wanted."

"Oh, she understood, all right. But I'll bet she's hoping to win the class herself. Maybe she wants to prove to Rick that she's just as capable of handling a dog as he is."

The finer points of presentation often went right over my head. I decided to seek a wiser opinion. "And is she?"

"No. She doesn't have Rick's finesse, or his experience.

Not only that, but Harry Flynn's in there and he can handle rings around her, if you'll pardon my pun. Which doesn't necessarily mean that Angie won't win. Charlie's the best dog and he's been on a winning streak. They may pull it out yet."

As if agreeing with Aunt Peg's assessment, the judge pulled Charlie and Harry Flynn's Cocker out of the line for further work. Still holding the Pointer, Rick moved over to stand next to a tiny older woman who was leaning heavily on a cane and glaring into the ring. She and Rick seemed to be discussing the class in progress and he was shaking his head vehemently.

"Who's that?" I asked, pointing.

"Florence Byrd, Charlie's owner. Come to watch her Cocker win, I'd imagine. And paying top handling rates to make sure it happens. It's got to be damn awkward for Rick to explain why he isn't in the ring on the dog. And if Charlie loses—"

All hell would break loose, I imagined. I watched that pair, who were at least as interesting as what was happening in the ring, and realized that a third person had joined the group. He was a man in his late thirties, tall and massively built, with short black hair and thick, blunt features. His size alone would have been enough to make him stand out; but unlike the majority of the casually dressed crowd, he was wearing a dark suit, white shirt, and narrow-striped tie.

"Who's the suit?" I asked.

Aunt Peg frowned at having her attention diverted. She was much more intent on the action in the ring. "That's Dirk, Mrs. Byrd's driver. As you can see, she's not in the best of health. He goes everywhere with her."

"Hey!" cried Davey. "Why is everybody standing over there? I want to see, too!"

I went over and scooped him off the top of the crate then walked back to where Aunt Peg was standing. He was a little heavy to be cradled on my hip but he clung like a monkey as I pointed toward the Cocker ring.

"Big deal," sniffed Davey, obviously disappointed. "More dogs."

"More dogs, indeed," said Aunt Peg. "What did you think we were looking at?"

"Cars?" Davey tried hopefully. They'd been his passion since he was a toddler. On the way out, I'd take him for a stroll through the back parking lot where the motor homes and big rigs were parked. That always made his day.

"Ooh!" Aunt Peg cried suddenly. "I think Angie's pulled it off."

In the ring, the judge had placed Charlie at the front of the line. Harry Flynn's Cocker was behind him. The judge sent the dogs around one last time, then pointed to Angie's Cocker for Best of Variety. Most of the other exhibitors stopped to congratulate her, but not Harry. He snatched up his dog, strode angrily to the gate, and disappeared into the crowd.

"I guess Flynn thought he should have won," I said.

"Nobody ever wants to lose. Some people handle it with better grace, that's all."

"Better grace? Try no grace. He looked livid."

"Harry Flynn's an excellent dog man. But he hasn't the best manners. You saw that for yourself at the wake. This is the first time that Charlie's been shown since Jenny died. And to find him in the ring with Angie . . . well, let's just say Harry must have assumed he'd be vulnerable."

"You make it sound like these handlers are after each other's throats."

"They're pros and they're here to win," Aunt Peg said simply. "That's what it's all about."

Davey went back on top of the crate with a book about cars and a box of juice. I'd stood Faith up and was fluffing through her coat with a comb when Angie and Rick arrived back at their set-up. She was grinning like a cat covered with canary feathers. Rick, however, did not look pleased. He put the hapless Pointer in a crate and continued on with a conversation that must have started at ringside.

"I don't want you ever doing anything like that to me again!"

"I don't see what you're so upset about," Angie replied. "I won, didn't I?"

"That's not the point—"

"Pardon me, but I thought it was. Did you see the look on Harry's face? It was priceless."

Rick's frown softened. "I'll admit that watching Flynn lose had a certain appeal. But I'd intended doing that from inside the ring, not out. Clearly that's where Mrs. Byrd expected me to be, too."

"Oh, that old biddy." Angie waved a careless hand through the air. "What does she know, except how to sign checks? She always left all the important decisions about Charlie's career up to Jenny. Now I'd say that means they're up to you. As long as the ribbons are the right color, she doesn't have a thing to complain about."

Rick spun around and looked behind him. Mrs. Byrd was nowhere in sight. "Damn it, Angel, keep your voice down, would you?"

"Don't worry." Angie dropped her voice to a whisper,

and snickered like a rebellious teenager goading her parents. "I think she's deaf, too."

Rick sighed. As a mother myself, I knew just how he felt. "She's not deaf," he said, "and neither is Dirk. So watch your mouth."

"Dirk. Ugh." Angie shuddered. "That guy gives me the creeps. He's always hovering in the background somewhere. He reminds me of that butler in the Addams Family. What was his name, Lurch?"

"Angie!"

Rick's frustration was palpable. Eavesdropping shamelessly, I smothered a chuckle.

"He was always watching Jenny, did you ever notice that? It was really weird."

"Don't be ridiculous," Rick said firmly. "You're letting your imagination run away with you. He was probably watching Charlie."

"It's not my imagination. I tell you he's a spook."

Aunt Peg came over to stand beside my table. She had a long comb in one hand and her best pair of Japanese scissors in the other.

"Hold her head here," she said, placing her hand under Faith's chin and lifting so that the Poodle's head was high and back over her shoulders. "Otherwise you'll spoil the lines."

"Yes, sir." A moment ago, I'd sympathized with Rick. Now I was feeling a bit like a rebellious child myself. I knew from experience that once Aunt Peg got started scissoring she could go on for an hour, perfecting the puppy's trim. Faith didn't seem to mind. Sometimes she all but fell asleep on her feet. I was the one whose arm kept getting cramps. A human hitching post, that's all I was.

I tuned back into the conversation next door.

"Now about the group . . ." Angie was saying.

"Don't even think it!"

"Why not?" She placed both hands on her hips and jutted out her chin. "I won the variety. I can win the group too. Admit it, you never would have given me a chance to show Charlie. But I did show him and I did great."

"You won the variety by the skin of your teeth. And you weren't great. You were good enough to win on the day, that's all. Mr. Dean's judged Charlie with Jenny, and he knows you were sisters. This was probably his way of expressing his sympathy."

Angie's lips drew together in a tight line. Clearly she didn't agree with Rick's assessment. "Mr. Dean's doing the group, too. Whatever the reason, he liked Charlie with me this morning. He's already put us once. It would be stupid to try something different later."

"We'll see." said Rick. "Right now I've got to get over to Beagles. You start working on Rugby."

"No prob, Bob." Angie was grinning again. No doubt she figured she'd won the argument. I wasn't so sure. The Sporting group would be judged in early afternoon. If Davey didn't get too bored, I wouldn't mind staying to see what happened.

There was one good thing about the events playing out next door. They were interesting enough to make me forget just how nervous I was about taking Faith into the ring for the first time. But when things slowed down at the Shamrock set-up and Aunt Peg finished trimming, the butterflies returned in a rush.

"I'm not ready," I told her. "This was all a big mistake."

"Nonsense. Turnbull women can handle anything. Besides, this is only a puppy class at a small show. What's the worst that could happen?"

"I could trip and fall down. No, I could trip over Faith and we both fall down. Even worse, I could trip over the judge—"

"You could try tripping over the tent post," Aunt Peg said dryly. "That way you might be able to work a falling tent into your path of destruction."

"Maybe I could," I said stubbornly, even though we both knew that the tents were held in place by dozens of sturdy spikes.

Aunt Peg looked over my shoulder, her eyes focusing on someone behind me. "Good, you're just in time. Melanie's suffering from a severe case of cold feet. Maybe you can prod her along."

I turned and saw Sam approaching. "What are you doing here?"

"You didn't think I'd miss your debut, did I?"

Actually, that's exactly what I'd been thinking. I knew from handling class that this dog showing business was something that took practice. And while I'd resigned myself to the fact that I'd probably look like an idiot on the first several tries, there was no way I'd intended to do so in front of Sam Driver, a man for whom I was trying to showcase only my best attributes.

But when Aunt Peg got a notion in her mind—like the one she currently had, that Sam and I ought to be together—denying her what she wanted was like standing in the way of a steamroller. Either way, you were bound to get flattened.

Sam stepped past me and had a look at Faith. "Want some help with your topknot?"

I mustered a smile. At least with Sam's expert help, the puppy would look first-rate. "Sure."

"You can spray her up, too," Aunt Peg offered. "I'm going to be pressed for time."

Pressed for time, my fanny. The schedule she'd laid out for our preparations was more detailed than the one Rommel had used to invade Africa. "You're not very subtle, Aunt Peg."

She watched me move in close to Sam as he began parting the hair for topknots on Faith's head. "I'm not trying to be, dear."

In principle, I'm against hitting old ladies, but if I'd had a free hand, I might have considered it. Sam, who'd placed one of my palms under Faith's muzzle and had the other tamping down the hair behind her occiput, just whistled under his breath and kept right on working. He parted, he banded; he fluffed and sprayed. And when he was done, even I had to admit that Faith looked gorgeous.

"Got your number?" he asked.

I gulped and nodded.

Showtime.

❧* Eleven *❧

After all that it turned out I'd done a lot of worrying for nothing. Faith was fine. I was fine. It wasn't an accomplished performance, but we didn't bring the tent down either. Or the house, for that matter. Aside from Davey and Sam who stood at ringside and cheered our puppy class win with total lack of dignity, I doubt that anyone else even noticed us.

Did I mention we were the only ones in the class?

Even so, the blue ribbon looked pretty good to me. It also meant we got to go back in the ring again to try for Winners Bitch. Six-month-old Standard Poodle puppies have a lot in common with Gumby. The chances of winning with one are roughly comparable to those of finding comfort in a pair of stiletto heels.

Still, once I'd decided the whole exercise wasn't going to kill me, it even became kind of fun. Aunt Peg won the open class with Peaches and when she took the points, I was the first to congratulate her. After the rest of the judging was over I stood by the gate with Sam and

Davey, watching as she posed her Poodle for a picture with the judge.

"Feel better now?" asked Sam.

"Much."

"What's the matter?" asked Davey. "Did you have a tummy ache?"

"Kind of." I smiled down at him. His small hand was tucked trustingly inside Sam's larger one and the sight gave me a pang. How could I feel my way through relationships with men when my feelings weren't the only ones involved?

"Do you want to hold Faith's leash?" I offered.

"Yeah!" cried Davey, his eyes lighting up. "Can I wear your number, too?"

I slipped off the armband and fastened it on over his sleeve, then handed him the looped end of the lead. "Use both hands, okay? We wouldn't want her to get away."

He was happy to comply. Sam was holding a comb and a can of hair spray in one hand. The other, newly freed, he slipped into his pocket. So I was the one left standing there twiddling my thumbs. That annoyed the hell out of me, which made no sense either. I wasn't happy when Davey and Sam were holding hands, and I wasn't happy when they weren't.

What kind of person did that make me? Hormonal, probably.

"I'd say we did rather well for ourselves," said Aunt Peg, exiting the ring.

"You would," I teased as we all headed back toward the grooming tent. "You're the one holding the purple ribbon."

"Nonsense. Faith acquitted herself quite well for her first try. And so did you."

Coming from Aunt Peg, that was high praise.

"Really?" I asked, eager to hear more.

"Which isn't to say there aren't a few things you could work on for next time. . . ."

I never should have pressed my luck.

"I'm hungry!" Davey announced. We were passing by the food tent. The aroma wafting from the large grills had no doubt cued his remark. "When are we having lunch?"

"Soon," I told him. Faith had to have the tight, show ring topknots taken down and replaced with looser, more comfortable ones. Her ear hair needed to be wrapped in its protective plastic wraps; and the hair spray in her neck hair needed to be broken apart and brushed out.

"But I'm hungry now!"

I hesitated just long enough to check out the length of the lines. They wrapped twice around the tent.

"You two go on," said Sam. "Start brushing out. Davey and I will pick lunch for everyone and meet you back at the set-up."

"Yeah!" cried my son, the shameless manipulator.

"You don't have to do that—"

"I know I don't." Sam piled his grooming supplies into my arms as Davey handed me Faith's leash. "See you in a few minutes."

"Well?" Aunt Peg said as we continued walking.

"Now what?" I snapped. She was about to reel off a list of Sam's virtues, I just knew it.

"Nothing," Aunt Peg permitted herself a small smile. "Nothing at all."

We went back to the grooming tent and got the Poodles undone. Now that we were finished showing, tension dissolved and nerves went back to normal. Over at the Shamrock set-up however, the maelstrom of activity continued.

From the look of things, Angie and Rick had brought more than a dozen dogs to the show. I knew that the large strings were necessary since professional handlers got paid by the dog. But without Jenny on the team, not only had they cut their manpower by a third, but they'd also lost their most valuable member.

Every handler works to present a facade of calm and capable efficiency. But at the Shamrock set-up the cracks were showing. Rick had two Brittanys out and ready to go up to the ring; but Angie who would normally have provided the extra hands he needed, was doing Jenny's old job of scissoring a Bichon Frise.

Aunt Peg was still working on Peaches. Faith who had much less hair was just about ready to go back in her crate. Sam and Davey weren't back with the food yet. From the look of the lines, they'd probably still be a while.

"Can I help?" I asked.

"Would you?" Rick said gratefully. As I stepped around the crates separating us, he was already thrusting a leash into my hands. "All you have to do is come up to the ring with me and hold the bitch while I show the dog, then hold the dog while I'm in with the bitch. It shouldn't take more than ten minutes, tops."

Easy as pie. Even a novice like myself could handle that. Rick took off at a jog and I fell in behind him. The leggy, compact bitch he'd handed me came just to the middle of my thighs. She was liver and white with a short tail and high-set ears. Not at all perturbed to have been consigned to a stranger, she bounded energetically across the field.

At ringside, Rick picked up both numbers. His class was called almost immediately and all I had to do was mind the bitch and watch. In handling class, Jenny had done most of the handling demonstrations and I knew how good she was. But now I realized that although Rick lacked some of her magic, he was an excellent technician.

Though the dog went reserve which meant that it didn't win any points, Rick accepted the ribbon with a smile and a nod. We switched Brittanys at the gate and he went back in with the bitch. The entry in females was larger and Rick looked more determined. Time and again, he used subtle shifts in positioning and graceful cues from his hands to draw the judge's attention to his bitch's best points. Watching his masterful performance, I wasn't at all surprised when the judge awarded him Winners Bitch and then, in the Best of Breed competition, Best of Opposite Sex over two specials.

"That's good, right?" I said when he came out. Even though Aunt Peg wasn't around to jab me, I still didn't want to repeat my earlier mistake.

"It's great!" Rick was beaming. "Going Best Op from the classes gave her a major. Her owners will be thrilled."

"Congratulations, then."

"Thanks." Rick glanced over at the schedule posted by the gate. "You can take the dog back if you want. I'm going to wait and get a picture. The judge will break after she finishes Gordon Setters and I'm sure the owners will want one."

"I've got time to wait with you," I said. This was just

the opportunity I'd been looking for. "You look pretty busy today."

"It's always hectic at a show."

"I guess most of your clients must have decided to hang on after . . ."

"After Jenny died?" Rick faced me squarely. "Don't be afraid to say it. I'm not. In the beginning I thought maybe if I didn't talk about it, it wouldn't really be true. But then I realized it was, and nothing I could do or say was going to change that. And yes, thank God, most of the clients did stick with me. I'd rather be busy. It's the only thing that helps."

Rick glanced around and checked the ring. The judge was taking her time deciding between two Open bitches.

"I met a friend of Jenny's the other day," I said casually. "A woman named Crystal Mars. Maybe you know her."

Rick's features tightened. "She may have been an acquaintance of my wife's, but she certainly wasn't any friend."

"You sound very sure of that."

"I am."

His vehemence was surprising. Especially in light of the fact that Crystal had Jenny's dog. She had said Rick knew nothing about Ziggy and at the time I hadn't really believed her. Now it looked as though she might have been right.

In the ring, the judge had finished with the Open Bitch class in Gordon Setters. Winners came next, then Best of Breed. I only had another minute or so and I needed to make it count. "Were you there the day that Ziggy got run over?" I asked.

"No, I wasn't. I've thought about that a lot. Who knows

if maybe there was something I could have done. But Jenny was home by herself." Rick's frown deepened. "God, I can't believe I lost both of them at once. Sometimes life really stinks, you know?"

Score one for Crystal.

"But Ziggy was Jenny's dog, right? So it's not like you were really attached to him."

"How can you say that?" Rick looked surprised. "Ziggy was Jenny's and my pet. We had a running joke about how he was our only child. That Mini went everywhere with us and I wouldn't have had it any other way. Did Jenny ever tell you where Ziggy came from?"

I shook my head.

"I got him for her as a wedding present. I knew she'd always wanted a Poodle, but she felt she had too many other dogs to take care of to be able to afford the luxury of having one of her own." Rick half smiled as he thought back. "I didn't know the first thing about Miniature Poodles and I spent six months researching lines until I'd found just the right puppy.

"Then I tied a big blue bow around his neck and delivered him to her in a basket the morning of our wedding. He got all excited and peed on the new shoes she'd bought to go with her dress. Jenny just laughed and laughed. She said that seemed like a fitting way for us to begin our lives together."

The Brittany nudged against my legs and nosed my pocket for liver. I reached down and scratched beneath its chin, grateful for the distraction.

"Over time I guess Ziggy became more Jenny's dog than mine," said Rick. "But that was his choice, not ours. We both loved him. After he died, I was looking into buying another puppy."

"You were?"

"Yeah." Rick shrugged. "Some couples have babies to keep them together. I guess we had dogs."

"Sir, are you waiting for a picture?" While we'd been talking, the Gordon Setters had finally finished. Walkie-talkie in hand, the steward was leaning out of the ring and beckoning to Rick. "I've called for the photographer if you want to come in and get set up."

"Thanks." He smoothed the Brittany's coat. "Be right back."

I watched him walk away. Why didn't anyone give me any answers? I wondered. All I ever got was more questions.

When we got back to the grooming tent, lunch had arrived. Aunt Peg was munching daintily on a hamburger. Sam was sharing a hot dog with Peaches; and Davey was up to his elbows in a sausage and onion grinder.

"Look what Sam got me!" he said happily.

Another case of good intentions run amok. I knew I was the only parent in the group, but was I also the only one with any common sense?

"Sausage and onions?" I tilted a brow in Sam's direction.

"Sure. My nephews love them."

Ah yes, I remembered these children. The nephews who lived at other ends of the country that he only got to see once or twice a year. Presumably their mothers spent the other eleven months recovering from his visits.

"You'll be up all night," I told Davey.

"Yippeee!" he cried. So much for suffering the consequences.

"He'll be fine," said Sam. "Trust me."

"She doesn't trust anyone with that child," Aunt Peg confided. "She's over-protective."

"Can't you at least wait until my back's turned to talk about me?"

"How do you know we weren't?" Aunt Peg said mildly.

Well, that made me feel much better.

I thought I heard Sam chuckling, but when I turned to look, he merely pointed to a cardboard box that was sitting on top of my grooming table. "We've got a hamburger and a hot dog left. Which do you want?"

"Hot dog. Thanks." I helped myself and Sam took the last burger.

"Is it time to go home yet?" asked Davey.

"Almost. There's just one more thing I want to see."

"What's that?" asked Peg.

"The Sporting group." I glanced toward the Shamrock set-up. For the moment, Angie had disappeared and Rick was busy talking to a client. "It's scheduled for two-thirty, right?"

Sam consulted the judging schedule. "Right. When did you develop an interest in sporting dogs?"

"Fairly recently." Rick didn't seem to be paying any attention to us, but I still had no intention of explaining while he might overhear. "I'll tell you all about it later."

After we finished eating, there was just enough time to hop Davey down off the crate, clean off the worst of the sausage and onions that now decorated his shirt, and take him for a walk around the back parking lot. When I was little, I was fixated on horses. For Davey, it's cars and trucks. He loves everything about them. And as far as he's concerned, the best thing about dog shows are the fancy vans, motor homes, and converted buses that many of the professional handlers use to transport their dogs.

He and I have a deal. When he comes to a dog show, he'll be patient while I do what I need to do; then I'll be patient while he oohs and aahs over the big rigs. The arrangement suits both of us pretty well.

We got back to the rings just as the Terrier group was finishing. Harry Flynn won it with a Scottie, then reappeared only moments later in the Sporting group with a Springer Spaniel. The group dogs arranged themselves in size order. Several places in line behind Harry stood Angie and Charlie.

"So Rick did let her show the dog," I said, coming up to stand beside Sam and Aunt Peg.

"Looks that way," said Aunt Peg. "Now let's see if it pays off."

"Let me see! Let me see!" Davey elbowed his way to the front. I stood him by the rail and kept a hand on his shoulder to discourage any thoughts he might have of disappearing.

"Rick Maguire?" Sam asked under his breath. Clearly he was experienced in the way of ringside chit-chat. Rule Number One: never talk about a dog in the ring in a voice loud enough to be overheard because without fail someone attached to the dog is standing within earshot.

I nodded. "The ascob Cocker is his. Or to be more precise, he was Jenny's dog to show. That's Jenny's sister, Angie, in with him now."

Angie was nervous. Even from ringside, I could see that. But while nerves fluster me, they seemed to energize her. The first time around the ring, with all the dogs gaiting together, she was a mess. But from there, her performance improved steadily. As for Charlie, the Cocker knew he had a job to do and he did it.

None of us were surprised when the pair made the cut. And by the time the final placements were made, Charlie was putting on such a show that winning seemed almost inevitable. The applause, when the judge pointed to the buff Cocker for first, was long and sustained.

Angie accepted the rosette and the trophy that went with it. She left the ring and walked straight over to where Rick and Mrs. Byrd were waiting. The older woman was smiling with satisfaction. Rick enveloped Angie in a hug. Charlie leapt up and down, clamoring for attention.

They all looked so happy. Dog, handler, and owner celebrating the success their efforts had achieved. Except that one vital member of the team was missing. Gone, never to return. Why was I the only one who was thinking about her?

❧❀ *Twelve* ❀❧

The day had gone so well up to that point that I decided to prolong it by inviting everyone back to my house for pizza. Sam accepted immediately. That made me feel terrific, until I remembered the dirty breakfast dishes in the sink and the toys scattered around the living room floor.

Aunt Peg accepted too, but I'd known she would. All day long, she'd been watching me watch Rick and Angie. She wouldn't ask any questions at the show—Aunt Peg was much too savvy for that—but I knew she was dying to find out what was going on.

We formed a caravan heading home. Aunt Peg led the way because she can't stand to drive behind anyone else. The sight of a traffic-filled highway brings out all her competitive instincts and woe to the driver on the road with her who doesn't ignore the speed limit in the passing lane. I'd ridden with her often enough to be glad Davey and I were safe in the Volvo, following along behind.

Once we crossed the Whitestone Bridge, Aunt Peg took

off and I knew we wouldn't see her again until we got home. But there in my rearview mirror was Sam's Bronco, its steady presence a curious comfort. A woman alone can find pleasure in the most mundane things.

Davey had had plenty of stimulation at the show. By the time the pizza arrived, he was having trouble keeping his eyes open. He gulped down a slice and a half, extracted a promise that I would save the leftovers for him, then trundled off to bed with Faith and Peaches trailing in his wake.

By common consensus the conversation had remained light while he was with us. But no sooner had his pajama-clad feet padded up the stairs than Aunt Peg got down to business. "I want to hear everything," she said. "What in the world is going on?"

"For starters, Ziggy's alive."

"He's not!"

"He is."

"Who's Ziggy?"

This last was from Sam. He helped himself to his third slice of pizza while Aunt Peg and I filled him in on the background, including the fact that nobody seemed to think that Jenny's death was an accident anymore.

"But Ziggy can't be alive," Aunt Peg argued when that was done. "Jenny said he was dead."

"Jenny was lying."

"Or mistaken," said Sam.

"This was no mistake. Ziggy was never hit by a car at all. Jenny took him up to a boarding kennel in Stratford. She paid two weeks in advance and told the owner she'd be back for him."

"You mean two weeks later she was suddenly going to

produce the dog alive?" Aunt Peg frowned. "That doesn't make sense."

"It gets worse. Crystal Mars—the woman who owns the kennel—told me that Rick hated Ziggy. Jenny hadn't exactly said as much, but Crystal assumed that's why the Mini was there. But today when I asked Rick about Ziggy, he said the dog was his pet, that he was the one who bought him in the first place as a wedding present for Jenny."

"What a sweet idea," said Aunt Peg.

Sam ignored the sentiment and went straight for logic. "If Rick feels that way, why is Ziggy still with Crystal Mars?"

"Because apparently, like everyone else, he thinks the Mini is dead." I lifted the box top and took my time, deliberating between the two sides of the pizza: pepperoni and onion or mushroom and sausage.

"That's crazy!" cried Aunt Peg.

"Tell me about it." Sausage and mushroom won out. I slid a thick slice onto my plate. "And here's something else."

"There's more?" Aunt Peg laid down her fork.

"See? I told you you should have answered those phone messages."

"You should have tried me," said Sam. "I would have called back."

It's hard to smile with pizza in your mouth, but I managed it. Did I mention he has the bluest eyes I've ever seen . . . ?

"Oh pish," said Aunt Peg, looking back and forth between us. "You two can save that for later. I want to hear the rest of the story."

It was like trying to sneak a kiss under the watchful eye of the prom chaperone. This was no way to conduct a relationship. I chewed and swallowed slowly. "Where was I?"

"Promising me more, I believe."

"Right. Remember how Angie told me at the wake that Jenny had been unhappy? She implied that maybe her sister had committed suicide?"

"You didn't tell me that," said Sam.

"At the time, I didn't believe it. But now Angie says she's found a suicide note."

"A note?" Aunt Peg shifted in her seat. "What did it say?"

"I don't know all the details, but it was something about how Jenny felt she had nothing to live for and losing Ziggy was the last straw."

"Except she hadn't lost him!" Aunt Peg cried. "Didn't you just tell us that?"

"Don't yell at me. I'm just telling you what I know."

"Try this on for size," said Sam. "Maybe Jenny *was* desperately unhappy. The fact that you weren't aware of it doesn't necessarily mean it wasn't so. Her sister seems to believe that."

"Rick doesn't," I pointed out.

"Rick might have been the problem. And if so, he's hardly likely to admit it. Suppose Jenny *was* planning to commit suicide. Everything you've told me suggests that she adored that Miniature Poodle."

Aunt Peg and I both nodded.

"So she'd have wanted to make sure that he was very well provided for. For one reason or another, she doesn't seem to have trusted Rick to provide that care, so she took him up to Stratford and left him with Crystal Mars."

Before he was finished, I was already shaking my head. "You should have seen the way Rick looked when he talked about losing Ziggy. He was all broken up."

"Then why didn't you give him the good news and a set of directions to Stratford?"

I had to admit, Sam had me there. "Because there are still too many unanswered questions for me to be entirely convinced about anything."

"I think you're wrong, Sam." Aunt Peg picked up a piece of crust and nibbled around the edges. "Because Jenny really did care about that dog. And if she didn't tell Crystal what she was doing, how could she know for sure that Ziggy would continue to be cared for? What if when the bills stopped being paid, Crystal had just turned the dog out? There are a lot of kennel owners who'd do exactly that."

"Then you think that when Jenny dropped Ziggy off, she had every intention of going back for him. And if that's the case, she couldn't have killed herself."

"Then why did she write a suicide note?" asked Sam.

I propped my elbows on the table and covered my face with my hands. "It's all impossible, every bit of it. This whole thing is giving me a headache."

"Have another beer, dear." Aunt Peg patted my arm comfortingly. "That will help."

"Three straight shots of tequila couldn't help this," I said, but I got up, went to the refrigerator and served another beer all the way around.

Aunt Peg looked longingly at the last remaining slice of pizza, then pushed her plate away. "Why do you suppose Jenny felt she had nothing to live for?"

Since Aunt Peg hadn't taken it, I split the piece and put half on Sam's plate and half on my own. "You know Rick said something today that made me wonder. He was talking about how after Ziggy died, he had looked into finding another puppy for Jenny. He said other couples had babies to keep them together. He and Jenny had dogs."

"So there *was* trouble in that marriage," Aunt Peg mused. "Maybe he was thinking about leaving her."

"Maybe she was thinking about leaving him," said Sam.

"Then why didn't she just go? Why kill herself instead?"

"Because she felt she had nothing to live for," said Sam, quoting the note.

We'd talked ourselves around in a circle. And if things had become any clearer along the way, I certainly hadn't noticed it.

We finished off the last of the pizza and I dumped the dishes in the sink on top of those from breakfast. I offered to make tea, but Aunt Peg shook her head.

"No, thank you. Dinner was lovely, but Peaches and I should be getting home." She pecked each of us on the cheek, whistled for her Poodle and let herself out the front door.

"Well . . ." I said, knitting my fingers together. Alone at last. Now what? "I should go up and check on Davey."

"Go ahead," said Sam. "Do you want me to start coffee?"

I shook my head and made my getaway. Or was it runaway? And why did I suddenly feel so skittish? Like if I stayed one more moment in that kitchen we were both going to spontaneously combust. The trouble was, half of me wanted that like crazy. The other half was scared to death.

Davey, of course, was fine. He'd kicked off his covers but his breathing was deep and even. Faith, who'd draped her body along the length of his, supplied all the warmth he needed. She looked up as I entered the room and thumped her tail quietly, then laid down her head and went back to sleep. So much for finding any excuses upstairs.

Back downstairs, I passed through the living room. I half expected to find Sam there, arranging for some soft lighting or slipping a CD in the player. The room was empty and I followed the sound of running water to the kitchen.

Sam was standing at the sink washing dishes.

Relief had me laughing. And once I started, I couldn't stop.

Sam glanced back over his shoulder. "What are you laughing at?"

"Myself, I think."

"Oh?"

"This isn't where I expected to find you."

Sam rinsed off the last plate, then stacked it in the drain board and dried off his hands on a towel. "I thought you might take some time upstairs."

"Maybe slip into something more comfortable?"

He crossed the room and wound his arms around me. "A man can always hope."

"Sam, I . . ."

He silenced the thought with a kiss. That was just as well, because I had no idea what I intended to say. Sam, I want you? Sam, I don't want you? Well that was a lie. But when he drew back, at least I knew what I needed to say.

"Sam, I'm not ready."

"For what?"

His fingers were tracing lazy circles over my back. Points of heat spiraled outward from his touch. If I didn't get the words out soon, it was going to be much, much too late.

"For this . . . for something serious . . . something irrevocable."

"Nothing's irrevocable." His voice was low and husky. It made me want to believe everything he had to say.

I braced both hands against his shoulders and pushed gently away. "I can't. I just need more time."

"Okay." He released his hands and I stepped back. I was almost sorry he'd let go so easily. "Let's see," he said, considering. "Something that isn't serious. How about if we sit on the couch and neck like teenagers?"

"When I was a teenager, we did our necking in cars."

His brows waggled comically. "I'm game if you are."

I giggled at the expression on his face. For a moment, it almost was like being a teenager again. I felt giddy, light-headed, and more than a little tempted. "How about if we sit on the couch and talk?"

He took my hand and we went into the living room. The lights were off and we didn't turn them on. Luckily neither one of us tripped over any toys. Sam sat down first, then pulled my hand so that I ended up close beside him. Very close. I felt his lips on the side of my throat. My pulse began to race.

"I thought we were going to talk."

"Go ahead," Sam murmured. "I'm listening."

Okay, so I gave up. But just for a few minutes. Just long enough to discover that kissing Sam could reawaken every nerve ending in my entire body. Long enough to wonder if I was fighting the inevitable. And if so, wouldn't it make more sense to simply give in. . . .

That's when Sam stood up.

"I've got to go," he said.

"But—"

He leaned down for one last hard kiss. "If I don't leave now, I won't leave at all."

That was my cue to tell him to stay. That was my chance to satisfy the part of my soul that yearned for him like a flower tilting toward the sun. But instead, I let him go. Instead, I said nothing at all.

I sat on the couch, listened to the sound of my own breathing and watched out the front window as his taillights disappeared down the road. Why should I think I can figure out what happened between Rick and Jenny?

Sometimes I don't even understand myself.

⌘❀ *Thirteen* ❀⌘

Davey was going to be a fireman for Halloween. The year before he'd been a clown and the costume, bought big, still fit. But what was appropriate for preschool and what would impress his peers in kindergarten were, apparently, two different things. My child was aiming for a more grown-up image; and after I'd ruled out Dracula, who could drip blood, and the Creature from the Black Lagoon, who could drip gore, we'd settled on the fireman idea. The costume didn't drip anything—although I'd volunteered to spray him with water—but it did have a helmet with an ear-splitting siren and Davey seemed to think that was almost as good.

On Halloween, the children were to bring their costumes to school in a bag and then change at noon for the costume parade and party. The older kids could take care of themselves, but those in the younger grades all seemed to need help at once. Every available adult was pressed into service.

I started in Davey's room, helping with snaps and zippers and applying make-up, most of which consisted of dripping blood and gore. Three Cinderella wands had to be found and sorted out, and I rescued a bent tiara from beneath a pile of blocks.

Then I made the mistake of telling my son he looked cute in his costume and snapping a picture. He fussed, his friends laughed, and I decided it was time to move on. When I was his age, cute was a good thing. When did five-year-olds become so sophisticated?

I'd promised Betty Winslow some back-up, so I headed to her room next. The kindergarten classroom had been a study in controlled chaos; the third graders were aiming for total pandemonium. The decibel level alone was enough to rattle the windows. Batman and Superman were leaping from desk to desk. A dinosaur with a long, spiked tail had knocked three plants from the windowsill; and a laser gun fight had broken out near the sinks.

None of which seemed to particularly perturb Betty, who was sitting in a corner with a tear-streaked fairy princess on her lap. She had a needle and thread in one hand and several pins in her mouth, and she was busy repairing a rip in the back of the costume. A swashbuckling pirate with eye patch and tin foil sword, who looked suspiciously like he might have been responsible, was hovering anxiously in the background.

"Feel free to jump in anywhere you want," said Betty, mumbling around the pins. "But watch out for that Samurai over there. He kicks."

"Got it."

I made my way cautiously into the room, thinking it was a good thing I wasn't going to be around after the party when all the little darlings would be buzzed on a sugar high. Amazingly, despite the state of general upheaval, everyone seemed to be in pretty good shape.

I had an extra look to make sure "my" kids were all okay, and had to scan the room twice before I found Timmy Doane. Then I was working by process of elimination. There were three ghosts, all appropriately draped in white sheets with holes cut out for the eyes. Two were chasing each other around the room, one of them stopping every so often to lift little girls' skirts. The third ghost was sitting off by himself, staring out the window and waiting patiently for the parade to start.

Timmy, it had to be.

As a mother, my heart went out to him. It wasn't just that he was shy. In the work we'd done together so far, I'd also found him slow to offer input, and easily swayed from those few opinions I'd managed to draw out. His self-esteem was at such a low ebb that he couldn't imagine how anything he had to say could possibly be of value.

I walked over at sat down beside him. "Hi, Timmy."

He turned and looked. "Ms. Travis." He sounded pleased and I wondered if he was smiling. "How'd you know it was me?"

"I'm a good guesser. I like your costume."

"It isn't much." His hands fiddled with the folds of cloth.

"It's perfect. What could be better than a ghost on Halloween?"

"I guess it's okay."

"Are you looking forward to the parade?"

"Not really."

He looked so small and defenseless sitting there, I wanted to gather him into my arms. "How come?"

"When I walk, my sheet drags. Then the other kids step on it and it moves around and I can't see."

He stood so I could check out the extent of the problem. The sheet was definitely too big and its excess fabric pooled around his feet. I lifted the material and rearranged it over his narrow shoulders, but as soon as I let go, the ends still fell in soft folds to the ground.

I tried making some gathers at his waist. "How about a belt?"

Timmy made a disgusted sound. "Ghosts don't wear belts."

I thought some more. "How about a sword?" With all the pirates and knights and ninjas running around, there was bound to be an extra weapon somewhere.

"How's that gonna help?"

"I was thinking that if you had a sword and waved it around a little bit and yelled "Get back! Get back!" like you were a very fierce ghost, maybe no one would come close enough to step on your sheet."

Timmy pondered that. "It might work. Do you have a sword?"

"I can get one."

I stood up and went to have a look. I liked the idea that Timmy was willing to take positive action to solve his problem. I also thought there was a small chance that having a sword to wave around might bolster his confidence a little. At the very least it would force him to interact with the other kids. Bearing all that in mind, I figured I was going to come up with a sword if I had to knock the samurai down and steal his.

Fortunately that wasn't necessary. Betty had a box of props in the closet and halfway down, I found a perfectly serviceable plastic lance. By the time I got back to Timmy, the kids were already forming a line. Predictably, he was near the end. I handed the weapon over.

"Don't come too close," he warned, shaking it at the sheriff behind him. "I wouldn't want to have to poke you."

"You poke and I'll shoot," the sheriff replied.

If these two kids grew up to be terrorists, I supposed they'd have their third grade special ed. teacher to blame.

"Go ahead," said Timmy. "Make my day."

Then the line lurched forward. As Timmy started to walk, the sheriff dropped back respectfully. Just before he reached the end of the hall, Timmy gave me a thumbs up.

At least I think that's what it was. Mostly it just looked like a sheeted arm poked in the air. I returned the gesture and he turned the corner and was gone.

If only the rest of life's problems could be solved so easily.

After two weeks off, handling class started up again that Thursday. I fed Davey an early supper, left him in the baby-sitter's capable hands, and met Aunt Peg there. I'd expected there to be some initial awkwardness as the class had been very much Jenny's domain; but Rick and Angie had obviously worked everything out ahead of time in an effort to make the transition go as smoothly as possible.

Angie was waiting by the door just as her sister had, taking the fees, marking attendance and joking lightly with the students. When the class started and the line split in half—big dogs in front, small dogs to the rear— Angie handled Jenny's duties at the other end of the room as if she'd been doing it all her life.

At times, she'd lift her hand to make a correction just as Jenny had done, or use one of her sister's phrases to make a point. Angie's hair was floating loose around her shoulders and the family resemblance was suddenly much more striking than I'd ever noticed before. Or maybe it was just that this was the first time I'd seen her in a capacity I associated so strongly with her sister.

I looked around at the rest of the class. Everyone else seemed to be taking the switch in stride, and even I had to admit that Angie was doing a fine job. The problem was that as effortlessly as she slipped into Jenny's shoes, Angie couldn't make me forget her sister. Or the little black Miniature Poodle that should have been sitting on the stage, chewing on a stuffed rat and overseeing the proceedings.

As soon as class ended I rushed Faith out and locked her in the car. When I got back inside, Rick was over in one corner working out some aggression problems with an overeager Rottweiler. Angie had started to roll up the mats.

"Here," I said, squatting down beside her. "Let me help you with that."

Angie blew a cool stream of air upward to ruffle her bangs. "Thanks."

The wide green rubber mats had been laid out in a square around the outside of the room, with one long mat bisecting the middle to form two triangles. Their purpose was to give the dogs traction on an otherwise slippery floor, and most handling teachers tended to bring their own. In theory the mats, once rolled, were portable; but only a longshoreman could have carried them comfortably.

I placed both hands on my side of the partially rolled

mat and began to push. On the other side, Angie did the same.

"What did you think of class?" she asked.

"It went very well. You do a good job."

Her smile was quick and pleased. "Thanks."

"You seem to get along well with Rick."

"Yeah." The smile widened. "He and I are buddies."

We reached the end of one mat, pushed the finished roll aside, then turned the corner to begin again. I waited until we'd got the new end tucked under and started rolling, then said, "I guess he and Jenny were having some problems, huh?"

"What makes you say that?"

"It just occurred to me during class. It seems easier now, you know? Like there's less tension around." It was a lie, but I was hoping Angie was self-centered enough to fall for it. She was.

"I guess there is," she agreed. "Rick and I work together pretty well. And it's different living together, when you're not married."

Interesting choice of words. Although Rick and Angie were indeed living in the same house, I hadn't thought of them as "living together." I couldn't imagine Rick did either. He'd always treated her very much as a little sister.

"Being married is hard," I said. "I was married once, briefly."

"Yeah." Angie looked up as we inched the mat along the floor. "I saw your kid at the show. He's cute."

"Thanks."

"Are you divorced now?"

I nodded. "Four years."

"That's tough. Jenny and Rick almost got divorced once."

I over-balanced, nearly fell, then managed what I hoped was a graceful recovery. "Really?"

"Yeah, it was supposed to be a secret, but I don't see how it matters now. Jenny filed and everything, but Rick just went crazy. He said he loved her too much to let her go."

We reached the end of another mat, shoved that one aside, and went on to the next. Now that I'd gotten Angie started talking, I was determined she wouldn't get distracted. "Then what happened?"

"Rick convinced her to come back. He told her they could work everything out."

"And did they?"

"I guess. I mean, they stayed together, didn't they?"

"If Rick and Angie had divorced, what would have happened to the dogs?"

Angie considered before answering. "Things never got that far. But I think Jenny would have just left the whole thing to Rick."

"But it was her business, too!"

"It was," Angie agreed. "But Jenny was getting pretty tired of all that. Even way back in the beginning, she never became a handler because she loved it so much. She started handling because she was eighteen years old and out on her own and it was the only thing she knew how to do."

I remembered the story. The version I'd heard hadn't contained many details. "She left home pretty young, didn't she?"

"Yeah, I guess."

I guess. That seemed to be Angie's stock answer to just about everything. Maybe it was time to try shaking things up a little.

"You were even younger, but you moved out, too." I waited a minute, but Angie didn't offer any comment. "How come?"

I wasn't looking at Angie, but I knew she'd stopped pushing when the mat suddenly became twice as heavy in my hands. I stopped too, and looked up.

"It was no big deal," she said carefully. "It was just time."

We finished rolling the rest of the mat in silence. Then Rick came to help us and I left the two of them to it. They hoisted the rolls and carried them out to their van. I sat in my car and watched, frowning.

According to Angie, Rick had told Jenny that he would never let her go. Now she was gone and in her place he had Jenny's sister, a younger, more tractable version of the woman he had loved. A woman he was already living with in the house he'd shared with his wife. A wife who apparently had begun to rebel against some of the restrictions in her marriage.

It gave me plenty to think about.

ᐁ✻ *Fourteen* ✻ᐁ

Aunt Peg and Sam both had Poodles entered in the shows that weekend in Massachusetts. My puppy was staying home. At her age, she was only showing to get experience and once a month was plenty.

Saturday, Standard Poodles had been scheduled for early in the morning; but Sunday the judging time was at a reasonable hour and Davey and I had promised to take a ride up and cheer for the home team. There was little doubt in my mind that I'd feel vastly more comfortable with Sam inside the ring and me out. That way he could put on the performance while I carried the supplies and stood at ringside looking knowledgeable.

Saturday morning I called Alice Brickman to see if Joey could come over for the afternoon. The biggest problem with having an only child is the perpetual search for playmates. When they're by themselves, they're bored. Then when their friends come over, they spend half the time fighting. Your basic lose-lose situation. But I'm a mother, which means I keep trying anyway.

"Joey's cousins are here visiting for the weekend," said Alice. Judging by the noise in the background, he had a battalion of them at least. "Why don't you bring Davey here instead? When you've got six kids to look after, what's one more?"

Possibly the last straw, I thought, but who was I to argue with a woman who was clearly bucking for sainthood? I ran the idea past Davey and he thought it sounded great. That's another truism of childhood. They would always rather go to the other kid's house because, without fail, his toys are better.

That left me with the whole afternoon free, a luxury which doesn't happen often. I thought about raking some more leaves, but that wasn't nearly decadent enough. I checked the local movie listings, but the only Saturday matinees available were Disney cartoons and another sequel to the *Mighty Ducks*. I could have taken myself out to lunch, or soaked in a bubble bath with the newest Sue Grafton. But in the end, I got in my car and drove up to Ridgefield on a quest for knowledge. I liked the sound of that. It made it seem like I might actually learn something for a change.

The Ridgefield Police Department looked nothing like I'd expected. I'd been prepared for industrial gray cinder block, or functional one-story brick. But signs on the edge of town directed me down a small hill, then up a big one. At the top stood a big old Victorian House, painted white on white, with its lawns paved over for parking. Wow. Maybe they'd be serving tea in the front parlor.

Inside, those hopes were quickly dashed. The interior of the building had been transformed into a model of a suburban police department. There was a waist-high counter, large panes of bullet-proof glass, and a small waiting area where I sat after stating my business.

I didn't have long to wait, which was good because the magazine selection varied only in age. Old editions of *Field and Stream* or slightly newer editions of *Field and Stream*. Take your choice.

A door led from the back of the station directly into the waiting area and I stood as it opened. The detective was of medium height and broadly built. He had dark eyes beneath bushy brows and darker hair that was neatly combed back and liberally sprinkled with gray.

"Ms. Travis? I'm Detective Petronelli. I understand you're looking to talk to someone about the Jenny Maguire case?" He had large, beefy hands and he held one out to me.

I took it and had my arm pumped up and down. "Yes, I am."

"Come on in back. We may as well sit in my office and get comfortable."

His office was barely past cubbyhole size, though it did have a window. Stacks of papers covered the tops of two file cabinets, but the surface of his desk was scrupulously neat. The two chairs we sat in pretty much took up all of the remaining space.

"What can I do for you?" he asked when we were seated.

I hadn't thought about what I was going to say. Now with the detective staring at me intently, I felt as though I should have prepared. "Jenny Maguire was a friend of mine," I began. "I guess the reason I'm here is because I don't understand how she died, or why. Rick Maguire told me you'd been investigating . . ."

"That's right, ma'am. We have." Petronelli opened the top drawer of his desk and took out a pen and a pad of paper. "Why don't we nail down a few details, if you don't mind?"

He led me through name, address, and phone number, and I was explaining about how I'd met Jenny at handling class before I realized how deftly he'd taken control of the discussion. Not that I minded. I was more than happy to share my information with him, as long as he'd share his with me.

I told him about Ziggy, presumably dead and now alive. I speculated as to whether Rick and Jenny had been happy together and wondered aloud why she'd filed for divorce then changed her mind. I stated firmly that I had *not* thought her to be a woman on the verge of suicide, and yet her sister had found a note that clearly contradicted my feelings.

Through it all, the detective took plenty of notes. And when I was done, he still didn't say anything. Maybe he figured if he kept silent, I might just keep on talking.

"Well?" I said.

Petronelli looked up.

"I showed you mine. Aren't you going to show me yours?"

At least I found out he could smile. Then he cleared his throat and we were all business again. "Ms. Travis, I'm sure you realize that I can't give out a lot of information about an ongoing investigation."

"Ongoing," I said quickly. "Does that mean you don't think Jenny's death was a suicide?"

"At the moment we're exploring several avenues—"

"What about the note?" I stopped as I suddenly

thought of something. "Rick did give it to you, didn't he?"

"Yes, ma'am, Rick Maguire did deliver a suicide note to us, one purported to be in his wife's handwriting. We received it several days after Mrs. Maguire died. I believe it had been found by the deceased's sister."

"In a desk," I prompted. "Under a pile of stuff. That's what Angie told me. If you were going to kill yourself, wouldn't you leave the note sitting out where someone could find it?"

"Well, Ms. Travis, I don't like to speculate about something like that. However, I will tell you that in this case the possibility of suicide seems remote."

Now we were getting somewhere. "Why is that?"

"According to the medical examiner's report, Mrs. Maguire died of circulatory failure brought on by chronic arsenic poisoning."

Petronelli paused as though that should mean something to me. It didn't.

He stood up and picked up a folder from the top of the file cabinet, opened it and began to read. "Traces of arsenic were found not only in the victim's digestive tract, but also the hair, fingernails, liver, and kidney."

"So she died of arsenic poisoning."

"*Chronic* arsenic poisoning."

"What's the difference?"

"Acute poisoning would mean that she ingested a large quantity of arsenic and died as a result. Not the way I would choose to commit suicide, but an option people have chosen. In the case of Mrs. Maguire, however, traces of the element were found in her organs. Her red blood cells had been affected. It was the opinion of the medical examiner that the poisoning had happened slowly over a period of time. Now I've known people to do weird things but in my experience, someone who's looking to kill themselves just does it. It's quick and it's done. Why cause yourself any more pain than you have to?"

"Slowly over a period of time," I said, frowning. "Like maybe from handling the rat poison Rick said they kept in the kennel?"

"No, ma'am, we checked the product they had on hand. It contained warfarin, which is an anti-coagulant. A lot of the older rat poisons contained arsenic, but not anymore. Now it's pretty hard to come by."

I stared out his window. A squirrel, its mouth crammed with nuts, was running up the tree outside. "So she definitely was murdered."

"Right now, it looks that way."

"Jenny was at my house a few days before she died. She told me she hadn't been feeling well. She had cramps, some nausea and headaches too, I think."

Petronelli nodded and made a note in the folder. "That would be consistent with the medical examiner's findings. She was probably suffering from the effects of the arsenic in her system."

"What about the suicide note?"

"What about it?"

"If Jenny didn't commit suicide, that might be a clue to point toward her killer."

"I don't think so. The note was written, not typed and we've had our experts look at it. For whatever reason, it was written by Mrs. Maguire. Maybe it was some sort of game she was playing, or a fragment of a letter she intended to send to a friend. She mentions the dog you spoke about earlier and says she has nothing to live for. It doesn't say she was about to kill herself. It looked like a suicide note, true. But the contents are also open to other interpretations."

I glanced past him. The squirrel was on the way back down for another load of nuts. "Who do you think killed her?"

"I'm afraid I can't speculate—"

"Who are you investigating?"

"I'm not at liberty to reveal that information—"

"All right, don't," I said, thinking aloud. "But if Jenny was poisoned slowly over a period of time, that would point to someone who lived with her, wouldn't it?"

"I would say that's a possibility. On the other hand, according to her husband and sister, she attended dog shows weekly, where she came in contact repeatedly with the same group of people, many of whom she was engaged in direct competition with."

So much for trying to narrow the field.

Detective Petronelli saw me back to the front door and handed me his card as I was leaving. "If you come across any other information you think we should have, you be sure and call this number."

I took the card and tucked it away in my purse. All their resources, all their experts; and I suspected the police were just as baffled as I was.

In the Northeast, during the warmer months, dog shows are held outside. Dog clubs compete for the best sites: usually large grassy fields with ample room for parking, rings and tenting. But as winter approaches, weather forces the clubs to move indoors. Good locations are at a premium and clubs must become highly creative in their hunt for appropriate and available sites.

The show on Sunday in Fitchburg was the first indoor dog show Davey and I had attended. Accustomed as I was to big rings, spacious tenting, and wide open spaces, finding just as much action crammed into a room—albeit a very large one—came of something as a shock. Rings filled the center of the big hall, with space set up for grooming along the side where we came in.

The other half of the room was filled with a long row of brightly colored concession booths. A quick glance revealed stands hawking everything from grooming supplies to canine art. I even saw a blue and white banner proclaiming the presence of Crystal's All Natural Dog Munchies.

Poodles were scheduled to be judged in ring three and Davey and I found Aunt Peg and Sam set up in the grooming area nearby. Though there were several hours yet before the Standards would be called to the ring, both had their Poodles out on the grooming tables and were busy brushing. All around them, a bevy of other Poodle exhibitors were doing the same.

"There's my young man!" Aunt Peg said to Davey. "Do I get a hug?"

"Maybe." His eyes took on a speculative gleam. "What will you give me?"

"Davey!"

"I was only kidding."

"I should hope so." I nudged him firmly between the shoulders and he skirted around the legs of the grooming table to greet his aunt properly.

Sam had watched the exchange with amusement. "Do I get a hug, too?" he asked me.

"Maybe . . ."

"Like mother, like son, I see. Born negotiators. I like that in a woman."

"Really? What else do you like?"

"Intelligence and a sense of humor, for starters."

"Then you've come to the right place. I do believe you'll get that hug after all."

My ex-husband, Bob, had hated public displays of affection, so I'd intended to step up and wrap my arms around Sam, then quickly pull away. But no sooner had I ducked around two crates and a grooming table to reach him than he opened his own arms and drew me in.

"I'm glad you came," he said. His body was warm and hard and pressed against the entire length of mine before he released me.

"So am I."

Aunt Peg cleared her throat loudly. "I'm glad to see you two are finally taking the hint."

Sam looked over my shoulder at her and lifted a brow innocently. "What hint?"

She harrumphed under her breath and turned away to rummage in her grooming box. Knowing Aunt Peg, she probably had doughnuts in there, along with the leashes, combs and sprays.

The latest issue of *Dog Scene* Magazine was sitting on top of Peaches's empty crate. I pushed it to one side and put Davey in its place. The crate was standard sized, which meant it was just high enough to keep him in place. Left to his own devices on the ground, he'd be gone in a matter of minutes.

"What'd I miss yesterday?"

Aunt Peg came up with a pair of eight-inch curved scissors. She nudged Peaches to her feet. "Sam's Casey took the points in bitches."

"Congratulations! That's great."

"Not so great," Aunt Peg said pointedly. "*I* went reserve. He's told me today's my turn."

Sam slipped me a wink.

"I saw that," said Peg.

"I figured you might." Sam grinned. Not much got past Peg. "Today's judge should like Peaches better."

"Yesterday's should have too. She's the better bitch."

"Says who?"

Aunt Peg drew on the dignity of her nearly sixty years. "The voice of experience."

"Pardon me, but I think that voice is biased."

If I didn't step in now, they could quibble over the respective merits of the two dogs for the next half hour. "So Sam won with Casey," I said, wrapping up. "What else happened?"

"The Doberman went Best."

Not a Doberman, *the* Doberman. That meant he was currently one of the very top-winning dogs, one that was so well known to the show going fraternity that his name didn't even have to be mentioned. Of course, being relatively new to Poodles and totally lacking when it came to Doberman Pinschers, I had no idea who she was talking about. Not that that seemed to bother Aunt Peg. She simply plowed on without me.

"Harry Flynn's Springer won the Sporting group."

"What about Charlie?"

"Second."

"Who showed him?"

"Angie again," said Sam. By now he knew enough

about what was going on to be keeping tabs, too. "She and Rick must have worked things out because Charlie seems to be her dog now."

I leaned back against the edge of the grooming table, being careful not to crowd the Poodle. "What happened? Did Angie blow it?"

"Not really," said Aunt Peg. "Charlie simply got beaten by another very good dog. Every judge has a different opinion, and that's what makes every dog show different. The Springer's a nice one. There's no reason he shouldn't win, except that right now, Charlie's the one with all the momentum. He's got a very nice ad in *Dog Scene* this week." She gestured toward the crate. "It's a tribute to Jenny. Take a look."

I did and saw that Davey had decided to occupy his time by thumbing through the trade journal. "What are you doing?" I asked.

"Reading."

That was wishful thinking on his part. He barely knew the letters of the alphabet. I glanced down over his shoulder and saw that he'd stopped at a picture of a particularly large Great Dane. "About what?"

"A pony. See?"

"Yes, I do. Do you mind if I look for a minute?" He shrugged and I lifted the magazine away and thumbed through the pages.

Dog Scene was the bible of the dog show world. Published weekly and mailed free to judges, it contained news, gossip, updates on AKC rulings, and most importantly, advertisements about all the top-winning dogs. What was the point of scoring a big win under a good judge if only the people who were actually at the show knew about it? *Dog Scene*, with its large audience and its flashy ads, made sure that all the people who should have been in the know, were.

"Where did you get this, Aunt Peg?"

"Pat came around passing out freebies under the theory that every exhibitor is a potential advertiser. I'm too cheap to subscribe, so I was happy to get one. The ad's near the beginning. Go back, I think you've passed it."

Of course, I should have known. In ads, as in real estate, location is everything; and the big players paid a premium for preferred positioning. I flipped back and came very quickly to a picture of a buff Cocker Spaniel.

Champion Shadowlands Super-Charged, the headline read. The page might have been intended as a tribute to Jenny, but the dog was still prominently featured.

"Hey, wow!" cried Davey. "Great car!"

"Where?"

"There. See?"

Of course, now that he pointed it out, I did. I'd been looking at the picture which was of Jenny and Charlie winning Best in Show at Devon in early October, presumably their last show together. But Davey was right, the ad did contain a car. A cartoon model of a souped-up sports car was roaring along just below the words Super-Charged in the dog's name.

"That's Charlie's logo," said Aunt Peg. "It runs in all his ads."

"Why does a dog need a logo?"

"To make him stand out and to give people something easy to remember," Sam explained. "After a while all those pictures of dogs and judges begin to look pretty much alike. And don't forget these same dogs are adver-

tised week after week. Somebody started the idea a couple of years ago and now they all do it.''

I flipped though the next few pages and saw what he
was talking about. A Chow Chow named Ruxpin had a
teddy bear; and a Whippet named Lullaby featured a mu-
sical score. I turned back and read the rest of Jenny's ad.
The copy was indeed intended as a tribute. It had been
written with great feeling by Florence Byrd and there was
a catch in my throat before I'd finished reading.

I wondered if Charlie's owner knew that her handler
had been murdered. Or, as I was beginning to suspect,
that Jenny had been trying to escape from an unhappy
marriage. Letting out a deep sigh, I slapped the magazine
closed and put it back down on the crate.

"Can you watch Davey for a few minutes?" I asked
Aunt Peg.

"Sure. What's up?"

"There's someone I want to see."

∽❋ *Fifteen* ❋∽

Crystal Mars's booth was midway down the concession line in front of a large window. Bounded by two merchandising behemoths whose dog care supplies were stacked halfway to the ceiling, her stand looked small and almost spartan by comparison. Maybe she should have brought along some wind chimes.

Crystal's waist-high counter held two bowls offering free samples of kibble and biscuits. There was a stack of brochures and a chart displayed on a tripod, touting the nutritional value of her foods compared to the other leading brands. Behind the counter was a pile of twenty-pound bags, a small metal cash box, and a chair for Crystal to sit on.

It was no-frills salesmanship, but it seemed to be working because when I arrived at the booth, there were several people in line waiting to hear what Crystal had to say. One thing I'd learned about dog people in the last few months: they're always looking for a better way. Softer brushes, richer shampoos, healthier and more pal-

atable foods—they're willing to try just about anything.
Whatever they're using is the best they've found so far,
but they're always open to suggestion.

I browsed at the booth next door until Crystal had a
free moment. By the time the line had been dealt with and
she'd sat down to light up a cigarette, I'd purchased a
large nylabone and a braided leather leash, and was seriously considering the merits of a forced air dryer. And
they say raising children is expensive.

I walked the few feet over and found Crystal opening
quarter rolls into the cash box on her lap and inhaling
smoke as though she was wishing she could mainline it.

"Crystal?"

"Yes?" She set the cash box aside and reached to stub
out her cigarette.

"Melanie Travis, remember? I was out at your kennel a
couple weeks ago."

"Sure, hi. How's the kibble working out?"

"Great. Faith loves it." I looked around behind the
counter, hoping I might find a playmate for Davey.
"Where's Sarah?"

"Home with a sitter. Her team had a soccer game today
and I hated for her to miss it." Her hand hovered reluctantly over a disposable foil ashtray. "Listen, do you
mind if I smoke? I've been waiting all morning for this."

"Go ahead. Just blow in the other direction, okay?"

"You got it." She took another drag. "With only one
dog, you can't be out of the kibble already. Ready to try
some biscuits?"

"Sure." That would buy me some time. I glanced down
at the selection. "The medium size, I guess."

"Whole wheat, charcoal, or peanut butter?"

"You're kidding, right?"

Crystal looked offended. She leaned down under the counter and pulled out all three bags so I could have a look. Not surprisingly, they all looked like dog biscuits. I pointed to the peanut butter, that being one of Davey's favorite foods. Like child, like Poodle, I hoped.

"I wanted to ask you how Ziggy was doing."

"He's fine." Crystal laid the bag of biscuits on the counter and went to write up a slip. "Why wouldn't he be?"

"No reason. It's just . . ." I stopped, feeling an absurd desire to look back over my shoulder. "Did you know that the police think Jenny was murdered?"

Her hand stilled in mid-air. "I heard it was an accident."

"So did I, at first. But it wasn't. She was poisoned, apparently on purpose."

She finished quickly with the slip and shoved it to me across the counter.

"Crystal, Jenny must have had a reason for hiding Ziggy away. If we could figure out what it was—"

"I told you before." Crystal snatched up my five-dollar bill and made change. "Jenny wanted to get the dog away from her husband."

"That was her side of it. It isn't Rick's."

She stared at me accusingly. "Did you tell him where Ziggy is?"

"Not so far."

"I guess that's something." She was still frowning.

"Why did Jenny pick you to leave Ziggy with?"

"I guess she knew I'd take good care of him."

"Even though you two weren't friends?"

"Who told you that?"

"Rick."

"Rick Maguire doesn't know what he's talking about. It's not the first time he's gotten something wrong and I'm sure it won't be the last." Crystal reached over and stubbed out her cigarette. "Look, I don't have time for this. I'm trying to run a business here."

I looked around. I was the only customer standing at the booth and I'd just paid four ninety-five for a bag of dog biscuits. I figured that entitled me to one more question.

"Was Jenny thinking about divorcing Rick again?"

"How would I know the answer to that?" She looked exasperated now; but also resigned, like maybe she'd realized that I wasn't going to leave until I was ready.

"Her sister told me she didn't care about the kennel and the business. She'd have left all that behind. But she cared about Ziggy. Is that why she wanted to get him away?"

"Look." Crystal braced both hands on the counter and leaned toward me, lowering her voice. "All I know is what I saw. Jenny always had Ziggy with her. She took him everywhere. So you'd think she would have been unhappy when she left him with me, but she wasn't. Just the opposite. It was almost like she was excited or something. Then bang! A week later she's dead. Something weird was going on. That's all I know."

On the way back to the grooming area, I bumped into Harry Flynn outside the Springer Spaniel ring. I could say it was fate, or even an accident, but considering I had to manhandle three people out of the way in order to throw myself in his path, I'd say good timing had more to do with it.

He'd just won Best of Breed with his dog which should have meant I'd be catching him in a good mood.

"Why don't you watch where you're going?" he snarled as we both righted ourselves. Being smaller, I was the one who'd suffered more damage. Harry wasn't tall, but he was tough. He'd rolled over me like a bulldozer.

"Harry Flynn." I tried out a smile.

"Yeah?" Now that he was going again, he didn't even break stride. "Who are you?"

"Melanie Travis." I fell in beside him. "We met at Jenny Maguire's funeral."

"If you say so."

We were weaving a circuitous route through the crowds back toward his set-up at the other end of the grooming area. The throngs of people pushing toward the rings were too thick for me to remain beside him. Instead I dropped behind a step and let Harry run interference for me. We reached his set-up and he tossed the purple and gold rosette on top of a tack box and slipped the Springer into a wire mesh crate.

"I've been wanting to talk to you," I said. "Do you have a minute?"

"No."

"How about if I talk while you work?"

"Make it fast." He was already pulling another dog out. "I got Cockers coming right up."

"It's about Jenny Maguire."

"What about her?"

There was no use beating around the bush with this man. "Why did you hate her?"

He hefted the Cocker onto the table and slipped a grooming loop over its head to hold it in place. "Who says I did?"

"You did . . . sort of. At the wake you called her a bitch."

"Hell, lady, I call lots of people bitches. Sort of an occupational hazard, I guess you might say." He laughed heartily at his own joke. The rough and raspy laugh of a two-pack-a-day man, it was harsh enough to sound painful.

"You also implied you were glad she was dead."

"No crime in that, far as I know. Any time the competition wants to do itself in, more power to them."

"It seems like you've been doing more winning now that she's out of your way."

"Maybe," said Flynn. He took a spray bottle and spritzed the Cocker lightly with water. "What about it?"

"I guess you heard she was murdered."

"So somebody didn't like her."

"Somebody like you?"

Flynn turned on a hand-held dryer and smoothed the Cocker's coat. "I don't know why you're so interested, but as it happens, you're right. I didn't like her."

"How come?"

"How come?" He chewed on that for a moment. "How come? Because she didn't have to start from scratch and make her own way like the rest of us. With her parents' name behind her, you knew the judges were going to sit up and pay attention right from the get-go. And they did, too."

"You resented her success, then."

"No, I resented the way she got her success. Jenny Maguire made it look easy. And it isn't easy. It's never easy.

You're scrambling to win, and you're scrambling to pay the bills. You're going to bed at midnight and getting up at three A.M. to drive two hundred miles to some God-forsaken fairground in the hope that you can keep everything together one more day. Take it from Harry Flynn. Making a living showing dogs is no picnic. It's damn hard work."

He replaced the loop with the Cocker's lead and swept the dog off the table into his arms. "Does that answer your question?"

He was gone before I could tell him it had.

When I got back to the set-up, Aunt Peg and Sam were engaged in the last stages of preparation for the ring. Peaches and Casey were standing on their tables having hair spray applied to their toplines to make the coat stand up and look as lush and profuse as possible. This was one of those things that had baffled me in the beginning, like using clippers on smooth-coated Whippets and back brushing Old English Sheepdogs. But by now I was inured to almost anything exhibitors might do to get their dogs ready to be shown. I didn't even look twice.

I did, however, gaze carefully around the set-up. In my absence my son seemed to have disappeared. I hoped it was a good sign that nobody seemed concerned.

"Where's Davey?"

"He found a friend." Aunt Peg nodded back over her shoulder and I saw that he was in the next row of crates. He and another boy about the same age were zooming matchbox cars up and down the side of a tack box. "*That* child's mother thought to bring toys."

I'd been afraid toy cars might get in the way and had

packed extra juice boxes, crayons, and paper. Aunt Peg clung to opinions, however, like a subway straphanger during a New York rush hour. There was no use even trying to explain. "Do you want me to go pick up your armbands?"

"Yes, please. Number sixteen."

"Ten for me," said Sam. "And check and see if the ring is on time, would you?"

Half a dozen other exhibitors were already waiting for armbands at ring three. Bichon Frises were being judged. I read over a spectator's shoulder, checked the numbers in the ring against those in the catalogue and realized I was watching Best of Breed which meant that the judge was on time and that Standard Poodles were next.

When my turn came, I collected the numbers I needed plus rubber bands to go with them. In the next ring over, Ascob Cocker Spaniels were just finishing. Flynn was nowhere in sight and Angie and Charlie were once again at the head of the line as the judge made her selection for Best Of Variety. Angie got her ribbon, picked up Charlie and strode from the ring. Last time I'd seen her win with the Cocker she'd been elated; now she accepted the prize as her due.

Glancing around, I realized that Rick hadn't come to oversee her performance. Obviously things had progressed to the point where he trusted Angie to show their most valuable client's dog without his supervision. And why not? Angie seemed to be doing just fine. In the month since Jenny had gone, she'd blossomed from being the shy assistant to holding center stage. She was taking on the top sporting dog handlers and, for the moment, beating them handily.

"Congratulations," I said as she walked past.

"Thanks. I didn't see you over here. Charlie was great, wasn't he?"

"He was. And so were you. It's amazing, isn't it?"

"What?"

"A month ago, you'd barely even been in the ring. And now look how far you've come."

Angie frowned. "I could have been doing this all along. I had the talent, I just didn't have the chance. Jenny never let me try."

"It helps to have a good dog," I said dryly.

To her credit, Angie had the grace to blush. "Charlie's the best. He put Jenny on the map and he can do the same for me. All I need with him is time."

Time. The one thing Jenny hadn't had.

Crystal Mars didn't think that Rick knew much about anything. Since Ziggy was still in Stratford, it seemed doubtful that Jenny had confided in her sister either, but it wouldn't hurt to ask. "I was wondering, do you know a woman named Crystal Mars?"

"No." The denial came too quickly to be entirely believable.

"She lives in—"

"I told you, I don't know her." Angie shouldered past me and disappeared into the crowd.

I might have spent more time wondering about that if I hadn't turned back to ring three and seen that the first class in Standard Poodles was already being judged. I hurried back to the set-up.

"Puppy Dogs are in," I said, handing out the arm-bands. "And Angie just won the Variety with Charlie."

"That's seven in a row." Aunt Peg hopped Peaches

down off the table, waited until she'd shaken out, then did some minor repairs to the carefully coifed coat.

"If she's so good, how come Jenny never let her handle?"

Aunt Peg looked up. "Who says she is?"

"Angie, for one."

Casey landed on the ground behind me with a quiet thump. She, too, enjoyed a leisurely shake. "Angie's adequate." Sam sprayed back a strand of fallen top-knot hair. "That's about it."

"Then why is she winning?"

"Half of it's Charlie," said Aunt Peg. "As for the rest, that girl's riding on her sister's coattails and reputation, that's all. Now lead the way and block for us. We've got to get going or we'll be late."

With me in front, arms spread wide to part the crowds so that the dogs wouldn't get jostled, we took the Poodles up to the ring. Puppy Bitches were in, followed by a Bred-By-Exhibitor class of two. The Open class, where both Sam and Aunt Peg were entered along with four or five others, came after that.

Crawford Langley was also waiting at ringside with his entry as were several other professional handlers I'd met during the summer. The judge was having a hard time deciding between two puppies, a black and a cream, both of whom looked pretty similar to me. I sidled over to where Crawford was standing.

He looked up and smiled, the consummate pro. His gray flannel pants bore a sharp crease and his burgundy jacket was set off by a pale yellow silk pocket square that picked up the flecks in his tie. "Not showing your pretty puppy today?"

Complimenting people's dogs came as naturally to Crawford as breathing. He was smart and savvy and played the game as well as anybody; and he had a long list of satisfied customers to show for it. He'd also been around long enough to know where most of the skeletons were buried. The problem was getting him to talk about them.

"No, I'm just here as a spectator. Crawford, you're friends with Roger and Lavinia Peterson, aren't you?"

"Used to be." He slipped a comb out of his pocket and smoothed it through the Poodle's long ears. "Since they moved south, I don't see that much of them anymore."

"Did you know Jenny and Angie when they were little?"

"About as well as I knew any kids." Crawford crooked a brow meaningfully. He was gay and kept his relationships discreet. "Which is to say, probably not very well at all."

"Jenny moved out when she was still a teenager and Angie followed soon after. Do you know why?"

He gazed over my shoulder into the ring. The Bred-By-class was in. "What does it matter now?"

"It matters because Jenny was murdered."

His eyes met mine. "Roger and Lavinia didn't have anything to do with that."

"Aunt Peg said Jenny and Angie were estranged from them. How come?"

Crawford hesitated. I knew he was hoping the steward would call his class and save him. Thankfully the judge was still taking her time. "It probably wasn't the easiest house to grow up in." he said finally. "Roger got around pretty good."

"Got around. You mean with other women?"

Crawford nodded. "It wouldn't have been so bad except he did it right under Lavinia's nose. And she wasn't the type to take anything lying down."

"Did they fight about it?"

"I'd say so."

There was something in his tone. . . .

"How bad?"

The judge was handing out the Bred-By ribbons.

"There's my class—"

"How bad, Crawford?"

"Bad enough." He started for the gate.

I followed right along behind. "How bad?" I hissed in his ear.

There was a jam-up at the gate. Poodles coming out, Poodles going in. Crawford had to stop for a moment and when he did I was right beside him. He gave me a furious look, but with it came the answer I was after.

His voice was so low that even in the crush of bodies, I had to lean in to hear him. "Bad enough to put Lavinia in a cast once or twice, okay?"

Okay.

At least now I knew.

❧❖ *Sixteen* ❖❧

It was a shame for Aunt Peg's sake that I'd lit a fire under Crawford like that, because when he finally got into the ring, he showed his Open bitch with a vengeance. And when Crawford Langley was hot, nobody else even stood a chance. The judge, who'd been dithering over every decision she made all afternoon, couldn't hand him the Winners Bitch ribbon fast enough. Not only that but since there was only one mediocre champion in attendance, she gave him the Variety too.

"Too bad," I said to Aunt Peg, who was holding the striped ribbon for Reserve.

"Luck of the draw," she said with a sigh. "Crawford's bitch is pretty. Sam was lucky to beat her yesterday."

Today he'd gone third in the Open class behind the two of them. "Luck?" he said, coming up behind us. "I assure you it was all skill."

"Really?" Aunt Peg teased. "Then what happened today? Lose your touch?"

We reached the set-up before Sam could come up with an answer. While we were gone, Davey had taken command of Aunt Peg's grooming table. His new friend was beneath Sam's and their matchbox cars had become guided missiles which they were lobbing at each other across the aisle. The boy's mother, who was brushing an Afghan, had the frazzled look of somebody nearing the end of her rope.

"Johnny!" she cried as we approached. "If you throw one more thing, I'm going to lock you in a crate!" She glanced over and saw us coming. "Thank God you're back. I've got to get up to the ring. Do you suppose . . . ?"

"I'd be happy to." With practiced ease, I swung Davey down off the table top, removing him from his source of ammunition. "I was about to get Davey some lunch. Does Johnny like hot dogs?"

"Loves them," his mother said gratefully. She hopped the Afghan off his crate and hurried down the aisle. "I shouldn't be more than twenty minutes, okay?"

While Sam and Aunt Peg began the work of undoing the Poodles, the boys and I went off to get lunch. I'd thought Davey had plenty of energy, but Johnny was a miniature dynamo. He ate two hot dogs, blew bubbles through his straw until his soda overflowed, and painted several long smears of mustard down the front of his shirt. All this while taking aim and pretending to shoot his finger at everyone who walked by. I jumped with the first round of sound effects, and was still jumping fifteen minutes later.

I'm not only a mother, I'm a teacher. I should be able to cope, right? It pains me to say it but I couldn't give him back soon enough.

Sam, who'd kept himself carefully removed from the fray, was laughing by the time I returned Johnny to his mother. The two of them immediately began haggling over whether or not he'd been good enough to deserve an ice cream cone. I wondered if they wanted to hear my vote.

"It makes you want to run right off and have more, doesn't it?" he asked.

I gave him the look that comment deserved as mother and son walked off, presumably in search of ice cream.

"The Non-Sporting group should just about be ready to start," said Aunt Peg, consulting her schedule. "Let's go see how far Crawford manages to get with his bitch."

We left the Poodles in their crates and trooped up to ringside. I was holding Davey's hand, and Sam had his arm around my waist. Aunt Peg was beaming happily, looking as though she wished she had a camera to record this Hallmark moment for posterity. Sometimes I just want to smack her.

Davey's patience lasted pretty well through the judging of the Non-Sporting group. A Bulldog won and Crawford's Standard bitch was fourth. As the Sporting dogs filed into the ring, however, he began to dance in place. I took a firmer hold of his hand and gazed up and down the line, finding Harry Flynn with his liver and white Springer in the middle and Angie with Charlie several places behind.

The buff Cocker looked first-rate. His coat was sleek and shiny and he was bouncing with excitement at being in the ring. Some dogs really love to show; and Charlie looked like he was ready to have a great time. Even though Angie was at the end of the lead, I still thought of him as Jenny's dog, so rooting for the Cocker was like pulling for a friend.

I nudged Aunt Peg. "Do you think Harry can beat him again?"

"There's a whole ring full of dogs in there," she said mildly. "In theory, any one of them could beat Charlie on the day."

On the day. It meant that judges were supposed to consider the animals only as they appeared before them at the moment of judging. If a dog was having an off show, they were not to remember how well he'd appeared on another occasion. If a dog was young, they were not to excuse the immaturity or speculate what the finished product might look like. The dogs were to be judged solely by their appearance on the day.

But as the judge sent the line of dogs gaiting around the ring for the first time, I could see that, by any criteria, this was clearly Charlie's day. The buff Cocker was super charged, just like his name said. He bounded around the ring, moving out and covering ground and hamming it up for the ringside.

"There's Mrs. Byrd," said Sam.

He pointed and I saw Charlie's owner seated front row center on the other side of the ring. Up close, she was older than I'd realized before; perhaps mid-eighties, judging by the carefully styled white hair and the birdlike fragility of her frame. Her narrow face was lined with wrinkles, but her blue eyes were clear and sharp. She'd braced her cane on the ground in front of her and was leaning forward on it from her seat as she took in the action in the ring. Behind the chair, Dirk hovered protectively.

"Mom?" Davey tugged at my hand, pulling downward until I squatted beside him. "I have to go."

"Now?" The judge was making her first cut.

Davey nodded.

"Can you wait just a few minutes?"

He clutched the front of his pants. "I don't think so."

Right. I stood back up.

"What's the matter?" asked Sam.

"Davey and I are going to the ladies' room."

"The *ladies'* room?"

"He's five, Sam. It's not like he can go into the men's room by himself."

Sam held out a hand. "Come on, sport. I'll take you."

"Into the men's room?" Davey's eyes opened wide. "Wow!"

"Are you sure you don't mind?"

"A man's gotta do what a man's gotta do. Right, Davey?"

"Right!"

I thought they were carrying things a bit far but I didn't say another word as they marched away. At least it meant that I got to watch the end of the group and see who won.

The judge had pulled out four finalists and lined them up in the center of the ring: Charlie, the Springer, a Clumber Spaniel, and a Flat Coated Retriever. He sent each on a final lap of the ring and the spectators responded by enthusiastically endorsing their favorites with applause. Just like Queen For A Day, except without the meter.

When the judge made his final arrangement, Charlie was in front. As he pointed to confirm the decision, Angie whooped with joy and gathered the Cocker up into her arms. Harry Flynn, with his Springer, had to settle for third.

Sam and Davey weren't back yet and Aunt Peg was engrossed in a conversation with some people standing behind her so I went to congratulate Angie. Clutching the big blue rosette and silver trophy, she left the ring by a gate on the other side. As I hurried around to catch up, I realized she was taking the prizes to Florence Byrd.

When the two women met, Mrs. Byrd was already on her feet. I was half a side of the ring away but I could see the older woman quite clearly. Whatever pleasure she'd felt in the win was being contained behind a wall of strict reserve. She accepted the ribbon and the silver plate and spared Charlie a pat on the head. Meanwhile Angie was bouncing up and down in place, joyously exuberant enough for both of them.

"We're hot now. Nobody can touch us," I heard her say as I drew near.

"You all say that when you win. Yesterday you lost."

"Yesterday was a fluke. I bet I don't lose another group all year. Charlie's a super dog."

"Good breeding will always tell," Mrs. Byrd said sternly. The Cocker jumped up against her leg. He couldn't have weighed much but it was still enough to stagger her slightly. Dirk moved in quickly from behind but the old woman waved him away. "And of course, Jenny made sure he was beautifully trained."

"Yes . . . of course." Angie's smile faltered a bit, then quickly recovered. "But he shows great for me, too. And we're just getting started together. Next year—"

"Next year, he'll be retired. The dog's coming home in December."

"I know that was the plan, but he's doing so well—"

Caught up in the crowds near the ring, Harry Flynn pushed past them rudely. He was glowering about something. Or maybe, as I was beginning to suspect, that was just his natural expression. Neither woman paid any attention.

"Charlie's done well all along," Florence Byrd said.

"But he's a dog, not a machine. He's had a long, hard year and at the end of it, he'll come home."

"Of course it's your decision, but I hope you'll think about letting him go on."

"There's nothing to think about," Mrs. Byrd said firmly. "That's the plan I made with Jenny, and that's what we're going to do."

By now I was standing right behind them. I'd thought I'd catch Angie when they were finished, but I never got the chance. Her features arranged in a sulky pout, the handler snatched up Charlie and stalked off. I was left facing Florence Byrd who looked as though she knew full well I'd overheard most of their conversation.

"Congratulations on your win," I said lamely.

"Thank you." Her wispy brows lowered as she stared at me intently. "Who are you?"

"Melanie Travis." Feeling a need to justify my presence, I added, "I was a friend of Jenny's."

The news didn't soften her frown, nor her stare. "That's easy to say after the fact, isn't it?"

"What do you mean?"

"Exactly what I said," Florence Byrd snapped. "I'm old. I don't have time to prevaricate. Jenny Maguire was a good person. She needed friends and I got the impression she didn't have nearly enough."

Dirk stepped up beside her and laid a hand solicitously on her elbow. Irritably she shook him off. "When I'm darn good and ready. Don't try to tell me what to do!"

"No, of course not," he murmured. His eyes, looking me over carefully, were a flat, cool shade of gray.

Mrs. Byrd moved back to my side. "It doesn't do any good now to call yourself a friend of Jenny's. You weren't much use to her, were you? If Jenny had had better friends, maybe she wouldn't be dead."

I wished I could argue with that, but I couldn't. The truth was I'd spent more time thinking about Jenny now that she was gone than I ever had when she was alive. But whatever Jenny had needed, I hadn't known her well enough to supply it.

I watched the tall, hulking man lead his fragile charge away and wondered if it was only a coincidence that Dirk had stepped in on our conversation when he'd heard me mention Jenny's name. Had he been more interested in sparing Mrs. Byrd from a painful topic, or in hearing what I had to say?

Angie had called him a spook, and while I wouldn't have gone that far, there was something disconcerting about being the object of his attention. And to hear Angie tell it, he'd paid a great deal of attention to her sister.

Jenny'd been perky and lively and pretty as a doll. And she'd worked for Dirk's employer as well. I wondered if that meant he'd felt some sort of a kinship with her. One she might not have shared.

No doubt about it, if I thought of all the people who'd surrounded Jenny and picked the villain from general casting, it would have been Dirk. Not that it was fair to condemn a man on the strength of his looks. But then, that was the whole problem. Life wasn't fair.

What had happened to Jenny Maguire was ample proof of that.

❧❀ *Seventeen* ❀❧

The problem with dog shows is that everything takes place in such close quarters there's no way to talk privately. Especially not about the kind of information I was beginning to pile up.

I'd started asking questions in the beginning because Jenny's death had shaken up my well-ordered notion of the world. At thirty, I'm old enough to know I won't live forever, but still young enough to believe there must be plenty of time left. Somebody had taken that away from Jenny.

Unfortunately the more I learned, the more confusing things became. Instead of slipping into sharper focus, I had a feeling that the picture of her life I was developing was growing hazier by the moment. I definitely needed a second opinion.

Monday, I went through my duties as teacher by rote. Sometimes it happens. When it does, I try not to think about the fact that the future of America's youth rests in my hands.

New facts fresh in my mind, I gave Sam a call that evening. Unfortunately the effort produced nothing save the opportunity to leave a choice message on his machine. And Aunt Peg thought our relationship wasn't progressing.

From the rumble of running feet I heard on the ceiling, I guessed that Davey and Faith were playing hide and seek upstairs. Davey was fed and bathed and wearing his pajamas. With any luck the puppy would wear him out enough so that in a half hour's time he'd drop straight into bed. I poured myself a cup of coffee, sat down in the kitchen and dialed Aunt Peg. Thankfully, she was home.

Now that I finally had someone to talk to, I went for maximum shock value. "I spoke to the Ridgefield police on Saturday. Jenny was murdered."

"For sure?"

"Ummhmm." I sipped at my coffee and filled her in on what Detective Petronelli had told me. I went from there to Crystal Mars, Harry Flynn, and Crawford Langley.

"You've been busy," she said at the end.

"That's not all. Angie and Florence Byrd are apparently arguing over how long Charlie will remain on the circuit."

"That will be a short argument. It's Florence's dog and Florence's money. That makes it her call."

"Maybe, but Angie's hoping to change her mind. I wonder how Jenny felt about the length of Charlie's career."

"Is this your way of saying you think that Florence might be implicated in Jenny's death?" Aunt Peg's tone clearly conveyed her skepticism.

"How about Dirk then? Angie calls him a spook. She says he used to spend a lot of time watching Jenny."

"Oh, that girl. I think she'd say anything that would

draw attention to herself. I'm more interested in what the detective told you. So Jenny was poisoned slowly over a period of time. Rather an odd choice of methods, wouldn't you think?"

"Of course it's odd," I grumbled. "Every single solitary piece of information I have is odd."

"Remember what I told you about the handlers who used to feed arsenic to their dogs to make them grow coat?"

"Right." I sat up suddenly. "A little bit at a time. Who else would have known about something like that?"

"Lots of people, unfortunately. It's an old handlers trick."

"Harry Flynn's an old handler."

"So he is."

"And Florence Byrd has been around forever."

Aunt Peg harrumphed at that. "Since you're running around talking to people, what about that kennel girl Jenny fired? The one she chased with a broom? She would have had access. Maybe there was more to that argument than meets the eye."

There was a loud crash from the living room, followed by a wail from Davey. The phone was a cordless, but as soon as I reached the doorway, I knew I was going to need both hands.

"Any blood?" Aunt Peg asked. She could hear Davey screaming through the line.

"No. A broken vase, a turned over table, and a puppy tangled in an electrical cord."

"Off you go then," Aunt Peg said cheerily. "Keep digging. And let me know what else you find out."

On Tuesday, Betty Winslow and I had set up an appointment to meet with Timmy Doane's parents. Despite Timmy's insecurities, I'd found him to be a bright and engaging child. Since he was new to the school system, Betty and I had wondered if there was anything in his history we should have been aware of. We knew about the move obviously; but if there'd been any other recent turmoil in the family, the parents were the ones to fill us in.

The conference was set up for after school Wednesday. It was a warm afternoon and Davey was outside waiting for me on the playground. I could see him from the third grade classroom where the meeting was to take place.

When I got there, however, Betty was the one who was missing. I found some adult-sized chairs, arranged them in a semi-circle and waited. She came flying in only moments later.

"I've got to go." Betty went straight to her desk and dug out her purse.

"What's wrong? Is it your kids?" Betty had three, two in high school, one in college. Their pictures decorated the window sill behind her desk.

"Sean's in trouble over at the high school."

Sean was her youngest, fifteen but trying desperately to be older; smart, sassy, and a heartbreaker in the making. "Can I do anything to help?"

"Care to hold him?" asked Betty. "I'm planning to whip his butt."

I grinned at her look of exasperation. "What'd he do?"

"Got busted for carrying a beeper in school. As if he doesn't know better. As if I haven't told him a thousand times that when you're black, if you want to be taken seriously, everything you do has to be above reproach. But no, he thinks he's too important for that. Mr. Track Star. Like he can't get in trouble like everybody else."

Beepers had been banned in most of the local schools. They were disruptive in class, and served as a handy tool for the area drug dealers who beeped their clients when they came on campus. Teachers had good reason to be suspicious of any student they found carrying one.

"Sean isn't . . ."

"Into drugs?" Betty answered my unspoken question with a vehement shake of her head. "Not on his life. I went through that with Kevin, my oldest, so believe me, I know the signs. Besides, Sean's too into his body—which we're both hoping will win him a scholarship to college—to even think of defiling it like that."

"What was he doing with a beeper?"

"Acting like a fifteen-year-old jerk." Betty sighed. "He thinks it's hip, and at that age, hip is everything. Now I've got to go bail him out and see the principal."

"The Doanes are due any minute."

"I know and I'm sorry. We've discussed everything so I know you can handle the conference on your own. Do you mind too much?"

"No, go on. Ten years from now when I'm bailing out Davey, you can cover for me."

"You got it," said Betty and she was gone.

She must have passed Rob and Wendy Doane on her way out because they entered the classroom just after she left. Rob Doane was tall and spare. He was wearing a double-breasted suit and highly polished loafers; clearly he'd come from work. Fathers are rare at mid-day conferences and I was pleased that he'd made the effort.

Striding a half step behind him, Wendy Doane was chic and slender. She wore chunky gold jewelry and had manicured hands that looked as though they'd never seen a sink full of dirty dishes. Neither she nor her husband was smiling.

I introduced myself and led them to the seats. Mr. Doane looked pointedly at the empty chair. "I believe we were to be joined by Timmy's classroom teacher?"

"Yes, that was the plan, but Betty was called away by a family emergency. Both she and I have spent considerable time with Timmy and I feel comfortable speaking for her in her absence."

"I see." He folded his hands tightly in his lap. "Then we may as well get on with it."

It was supposed to have been my meeting, but Rob Doane was not one to cede authority lightly. He started by quizzing me on my credentials, which were in very good order, thank you; and ended by saying, "You've been with the school system how long?"

"Seven years."

"All in the same position?" His tone suggested that if I was any good I would have been promoted by now.

"I am a special education teacher, Mr. Doane. That's what I do. My children are very important to me."

"None of Timmy's other teachers have ever been dissatisfied with his performance," said Wendy Doane, leaning forward in her chair. Her pink-tipped fingers drummed in her lap.

"I'm not dissatisfied either. It's just that I think he can do better. He's new to Hunting Ridge Elementary and we'd like to make his adjustment as smooth as possible—"

"Timmy's a very intelligent child," Mr. Doane broke in. "We've had him tested. His I.Q. falls just below genius range, which is why we were very surprised to hear that he had been singled out for special help. I assure you he has no learning disabilities, nor any other problems of any sort."

"I realize that Timmy is very bright, but he has had some trouble expressing himself in the classroom environment. Perhaps the move has unsettled him—"

Wendy was angled so far forward that her chair scooted up with her. "We explained to him that the move was necessary. His father took a different job—a better job—in New York. Certain adjustments would have to be made by everyone. His contribution would be to work a little harder."

"I don't think the problem is how hard he works."

"It must be, or why else would you have called us here?" Rob Doane demanded. "We know Timmy's a smart child. There's no question of that. Yet obviously you feel he's not living up to his potential—"

Now it was my turn to interrupt. I was growing more than a little tired of the Doanes' hard line approach to their son and his problems. Too bad Betty wasn't here to stomp some sense into them.

"The way I see it, at the moment Timmy's potential is not the most important consideration. His happiness and well-being are. Ever since he came to Hunting Ridge, he has been quiet almost to the point of being withdrawn."

"Quiet?" Wendy asked. "You brought us in here because Timmy's quiet? That's absurd."

"I brought you in here because I feel he's unhappy."

"Your duty as a teacher is not to feel," said Mr. Doane.

"It is to instruct. If Timmy's unhappy it is because he has not yet learned how to successfully apply himself in this new environment."

What a lot of jargon. What a lot of bullshit. I wondered if he talked that way when he wasn't wearing a suit. Come to think of it, I wondered if he talked that way in bed. *Now Wendy, dear, you must apply yourself. . . .*

I fought back a highly inappropriate giggle and said, "I see that Timmy's success is very important to you. Perhaps he feels your desires for him as undue pressure."

"I should hope he does," snapped Rob Doane.

"Excuse me?"

"Life *is* pressure, and productivity, and accomplishment. A child is never too young to learn the value of discipline and achievement. Maybe we do push him a bit, I don't see that as a negative. The work habits he builds today will take him on into the Ivy League and the work force after that. Right now, Timmy is laying the foundation for his own future."

Give me a break, I thought. Timmy was eight. Right now, he was struggling in the third grade. And with Mr. and Mrs. Upwardly-Mobile behind him pushing as hard as they could, no wonder. I'd seen kids just slightly older with ulcers from just this kind of pressure.

The meeting concluded on a thoroughly unsatisfactory note. Rob and Wendy Doane stopped short of questioning my competence as a teacher, but they certainly disputed my concerns. From their point of view, there was nothing wrong with Timmy's classroom performance that couldn't be solved by pressing their son to apply himself more strenuously. By the time they left, I was afraid I might have done Timmy more harm than good.

I sat at Betty's desk, watched Davey chase a soccer ball around the field outside, and wrote up my notes about the meeting. Maybe I should have Betty reschedule and the two of us could take another go at it. Or maybe that would only make things worse.

So far, Timmy was handling the pressure by retreating. If that worked for him, so be it. I wasn't about to be the one who placed a wall at his back.

∽✷ *Eighteen* ✷∽

The town of New Canaan is old-fashioned in the best sense of the word. The downtown area consists of two streets, Main and Elm. Many of the shops have been in place under the same ownership for decades; and half an hour's pleasant strolling will cover just about all there is to see. A sign on the railroad station says "The next station to heaven" and few residents would disagree.

New Canaan is also right next door to Stamford; close enough that I was able to slip out during lunch the next day, race home and pick up Faith, then drive over to the smaller of the two pet grooming establishments in town. Finding Jackie had been easy. I'd simply called both salons and asked if they had a new girl named Jackie working for them. One said yes; one said no. Good thing she wasn't trying to dodge the IRS.

The Canine Chateau was located at the end of a wide, mostly empty sidestreet. The two block stretch leading up to it boasted a few offices, a video rental store, a plate glass emporium and an auto body shop. Finding parking wasn't a problem.

I slipped Faith's collar and attached leash over her head and hopped her out of the car. She'd been shown only two weeks earlier and didn't look anything like the average pet in need of a clip or flea bath. Not only that but Aunt Peg would kill me if I let a pet groomer touch even a hair of Faith's carefully stylized trim. The puppy would, however, provide me with an entree and I was hoping that was all I'd need.

A trio of bells chimed as I opened the door and walked Faith into the shop. The outer room was small and mostly crammed with a selection of pet supplies that was heavy on rhinestone collars and light on quality kibble. There was a waist-high counter at the back of the room. A doorway behind it was covered by a ratty-looking curtain that wasn't pulled all the way shut. I could see two grooming tables and the edge of a bathtub. The hum of a forced air dryer made Faith's ears prick.

A bored-looking young woman was seated on a stool behind the counter. She was thumbing through a magazine, holding each page by the tips of her fingers as though her bright pink nails were wet. She glanced up, then turned another page. "Help you?"

"Yes, I'm looking for a groomer for my Poodle."

She roused herself enough to look over the counter at Faith who was sitting by my side. "We don't take walk-ins. You'll have to make an appointment. Rates are on the wall. If he needs a flea dip, that's extra."

"I'm looking for a particular groomer. I was told you have a new girl named Jackie who used to work in a show kennel. Faith is a show dog."

"All our groomers are good. We handle show dogs all the time."

Sure, I thought. And then you tie bows in their ears and send them home.

"Bunny? You busy?" The voice, coming out of the back room, was loud enough to make Faith look up inquiringly. I gave the caller the benefit of the doubt and decided she was probably trying to make herself heard over the dryers.

"Yeah. Whatsa matter?"

Of course that didn't explain why Bunny shrieked right back.

"Jackie's goin' out on lunch. You want anything?"

Faith whined softly under her breath. I scratched her poor ears for reassurance. Maybe their mamas had taken them to too many rock concerts when they were babies. Or maybe they were just dumb. From the decibel level of the conversation, you'd have thought they were trying to make themselves heard through a solid oak door rather than a flimsy curtain.

"Send her out here first, wouldja?"

A moment later the curtain parted. Jackie was a chunky girl in her mid-twenties with a prominent chin and wiry blond hair. She was wearing jeans and a tee shirt with the words, "If you can read this, you're too close" stenciled across her breasts. She had a flannel-lined denim jacket in one hand and was counting the money in her wallet with the other.

"What?"

Bunny waved in my direction. "Lady here wants to talk to you about getting her dog done."

Jackie's gaze slid over me and went straight to Faith.

She dropped her jacket on the counter, shoved her wallet in the back pocket of her jeans, crouched down, and extended a hand. "Hey, pretty girl."

Faith sniffed the fingers with polite reserve.

"I understand you used to work for a show kennel."

"Yeah, Shamrock in Ridgefield. They didn't show any Poodles though." Jackie frowned suddenly, regretting her honesty. "But of course I know how to groom them. I can do all the breeds. What you've got here is called a puppy trim."

"And you think you could maintain it for showing?"

"Sure. Make an appointment and I'll show you. I've got some time open at the end of the week."

Considering Aunt Peg had just devoted several hours to scissoring Faith's trim, I couldn't imagine what Jackie thought she might possibly do to improve upon it. Nor did I have any intention of finding out.

"I don't know." I pretended to consider. "Ridgefield's not that far away. Maybe I should take her to this Shamrock place instead."

"Bad idea. Real bad idea."

"Why is that?"

"The people that own the place, they're a little crazy."

"They are?" I leaned in closer and injected just the right amount of shock into my tone.

"That's the truth. I'll tell you, the things that went on there . . ."

"Like what?"

"Well it was a husband-wife team, see? And when they had fights, you'd think the roof was going to come off the kennel, it was that bad. Even the dogs would hide in the backs of their pens."

"Is that why you left?"

"Nah, I just got fed up. I don't like to stay in one place for too long, you know? Besides, at the Maguires there was another girl, Jenny's sister. I was too far down the totem pole. I needed to get away and get to a place where I'd have a chance to move up."

"Jenny Maguire? I've heard that name at the shows. Isn't she the woman who died?"

"Yeah."

"Were you there then?"

"Nah, I was already gone. Doesn't mean I didn't cheer when I heard, though."

"I guess you didn't like her much."

"You can say that again. Little Miss Priss, when the clients were around. Like butter wouldn't melt in her mouth. But when they were gone, watch out! Mostly Angie and I just tried to stay out of her way."

"I heard she was murdered," I mentioned casually.

Jackie's eyes lit up. "Really? Go on."

"It's true." Just to see what would happen, I threw out another name. "Crystal Mars told me."

"Is that the lady with the kennel in Stratford? The dog food lady?"

I nodded. "Do you know her?"

"We never met, but I heard about her. Angie—that's Jenny's sister—her and me were friends. She and Jenny got into an argument once and I asked her about it later. Seems the dog food lady had had an affair with their father, can you beat that?"

No, I thought, I certainly couldn't. "Did it happen recently?"

"Nah, it was old stuff. Something that was going on

back when Jenny and Angie first moved out on their own. Angie didn't want anything to do with Crystal Mars and she hated it that Jenny did. But once Jenny got an idea in her head, good or bad, nobody could change her mind."

Crystal Mars and Roger Peterson? If that had been the precipitating factor in Jenny and Angie's leaving home, then frankly Angie's attitude made more sense to me than Jenny's did. Why would Jenny have wanted to keep up with the woman who'd rivaled her own mother for her father's affections?

"Hey, listen," said Jackie. "I gotta get going. Bunny, write this lady down an appointment, would you? End of the week."

Bunny pulled out an appointment book, picked up a pen, and stared at me blankly.

"Janet Reno," I said. "R-E-N-O."

Neither one of them batted an eye. I guess current events weren't a strong suit.

I got to handling class early on Thursday evening and managed to snag Rick for a few minutes of conversation. I started by congratulating him on Charlie's recent successes. He accepted the praise modestly and like a true dog man, gave the Cocker all the credit.

"Harry Flynn didn't look too pleased on Sunday," I ventured.

Rick was setting up a card table near the door to hold the cash box and attendance list. "Good."

"He didn't like Jenny much, did he?"

"He doesn't like anyone at Shamrock. Flynn's lost two big clients to us since the beginning of the year. If you've met him, you know that public relations isn't his strong suit. And he can be just as surly with the people who are paying his bills. But Flynn never saw himself as being at fault. As far as he was concerned, Jenny stole his dogs."

The outer door to the building opened and an eager black Lab dragged its owner inside. A Borzoi followed, and the line to check in began to form. When Aunt Peg showed up, late as usual, I motioned her over to the space I'd saved beside me on the mat.

By the time she got Hope settled, Rick was already calling the class to order. He walked to the front of the line and began making his way slowly from dog to dog, looking at each, but not yet touching, like a judge taking a first impression of his entry.

I made a quick inspection of Faith's stance. Her front feet were facing forward and were set properly underneath her. Her rear feet were stretched just enough to highlight her hindquarter angulation. I balled the narrow show leash inside my fist out of the way and used the same hand to lift her head up and back over her shoulders. The other reached to hold her tail. When Rick passed by, she looked alert and ready. I relaxed and let her droop a little after he'd passed.

In a carefully modulated whisper, I brought Aunt Peg up to speed on what I had learned. She shrugged over Rick's opinion of Harry Flynn as if that was old news, but the information Jackie had given me made her smile.

"Roger Peterson and Crystal Mars?" Her eyebrows waggled at the thought. I hoped that meant ideas were percolating.

Rick finished his opening perusal and set the line in motion. The week before he and Angie had seemed to be making an effort to handle things smoothly in Jenny's absence. Now only one class later, the transition from one sister to the other was just about taken for granted. As Aunt Peg moved off to the side to chat with the woman handling the Borzoi, I played tug-of-war with Faith and her squeaky and listened to a conversation between two women holding Airedales behind me.

"What's the difference?" one was saying. "One sister's pretty much the same as the other."

The second woman was a redhead, just like her dog. "I disagree. Jenny always gave me good tips. She told me I was gaiting Rufus too fast and when I tried it her way, I realized I was. Angie has nice hands on a dog, I'll give her that. She's great at socializing puppies, but not nearly as good at picking up on my mistakes."

"She's young, that's all. Maybe she's a little intimidated."

"If that's the problem I hope she gets over it, or I may start looking for another class. It would be one thing if Angie were only filling in every now and again . . ."

Their two big terriers, who'd been sparring playfully, suddenly decided to take each other seriously. There was a throaty rumble from one and a snap of teeth from the other and the two handlers hastily moved apart. I brought Faith forward several steps where she'd be well out of the fray and thought about what the woman had said.

It would be one thing if Angie were only filling in every now and again . . .

The last time I'd seen Jenny she'd mentioned that Angie would be taking her place at class that week because she was planning to be away. I hadn't asked her where she was going; at the time, it hadn't seemed important. Then Jenny had died and class had been canceled and I'd forgotten all about it.

Up ahead Rick was going over Hope, which meant that my turn was next. As Aunt Peg completed her exercises, gaiting the puppy in the several different patterns while Rick watched critically, I moved Faith up and stacked her. When he finished with Hope and turned to her sister, we were ready.

"She's really improving." Rick approached Faith in the quiet and efficient manner used by the best judges. He held out his fingers for her to smell.

"Thanks. We've been working on it." Faith held her stance and wagged her tail.

Rick studied the puppy's head briefly, then lifted her lips to check the correctness of her bite. "Good girl," he murmured softly, and moved on to feel the shoulder.

"You know, I was wondering about something."

"Hmmm?" He was running his hands down Faith's front leg, checking the amount of bone, and didn't look up.

"Just before Jenny died, she told me she was planning to be away for a bit. Where was she going?"

"What?"

I repeated the question as Rick felt for spring of rib. He stopped then, and straightened. "I don't know what you're talking about. Jenny wasn't planning on going anywhere."

"But she told me she'd be missing class that week."

"You must be mistaken." He skimmed a hand quickly over Faith's hindquarter then stepped back, signaling that the examination was over.

"I'm not. Jenny told me she was going to be away."

"That's not possible," Rick said shortly. "I don't know anything about Jenny taking a trip and she never would have planned one without telling me. You must have misunderstood."

"Yeah," I said slowly. "I guess I did."

He waved a hand toward the outside mat. "Down and back. And be sure to keep her straight."

We managed to complete the rest of the exercise without saying one more word to each other than was absolutely necessary. In no time at all, I was back at the end of the line. It would be a good ten minutes before Faith and I were called upon to do anything else. That was fine because it gave me time to think.

Jenny had told me she was going away, I was sure of it. At the time I'd assumed she meant a short trip, but what if she hadn't? By then, Ziggy *had* gone away; with Jenny concocting an elaborate lie to cover his disappearance.

I'd speculated that Jenny might have been thinking about divorcing Rick, but maybe I hadn't considered all the possibilities. I thought back to the times I'd seen Rick and Jenny together; the way he'd always been watching her, touching her, speaking on her behalf. At his kennel, when he'd told me that Jenny was his whole life, I'd assumed he was merely waxing poetic; but what if he wasn't?

Maybe Jenny had found her husband's constant attention smothering. Maybe she'd been looking for a way out.

According to her sister, Jenny had thought of divorcing Rick once. Angie said he had changed her mind. How? By convincing her to stay? Or by forbidding her to go?

The talk I'd had with Timmy Doane's parents was

fresh enough in my mind to still rankle. Timmy was handling a manipulative relationship by running away emotionally. What if Jenny had decided to solve her problems with Rick by running away physically?

Trapped with a husband who loved her too much to let her go willingly, she'd concocted a plan to get away that didn't need his consent. I knew she'd faked Ziggy's death. It didn't take much of a leap of logic to see that she could also have been planning to fake her own. Was that why she had written the phony suicide note? Had the missing jewelry Angie had told me about been intended to finance her run?

It all made a terrible kind of sense. Poor Jenny. Before she could get away, someone had stopped her from ever running again.

∞✽ Nineteen ✽∞

It's a good thing class was almost over because I was dying to run my theory past Aunt Peg. The moment Rick dismissed us, I pushed her out the door and informed her I was following her home. She accepted that pronouncement with a lifted brow and a heavy foot on the gas pedal.

Aunt Peg's herd of house Poodles met us at the door. There were six of them, all retired champions and all bitches except for Beau, who was definitely king of his domain. Their chorus of barking and leaping went on for several minutes and was clearly meant to make Aunt Peg feel guilty for having left them. While she passed out biscuits, then let the troupe out the back door, I went and called Joanie the baby-sitter and asked her to hang on for another hour.

Aunt Peg was brewing tea when I returned to the kitchen. A box containing an all-butter crumb cake sat open on the counter. The woman has a sweet tooth like you would not believe. Obviously she was hoping to tempt me too, because she'd set out two plates. It was too late at night for coffee. I poured myself a glass of water from the faucet, pulled out a chair and sat down.

"Listen to this." I led her back through what we had learned so far, about Jenny hiding Ziggy away and claiming he was dead, the fact that she'd written a suicide note and then been murdered. I reiterated what Jackie the kennel girl had told me—that Rick and Jenny had been fighting long enough and loud enough that they apparently didn't care who overheard.

"Then tonight at class I remembered something Jenny told me the last time I saw her. She said she wouldn't be at class the following week because she was going away."

Aunt Peg lifted the crumb cake down from the counter and made the first cut. "So?"

"When I asked Rick about it he said I must have been mistaken, that Jenny didn't have any trips planned."

"At least not any trips that he knew about," Aunt Peg said thoughtfully.

"Precisely. I think Jenny was planning on leaving him. According to Angie, she'd tried once before. She'd even gone as far as filing for divorce, but Rick had convinced her to stay. Rick says she was happy and that everything between them was hunky-dory. But Angie and Crystal Mars and Jackie have a different story to tell. And then there's the note."

When she saw I wasn't going to help myself, Aunt Peg cut a large square of cake and slipped it onto my plate. I eyed it unhappily, but didn't push it away. "Not to mention the missing jewelry."

"You think she was going to fake her own suicide and then disappear?"

"That's exactly what I think."

"But what about the business? It was as much hers as Rick's. She couldn't just walk out on that."

"Why not, if it was what she wanted? Angie said once that Jenny didn't get into handling because she loved it so much, but rather because she was young and it was the only thing she knew how to do. According to Angie, Jenny would have been happy to leave it all behind."

Aunt Peg lifted a piece of cake to her mouth, chewed and swallowed slowly. She was halfway through a square twice the size of mine. With her metabolism, she was probably burning calories by chewing. "Suppose Jenny did fake her own death, how would she have explained that to Crystal Mars when she showed up alive to get Ziggy?"

"Ridgefield and Stratford are nearly forty miles apart," I pointed out. "It's possible that Crystal might not have heard what had happened for weeks. Neither Angie nor Rick have anything to do with the woman, so they wouldn't have told her. When Jenny did die, Crystal only found out by accident, and then not until after the funeral.

"Suppose Jenny staged a suicide then went directly to Stratford to pick up Ziggy. By the time Crystal got the news, she probably would have assumed that it happened sometime after she saw Jenny. There wouldn't have been any reason to be suspicious."

There was a rumble outside as the Poodles came bounding up the steps onto the back porch. Aunt Peg opened the door and let them in. Beau immediately went over and sat down beside her chair. She ruffled his top-knot and ears fondly. "Of course she'd have had to arrange her death in such a way that no body was ever found."

I plucked a round, sugar-coated crumb from the top of my cake and popped it in my mouth. "I'd have made it look like I jumped off a bridge. The Tappan Zee is popular for that."

"So she leaves her car there, presumably with the note inside. How does she get to Stratford?"

"Hitch-hike?"

"And you don't think Crystal would have found that a little odd?"

I hadn't thought about that. I sighed and dug into my cake. "Maybe she had an accomplice."

"Who?"

"Angie?" I offered, then quickly shook my head. "I doubt she's a good enough actress. Besides, Angie's still angry about the missing jewelry."

"How about Crystal?"

"Possibly. She certainly was the only one who knew that Ziggy was still alive. But if she was in on the plan, why didn't she admit it?"

"Maybe she wasn't sure whose side you were on."

"Could be." I thought back to the show the previous weekend. "And then there's Florence Byrd."

"What about her?"

"When I told her I was a friend of Jenny's, she said something about Jenny not having enough friends. That maybe if she'd had better people around her, she might still be alive today. Maybe Mrs. Byrd was planning to help Jenny, but she never got the chance."

"We ought to talk to her and see what she knows."

Faith came over and laid her muzzle on my lap. I scratched beneath her chin. "I already tried. I didn't get very far."

"She's a tough old bird, if you'll pardon the pun. I doubt she'd take being questioned lightly."

"Who do we know that could give us an introduction?"

Aunt Peg thought for a moment. "Maybe Crawford. He knows everybody. I'll bet he could get us together next week at Springfield."

The following week was Thanksgiving, too, but that wasn't the way dog people thought. They measured the weeks of the year not by the usual calendar but by the dog shows that held those dates, as in "The puppies are due right after Elm City" or "We'll be on vacation the week of Penn Ridge." Springfield was a four-day weekend of big shows held at the Eastern States Exposition Grounds in Massachusetts over Thanksgiving vacation.

Faith was entered for two days and Peaches all four. According to Aunt Peg, the weekend drew many of the best dogs from all over the country and would be a valuable learning experience for me. She, Davey, and I were planning to share a hotel room.

"Will you talk to him?" I asked and Aunt Peg nodded. "In the meantime, I'll call Detective Petronelli and tell him what we're thinking."

"Good idea."

I pushed back my chair and stood up. Between us, we'd finished nearly half the cake. I could just about feel the pounds sliding right down onto my thighs.

"You're coming next Thursday, right?"

Aunt Peg looked up. "Where?"

"To my house, for dinner. It's Thanksgiving. The whole family's coming, remember?"

"Oh. Of course."

Of course, my foot. Dog people.

On Saturday night, I had a date. For me, that was a big deal. I couldn't remember having had a serious date since high school. In college and graduate school, we'd socialized in groups. After that, I'd married Bob and had Davey. Since Bob left, there'd been only a couple of casual relationships with men who had turned out not to be nearly as interesting as I had hoped.

The problem was between working and motherhood, I had neither extra time nor energy to expend trying to bolster a faltering social life. I also tend to have very high standards. I can't see the point of wasting my time with some mediocre man when I could be home enjoying my own company and that of my son.

And then Sam showed up. I'd tried pushing him away once or twice, but he kept pushing back. I like a man with perseverance. Not to mention sky blue eyes and a tight butt.

He'd called on Wednesday and asked me out for Saturday night. No Poodles, no Aunt Peg, no Davey. In other words, no distractions. Just us. Who knew what might develop? Certainly not me, but I dressed with great care from the skin out, just in case.

Sam was punctual. He arrived right on the dot of seven and since I was still upstairs poking at my hair, Joanie let him in.

"Hey, Mom!" Davey yelled up the stairs. "Sam's here. And he's got flowers and everything. You better hurry up!"

Five-year-olds have no appreciation for romance. I left my hair and went downstairs. If I didn't get there soon, Davey might manage to convince Sam that he needed to tag along.

But as I turned the corner and started down, I realized there was little chance of that. Sam was waiting for me at the foot of the steps. Davey and Faith were playing tag around him, but with notable lack of concern for his own safety, Sam only had eyes for me. He was holding roses, creamy white ones with petals the color of pearls. Their heady fragrance filled the hallway. My heart began to pound.

"You look great," said Sam.

I was wearing a sleeveless black wool dress with a mandarin collar and a body hugging shape that ended well above my knees. The two inch heels that completed the outfit would have me begging for mercy by midnight but for the moment I felt long and lean and terribly sophisticated.

"Thanks," I said. "So do you." His blond hair was wind ruffled; the killer smile was firmly in place. Beneath the camel hair topcoat, I saw a navy blue jacket and a tie whose pattern, on closer inspection, consisted of dozens of intertwined Poodles.

He held out the flowers. I took the bouquet in my arms and inhaled deeply. "They're beautiful. Thank you."

For a moment I wasn't sure what to do next. I'd known Sam for months, but suddenly everything seemed strange and new.

"Hey!" cried Davey, rounding the corner with Faith hard on his heels. "I thought you were leaving."

"We are." I leaned down and brushed a kiss across his curls.

Joanie was right behind him. From the way she kept staring at Sam with her mouth hanging open, I figured he was having the same effect on her that he was on me. "Do you want me to put those in a vase?" she asked.

"That would be great." I handed over the roses and got my coat out of the closet. "We won't be late."

"Yes, we will." Sam looked at Joanie. "Do you have a curfew?"

"I'm sixteen," she said, trying to sound very grown-up. "I can stay out as late as I want."

"Good."

Before I could say another word, Sam had bundled me into my coat, out the door, and into his car. Or maybe I was just speechless. Up until now, our times together had been casual, impromptu: pizza and Poodles. But not tonight. Tonight was a night for white roses and champagne.

"Where are we going?"

"Le Chateau."

"You're kidding!"

He looked over, amused. "No, I'm not."

"I've always wanted to go there."

"Good. Then it will be a special occasion."

Le Chateau was one of the finest restaurants in the area. Housed in an old stone mansion in the countryside of South Salem, it was a bit of a drive from almost everywhere. The fact that reservations were essential and hard to get was a testament to its excellence.

Oh my.

In the car on the way, Sam talked about his work. He'd started his own business in the spring and was designing a new type of interactive software for a client on the West Coast. Since going out on his own, work had been coming in even more quickly than his most optimistic projections had predicted. Modestly, he ascribed his success to a thriving market; but I knew better. He was just plain good.

It was inevitable that the conversation would eventually work its way around to dogs and dog people, but that didn't happen until we'd been seated in the shadow of a large Palladian window overlooking a lighted terrace with gardens beyond. At the other end of the room, a fire burned cozily in a stone fireplace. Though most of the tables were full, they were so well spaced that we might as well have been alone. The room was hushed, softly lit, perfect.

The sommelier poured the Bordeaux that Sam had chosen and discreetly withdrew.

"Peg tells me that the Ridgefield police are quite certain Jenny Maguire was murdered," said Sam.

I sipped at my wine, and nodded. It didn't surprise me that Peg and Sam had been talking about what I'd found out. Aunt Peg was just old fashioned enough to enjoy having a man's shoulder to lean on when the going got tough.

"Do you really think Jenny was planning to fake her own suicide?"

"I think there's a good possibility. That would explain the note, the missing jewelry, and why she did what she did with Ziggy."

"I don't know Rick Maguire except to say hello to. He seems like he can be pretty intense at times, but I'm not sure I can imagine his wife feeling she had to go to those lengths to escape him."

"Jenny had filed for divorce once before, but apparently Rick convinced her to change her mind."

"There you go." Sam lifted his wine goblet and light from the fire flickered across its facets. "Maybe she didn't know what she wanted."

"Maybe she knew what she wanted and was afraid to go after it. Jenny told me she was going away, Sam. At the time, I thought she meant she was taking a trip. But now I'm sure she meant to run away for good."

"Not everybody runs, Melanie."

"What does that mean?"

"Just what I said. Some relationships are better than others, but everyone doesn't solve their problems by running away."

"You think I'm taking this too personally."

"A month ago, you told me you didn't know Jenny that well. Now I'm wondering how you got so involved."

I shifted in my chair. "It just happened."

"I see."

The waiter came and took our order and I thought after that the subject would be dropped. And it was, in a way. But Sam was sly, I had to give him that. Because when he asked his next question, I knew I should have seen it coming.

"Tell me about Bob," he said.

I stuffed a piece of buttered bread in my mouth and decided it was too full to speak.

"Davey's father," he prompted. "Your ex-husband."

Oh, *that* Bob.

∽❋ *Twenty* ❋∽

"There's not much to tell," I said.

"I think there is. I think there must be."

"Oh?" The word sounded hard and defensive. I reached for my wine and gulped it with less than proper respect. As soon as I set the glass down, it was refilled.

"There's been something standing between us from the beginning. You'd like to believe it's Davey, but it isn't. Peg tells me it's Bob."

"Aunt Peg should mind her own business," I said with feeling.

"She wants you to be happy. Is that so bad?"

"She wants me to be her version of happy, with a husband to take care of me and a house full of Standard Poodles."

"Not the worst thing that could happen. Tell me about Bob."

"You'll be bored."

"I'll cope."

I sighed then. It was his mistake, but I guessed I could humor him. "Bob and I met young and married too soon.

I had visions of swing sets and picket fences. He thought we were Wendy and Peter Pan."

"You clashed right from the beginning then."

"Actually no. The problem was, we didn't talk about our expectations at all. So for the first few years we thought we were doing pretty well."

"What happened?"

"I got pregnant. It was an accident. We'd agreed to wait. But I was delighted."

"And your husband wasn't."

"That's putting it mildly. Bob was shocked, dismayed, surprised as hell. How could this have happened? That kind of thing. As if he hadn't been right there at the time."

Sam's lips pursed at that. "And then?"

"One day when Davey was ten months old, Bob left while I was at the supermarket. Talk about being knocked for a loop. I had no idea. There I was being the proper little wife and mother, taking my son in the snugli to go pick up formula, while Bob was home packing up the stereo in the car."

I shrugged my shoulders angrily. I'd put these memories away a long time ago. Dredging them up again wasn't pleasant. "The really stupid thing was that I didn't even have a clue. I knew things weren't great between us, but I figured we'd work on it. I thought that was what couples who loved each other did."

"Where's Bob now?"

"Last I heard, Texas. That was three years ago, so the information's probably out of date. Not that it really matters. He has his life and I have mine. There's no need for us to be in touch."

"What about Davey? What about child support?"

"Bob didn't want Davey then, and I don't imagine anything's changed since. He could see his son if he wanted to. So far, he hasn't made the effort. He's never going to be Davey's father in anything but the biological sense and frankly, for Davey's sake, I think it's better that he stays away. As to financial support, let's just say it's lucky I have a secure job."

"You could take him to court."

"I could, but what would be the point? He's supposed to pay now, and he doesn't. Besides," I said defensively, "Davey and I are managing just fine."

"Just fine," Sam repeated. "Except that even though you claim to have put Bob behind you, you still manage your relationships in light of what happened with him."

"That's not true—"

"No? Then why do I get the impression you keep expecting me to take off? I'm not your ex-husband, Melanie. And for all you keep trying to throw up road blocks between us, I'm not going anywhere."

I wanted to believe that. I really did. But it just didn't jibe with what I'd known of life so far. In my experience women were the ones who threw themselves heart and soul into a relationship, who pledged undying love and really meant it. Men were looking for something easier; a commitment that wouldn't inconvenience Sunday football games or nights out with the guys. Davey and I were worth more than that, damn it.

Sam backed off after that and I was just as pleased to have the subject changed. Still, I found myself thinking about what he had said during the rest of the meal. Sam certainly wasn't Bob; and I was older and wiser than I had been. But maturity had brought with it caution, and also some finely honed survival instincts.

By the light of a dozen flame-tipped candles, I gazed over at Sam. We'd both been too full for dessert, but were enticed by the notion of vanilla mousse. He'd ordered one portion and two spoons. He dragged his through the thickest part of the whipped cream, then offered it to me with a grin.

If ever there was ever a man who tempted me to chuck survival to the wind, this was the one. Some women dive into icy cold water. I'm the type who works my way down the stairs, one agonizing inch at a time. I took Sam up on that offer of whipped cream, then I took a deep breath and dipped in my big toe.

Sam said he wasn't going to leave, so I invited him to Thanksgiving dinner.

"Thanksgiving?"

"You know, Thursday. Unless you have other plans."

He thought for a long moment, then said. "No, I'm free."

"You don't have to—"

"I want to."

"Good." I relaxed, feeling pleased. "I cook a pretty great turkey, if I do say so myself. I'm having the whole family over."

He paled slightly. "*Whole* family?"

"Don't worry, there aren't that many of us. Aunt Peg and Davey you already know, of course. Then there's my brother, Frank. He lives in Cos Cob. And my Aunt Rose. She was Peg's late husband's sister. My father's, too."

"That's all?"

"Oh, and Peter. Aunt Rose left the convent last summer to get married. He's her husband, the ex-priest."

A smile twitched around the corners of his mouth. "Sounds like an interesting group."

"You don't know the half of it. Rose and Peg have been feuding for years. Putting those two in the same room is like adding nitro to glycerin."

"Nitro to glycerin. I see."

"I figure you can help run interference."

"Of course. What about Frank? Where does he fit in?"

"Frank." I sighed. "He means well."

"That sounds promising."

"Then maybe I'm giving him too much credit. I wouldn't want to mislead you."

"I'm sure you wouldn't. Are we done yet? You're sure there's no razor-wielding uncle who's going to jump out of the closet? No long-lost cousin home from the institution for the holidays?"

"You're not taking me seriously."

"On the contrary, I'm taking you very seriously. You're trying to scare me away."

"I am not."

"Your aunt really left the convent to marry a priest?"

"Ex-priest," I corrected. "Peter's really very nice and normal. He's teaching college in New London now."

"Thanksgiving dinner," Sam said cheerfully. "Sounds great. What shall I bring?"

"Nothing alcoholic. Frank has a real appreciation for fine wine, and I'd just as soon he cut down."

"Problem?"

"Not yet. But they say alcoholism runs in families."

"So they do," Sam muttered.

I felt bad. All right, I felt terrible. But it was for his own good. Sam might as well know the worst right off the bat. Then if he wanted to, he could bail out gracefully. Davey and I might cry a little, but we'd recover.

We polished off the mousse and Sam called for the check. At least Joanie wouldn't have to worry about too late a night.

"Good news," said Aunt Peg.

It was early Sunday morning and I figured she was calling to see how my date with Sam had gone. Not that I'd told her we were going out, but when it comes to this particular relationship, Aunt Peg seems to have spies everywhere. In fact she'd gotten me when I was still in bed. Asleep. Alone. So what else was new?

"What's good news?"

"I talked to Crawford yesterday and he was happy to intercede." Aunt Peg chuckled. "I gather he was just as pleased to sic you in another direction. You and I are going to see Mrs. Byrd this afternoon."

"Where?"

"Pound Ridge. The shows are up in Boston this weekend, but Mrs. Byrd stayed home. We're expected at four for tea."

That conjured up images of white gloves and fine china. As Davey ran into my bedroom in his pajamas, bounced off the headboard and landed, laughing, on the pillow beside my head, I thought, what is wrong with this picture?

"I'd better start calling around for a baby-sitter."

"For who?" Davey demanded.

"You."

"I just had a baby-sitter."

"Well, now you're going to have another."

"No, I'm not!"

"Melanie?" said Aunt Peg.

I juggled the receiver to the other ear and fended off Davey's mock attack one-handed. "Right here."

"You can come?"

"Of course I'm coming. I wouldn't miss it." My son was glaring daggers at me. "I may have to bring Davey, though."

"See what you can do. I'll pick you up at three-thirty."

What I could do, as it turned out, was devote the morning and early afternoon to wearing Davey and Faith out. We had Joey Brickman over for a couple of hours in the morning, then went for a walk on the beach. By the time we returned from a game of Frisbee in Binney Park at two, I figured he was probably tired enough to insure his good behavior at Mrs. Byrd's. Of course, then he dropped off in a nap. When Aunt Peg arrived to pick us up, Davey was awake, alert, and once more raring to go.

Florence Byrd lived in a red brick Georgian mansion with tall, white columns, wrought-iron balconies and leaded windows. It took us a full two minutes to drive from the gate posts to the house on an elm-lined driveway that bisected several dozen acres of gently rolling meadow. Along the way, we passed two pheasants and a small herd of deer. Even Davey was impressed.

"Does Mrs. Byrd live in the town hall?" he asked as we climbed the front steps to the door.

"No, she just has a very nice house." I took a firmer grip on his hand. "Remember what we discussed about being on your best behavior?"

"Sure."

I'm always suspicious when capitulation comes that easily, but there was no time to dwell on the possibilities. Aunt Peg had rung the bell and the door was opened almost immediately by a maid in a starched navy uniform. She showed us into the library where Mrs. Byrd was waiting.

The room was massive and very beautiful. French doors opening to an outside terrace ran along one wall. Two others held mahogany bookshelves extending all the way up to a ceiling so high that a ladder was needed to reach the upper tiers. The remaining wall was dominated by a gray marble fireplace. Above the mantelpiece was an oil painting of pastoral fields and Thoroughbred horses. Richard Stone Reeves, I thought.

The room was large enough to contain several groupings of furniture. Mrs. Byrd was seated in a wing chair just in front of the fireplace, her legs covered by a plaid wool throw. Behind the brass screen, a fire burned and crackled, adding to the heat in the room. As the maid withdrew and closed the door behind her, Florence Byrd set aside the book she'd been reading and looked at her watch.

"You're punctual," she said. "I like that. It's better if I don't get up. I imagine you can find your way over."

We crossed the room and introduced ourselves. Mrs. Byrd extended a hand to Aunt Peg, then gave me a narrowed look. "We've met."

"Yes, last week at the dog show."

"Crawford didn't tell me he was sending me people I'd already met. I hate having to repeat myself." She turned to Davey. "Who's this?"

"My son, Davey." A sharp poke between the shoulder blades had the desired effect and he offered his hand.

"Nobody brings children to visit me," Florence Byrd said decisively. "I don't like children. Never had any of my own. I always had better things to do." Her foot tapped the floor beneath her chair and I realized she was feeling for a buzzer. "Dirk will entertain him while we talk. Is that all right with you, young man?"

Davey looked up at me and I nodded.

"Okay," he said. "Does Dirk know how to play games?"

"I don't think so. Maybe you can teach him some."

The double doors at the other end of the room opened. Dirk stood in the doorway. "Yes, Mrs. Byrd?"

"Young master Davey here is in need of entertainment. I thought perhaps you might know where to find a ball." Her gaze went back to my son. "You do know how to play catch, don't you?"

Davey nodded.

"Good. Run along."

Davey did, leaving Aunt Peg and me without even a backward glance. I was afraid he might have found Dirk's size or his stern dark suit forbidding, but he skipped happily across the Persian carpets and out of the room. "Hey," I heard him say as the door were closing. "Maybe we can find a bat, too."

Mrs. Byrd waved toward a sofa opposite her chair and Aunt Peg and I were seated. "I understand from Crawford that you want to discuss Jenny Maguire. To be perfectly direct, I don't see the point. The girl is gone. What difference could a discussion of the circumstances possibly make?"

"Are you aware that Jenny was murdered?" I asked.

"Murdered? That's not what I was told."

"It's true," said Aunt Peg. "The police are investigating the case as a homicide."

Mrs. Byrd looked back and forth between us. "What's your interest in this?"

The sofa we were seated on was plush and comfy. I had to shift my weight forward and perch on the edge of the cushions to fight being enveloped. "Jenny was a friend of mine. Aunt Peg and I both took handling classes from the Maguires. At first I thought that her death was just a senseless tragedy. But then I kept running across things that didn't make sense. Like Jenny's Miniature Poodle, Ziggy."

"What about him?"

The doors opened again. The maid entered, bearing a wide silver tray that she set on the table between us. Aside from the tea itself, there were blueberry scones and a plate of finger sandwiches. Lunch had been a hot dog grabbed from a concession truck at the beach. Too bad this wasn't the kind of place where you could dig in with both hands.

I got on with the story and contented myself to wait my turn. "Jenny hid him away and told everyone he was dead. Apparently she intended to go back for him, but she never got the chance."

"She also wrote a suicide note," said Aunt Peg. "Although both Melanie and I are convinced that she had no intention of killing herself."

"If you wouldn't mind pouring," said Mrs. Byrd. "My hands aren't as steady as they used to be." She watched with a critical eye while Aunt Peg complied. "And what conclusions have you drawn from these inconsistencies?"

I took my tea and the napkin that came with it. Any minute now, I'd be able to go for those sandwiches. "We think that Jenny was trapped in an unhappy marriage. She was desperate to escape from Rick and had made a plan to do so by faking her own suicide."

"You do, do you?"

Florence Byrd was glaring at me. I met her gaze calmly and squarely. "Yes, I do."

"And have you spoken about this to anyone else?"

"Nobody who's involved."

"I see." Mrs. Byrd took a long, slow sip of her tea, then set the delicate cup aside. "Well, as it happens," she said. "You're right."

❧❃ ❖ *Twenty-one* ❖ ❃❧

I was so surprised that for a moment I couldn't say anything. Aunt Peg, busy pouring the last cup of tea, was similarly speechless. Florence Byrd looked rather pleased with the effect she'd had.

"Eat," she said, waving toward the food on the tray. "I hardly have any appetite myself and Marie always makes too much."

I slid two of the small sandwiches onto my plate. "Jenny actually told you she was going to leave Rick?"

"Told me? It was my idea in the first place."

"*Your* idea?" Aunt Peg repeated.

"Jenny felt stifled by her husband. I could see it plain as day. She used to come here quite frequently, you know. It started because I wanted someone really good doing coat care on the show dogs. But as time went on, I could also see how much she enjoyed having a place to get away to.

"After she was finished in the kennel, Jenny would come up to the house and we'd take tea together, much as we're doing now. And don't you know, without fail there'd come a call from Rick, asking what was taking her so long and when she was coming home." Mrs. Byrd sniffed indignantly. "As if she wasn't entitled to a little free time of her own!"

"Angie told me that Jenny had thought about divorcing Rick."

"She did. That was several years ago. We didn't know each other then and she didn't have anyone who could give her the kind of moral support she needed to go through with it. Rick told Jenny that no matter what happened, he would never let her go and she believed him."

"Why didn't she reconsider divorce now?" asked Aunt Peg. "Why go to such extremes?"

"That was the way Jenny wanted to play it, and if you knew her at all, you'd know that she was very strong-willed." Mrs. Byrd reached a gnarled hand across the tray and added a dollop of cream to her tea. "I'm not without resources, if I do say so myself. I told her I'd be happy to hire a good lawyer, and we'd take out a restraining order if need be. But she said you only had to watch the tabloid shows on TV to know how ineffective those methods could be if a husband was determined to get to his wife.

"Jenny was tired of fighting with Rick. After all those years together, I think she was just mentally worn down. She was looking for the easiest way out and she decided that disappearing would be it. She didn't care how much she had to leave behind. The only thing that mattered to her was Ziggy. She wouldn't go without him."

I'm not a tea drinker, but I took a sip anyway. It was strong and tart and tasted of citrus; not nearly as good as coffee, but at least it would wash down the sandwiches. "Where was she planning to go?"

"I don't know the answer to that." Mrs. Byrd frowned. "Imagine, she wouldn't even tell me. I told her she could come here and be my kennel manager, but that wasn't far enough away to suit Jenny. I do know she was planning on making a clean break. She wanted to start out somewhere new and leave the dog show world behind forever."

I took a moment to ponder that and used the time to slather a scone with butter. "If you knew what she was planning, why didn't Jenny leave Ziggy here?"

"At the end, she was obsessed with keeping secrets. This is a large household, as you can see. It takes a lot of people just to keep things running smoothly. Jenny didn't want anyone to know what she was up to, especially not someone who might have a chance to talk to Rick."

"Someone like Dirk maybe?"

"Perhaps. I thought at that point that her concern bordered on paranoia. Of course, as things turned out, she was right to be afraid."

Aunt Peg shifted in her seat. "Do you think Jenny had any inkling she was being poisoned?"

"I knew she hadn't been feeling well," said Mrs. Byrd. "But she blamed it on stress. Concocting this plan, getting ready to set it in motion and trying to keep everything a secret. She was sure once she got away, she'd be fine."

"And she probably would have been," I said. "Except that before she could go, her system had already absorbed a fatal dosage of the arsenic."

"Rick must have guessed what she was going to do," Aunt Peg said softly. "He said he'd never let her go, and he meant it."

Finally the thought that I'd been grappling with for days had been voiced aloud. Even with so many signs pointing in Rick's direction, the notion that he might have been responsible for his wife's death just didn't seem possible. He was bright, energetic, filled with common sense; surely not a murderer. But then wasn't that what people always said when the police told them they'd been living next door to a serial killer? "But he seemed like such a nice young man!"

Obviously, he'd been obsessed with Jenny and although that idea was foreign to me as well, I'd seen enough to believe it was true. How much did it take, I wondered, to push someone over the edge from obsessive behavior to needing to take total control of another's destiny? Even if the only way to control them was to take their life in your hands.

"Do you know how Rick and Jenny got together in the first place?" I asked Mrs. Byrd.

"I know they met rather soon after Jenny had left home. Rick was always interested in her, right from the start, but Jenny was young and she wasn't in any hurry to get involved."

"What changed her mind?"

"I think it was several things. One that his ardor was so steadfast. Jenny was rather naive in the ways of the world. I'm sure she found Rick's attentions flattering. Another was that he was so different from her father. Do you know anything about her childhood?"

"A bit," I said and Aunt Peg nodded.

"Then you can see why Jenny would have been attracted to Rick. He seemed faithful and stable, and everything her father was not. Unfortunately in choosing not to duplicate her parents' own relationship, she went overboard in the other direction. And then Angie played a part, too."

"How?"

Mrs. Byrd's fingers smoothed the fine linen napkin she'd laid in her lap. "She was every bit as desperate to escape that turbulent home life as Jenny had been. And of course Jenny could understand that. She was happy to take her sister in even though I gather at the time she didn't necessarily have the resources to support them both."

"By teaming up with Rick Maguire, she was able to expand the business," said Aunt Peg.

"That's it exactly. It also helped that Rick and Angie got along like a house on fire. Oh, I'd imagine that what Angie really felt was a school-girl crush, but I gather she all but convinced Jenny she'd be crazy to let a man like that get away."

"So Rick and Jenny got married," I said slowly. "Angie moved in with them, and they all became one big happy family."

"One big dysfunctional family," said Aunt Peg.

I nudged her with my elbow. "You've been watching Oprah again, haven't you?"

Aunt Peg rudely elbowed me right back. Pointedly, I ignored her. "I've heard that at the time Jenny and Angie left home, their father was having an affair with a woman named Crystal Mars. Was that the reason they went?"

"It was certainly a contributing factor." Florence Byrd took a long, slow sip of tea.

"But Jenny has remained in touch with Crystal over the years. In fact, that's where she left Ziggy."

"It was."

I waited a beat, hoping she'd elaborate. She didn't. "Frankly, I found that surprising. I would think that the circumstances of their meeting would have made them enemies, not friends."

"On the surface of things, you're probably correct. But if you're hoping for further enlightenment, you've come to the wrong place. Jenny was a very private person. She had secrets she would not have wanted revealed when she was alive, and I feel no compunction to break her trust now that she's gone."

An uncomfortable silence followed. I selected another scone and bit off a large piece, leaving it to Aunt Peg to find another topic. As usual, she coped magnificently.

"There's one thing I don't understand," she said. "It's no secret Charlie was going for the Quaker Oats award. If Jenny had stayed through the end of the year, I imagine the dog would have been a shoo-in. Why would she make a plan to go when the goal was so close at hand?"

"That was my goal, not hers," Mrs. Byrd said firmly. "Don't forget, she was planning to leave handling behind forever. These awards that the dog show world finds so dreadfully important had pretty much lost all meaning for her.

"Of course, selfishly, I would have much preferred that she finish the job with Charlie. That was the way we set it up originally. But the sicker she began to feel, the more desperate Jenny became to get away, and I wasn't about to stand in her way."

"Besides," Florence Byrd added with a gleam in her eye. "Both Jenny and I doubted that her sudden disappearance at that stage of the game would harm the dog's chances. Fame or notoriety—when it comes to influencing judges, either one will do the trick."

"You've been proven right about that."

"Hardly." Mrs. Byrd's features tightened. "In the beginning, it looked as though Angie was going to work out. Good enough to coast through the end of the year, at any rate. The sympathy vote never hurts, you know. But now I'm having second thoughts. The dog was beaten yesterday up in Boston."

"By whom?" asked Aunt Peg.

"Harry Flynn, in the Variety of all things. Charlie hasn't lost a Variety since March. At this stage in his career, it's ludicrous. You better believe I let Angie know what I thought about that! I've waited half a century to win that award. I'm not going to get this close only to have her let it slip through my fingers."

Aunt Peg and Mrs. Byrd moved on to the rest of the results from the previous day's show, and I left them in the library and went off to find Davey. The house was so big, I took three wrong turns before I finally found the kitchen. Marie was there, shelling peas and watching a Spanish soap opera on a little TV on the counter. She led me past the pantry and into a small sitting room. Davey and Dirk were bent over a table by the window. Both were concentrating fiercely on the checkerboard between them.

"Who's winning?" I asked.

Dirk gestured toward the stack of checkers piled high in front of my son. "He is."

Davey made his move and looked up proudly. "I've won every game so far. I like playing with Dirk."

I could see how he might. Though I was a great believer in bolstering Davey's self-confidence, even I didn't
let him win *every* game.

"It's time to go, honey."

"Not yet. I'm having fun. Dirk said we could raid the
refrigerator after this. Did you know this house has three
whole floors?"

"I'm sure it does." I watched as my son jumped Dirk's
last two checkers with a flourish, then eased him up out
of the upholstered chair.

"I told him we could have cookies," said Dirk. Even
though he was sitting down, we were at eye level with
each other. "He's been real good."

I gave Davey's shoulders a squeeze. "I guess we could
manage a minute or two for cookies."

"Yea!" cried Davey. "Do you have Oreos?"

"Let's go see."

The kitchen was empty now, though the soap opera
was still playing. A colander filled with freshly washed
peas sat beside the sink. Dirk disappeared into the pantry
and reemerged with a bright yellow package.

"Better than Oreos," he said to Davey, tearing at the
wrapping. "Mallomars."

Watching him pop one in his mouth whole, it didn't
take much imagination to figure out who they were
stocked for. But when Dirk offered one to me, I didn't de-
cline. While Davey sidled closer to the counter, fascinated
by the characters on the TV speaking in a language he
couldn't understand, I followed Dirk over to the gleam-
ing sub-zero refrigerator.

"My aunt and I came here today to talk to Mrs. Byrd
about Jenny Maguire."

Dirk opened the refrigerator and got out a carton of milk. "That's really none of my business."

"I understand you were a friend of Jenny's, too."

"Not really."

"But you saw her all the time at the dog shows."

He opened a glass fronted cabinet, took out a faceted tumbler that looked as though it should have been holding Chivas Regal and poured milk up to the brim. "My job is to look out for Mrs. Byrd. I go where she wants me to go. I see what she wants me to see."

"I'd imagine you see a lot more than that."

The flattery didn't help. Dirk drained half his milk in one long draught and went back for another Mallomar without making any response.

"And of course she was here some days working in the kennel, too," I prodded.

"I don't do dogs."

"Excuse me?"

Dirk's lips parted in a toothy smile. "Everybody's got their limits. Marie, she doesn't do any climbing or heavy lifting when she's cleaning. Someone's gotta come in special for that. Me, I don't do dogs. Not these dogs, anyway. Other people want to go crazy over a bunch of spaniels too in-bred to earn their keep in the hunting field, that's their business. Not mine. I keep out of it."

That was a long speech for him. Dirk had to refuel with another swig of milk and an additional cookie.

"It must be hard for you then, having to spend so much time at dog shows when you're not that interested in what's going on."

"I'm getting paid." Dirk shrugged. "I find enough to do."

"And enough to look at?"

His fleshy brow drew downward though he stopped just short of frowning. "What's that supposed to mean?"

"Angie Peterson told me you were interested in her sister. She said you were always watching her."

"That's a crock."

"Jenny was very pretty."

"So what if she was?"

"There's no harm in watching, Dirk. I was just curious why, that's all."

"She worked for Mrs. Byrd, didn't she? That's my job, keeping an eye out."

"I guess you got to talk to her, too."

"Sometimes, not very often."

"Not as often as you would have liked?"

His voice lowered to a growl. "Jenny was a nice girl. Real nice. It wasn't my fault what happened to her. If I could have kept bad things away from Jenny, I would have."

"Nobody's saying it was your fault—"

"I want you to listen." Dirk leaned down over me, his size and sheer physical presence trapping me against the counter. "And listen good. No matter what anybody thinks, I never had anything but Jenny's best interests at heart."

"Mom, hey!" Davey was staring at the two of us with a bewildered look on his face. Distracted, Dirk straightened and I slithered out from behind him. "You said it was time to go."

"It is." I crossed the room and took Davey's hand in mine. "Say good-bye and thank you."

"Good-bye," said Davey. "You're not a very good checkers player."

Under the circumstances, it was close enough.

Aunt Peg was saying good-bye to Florence Byrd when we got back to the library, and Davey and I did the same. The older woman shook Davey's hand gravely. "Did Dirk take good care of you?" she inquired.

"Unhn. He gave me Mallomars."

She nodded crisply. "He's good at looking out for people."

An interesting thought occurred to me. "Did you ever ask him to keep an eye on Jenny?"

"Jenny Maguire?" One thin, arched brow rose. "Why would I have done that?"

"No reason. I was just wondering."

As we left I couldn't help but think that a lot of people seemed to think they knew what was best for Jenny. With everybody so concerned about her welfare, how had she ended up dead?

❧❖ *Twenty-two* ❖❧

The visit with Florence Byrd had answered some questions, but it had also posed others. Luckily Faith seemed to have developed a taste for peanut butter biscuits, so the next afternoon when I piled her and Davey in the car and set off for Stratford, the trip came with a ready-made excuse.

Now that I actually knew where I was going, it didn't take that long to get to North Moon kennel. For late November the day was unseasonably warm. As we neared the end of the long, rutted driveway we passed Sarah on a pink two-wheeler bike. She wore faded jeans, torn across one knee, and a hooded jacket that flapped loose behind her. Her dark hair was ruffled by the breeze. As I parked the car, she rode up beside us, hopped off her bike and waved.

"Hey!" cried Davey. "Who's that?"

"Her name is Sarah. She's Crystal's daughter."

My son, whose patience with running errands was notoriously short, was waving back enthusiastically. "Do you think she wants to play?"

"Why don't you get out and ask her?"

Faith and Davey spilled from the car together, converging on Sarah, who seemed delighted by the prospect of visitors. When Faith jumped up and licked her face, she cupped the puppy's head in her hands and giggled out loud.

"Her name's Faith," Davey said importantly. "She likes to play hide and seek."

"So do I," said Sarah.

I went inside when they began laying down the ground rules. Crystal was up on a small step ladder, tacking new posters to a section of wall. She had her back to the door, but turned as the chimes tinkled.

"Is this straight?" she mumbled around a mouthful of push pins.

I walked to the center of the room to view the poster head on. It featured a shot of a Shih Tzu with a pink bow in its hair. "Life's short," it read. "Bite hard."

"Looks good to me."

One corner had already been tacked to the wall. Crystal smoothed the poster flat and quickly attached the rest. "Thanks," she said, hopping down. "What can I get for you?"

"More biscuits?"

"Sure." Crystal grinned. "I knew your puppy'd go for the peanut butter. They always do." She walked into the other room and emerged with a five-pound bag.

"How's Ziggy doing?"

"Fine. Better every day. That be all?" She was already punching numbers into the cash register.

So much for that topic. There didn't seem to be any way to lead gracefully into the questions I wanted to ask.

On the other hand, if I didn't get started soon she'd have me out the door before I'd learned a thing.

"I know this is really none of my business, but I've been talking to a lot of people since Jenny died. I've been trying to make sense of what happened to her."

Crystal's hand stilled above the register's keys. She looked at me and waited.

"I've heard that you and Jenny's father were . . . involved."

"Roger Peterson was *involved* with a lot of women." She sneered over the euphemism I'd chosen. "It didn't mean much."

"Maybe not to you, but how about Jenny?"

"I wasn't the first, you know." Crystal's rough laugh held no humor. "Nor the last."

"But still, the fact that you would become friends afterward seems . . . unlikely."

"Hell, all of life's unlikely. Haven't you figured that out yet?" She fished beneath the counter and came up with a pack of cigarettes. "Jenny wasn't happy about what happened, but she'd seen a few women come and go. She blamed her father for what went on, not me."

The rationalization didn't ring entirely true. Yet Jenny *had* kept in touch with Crystal and she obviously trusted her enough to leave her most cherished possession in the woman's care. Why?

"Four ninety-five." With one hand, Crystal punched out the numbers hard. The other was shaking a cigarette loose from the pack.

"But why did—?"

"Four ninety-five," she said firmly. "And no more questions. You were right about what you said before.

None of this is any of your business. So just stay out of it, okay?"

There didn't seem to be much I could say to that. I opened my purse, pulled out my wallet, and handed over a five-dollar bill. The conversation must have really upset her. She didn't even try to sell me a tee shirt.

Thanksgiving is one of my favorite holidays of the year. There's a four-day weekend, you don't have to buy presents, and you get to cook the way everybody used to before words like high-fiber and cholesterol became part of our everyday vocabulary. Davey was already looking forward to Thanksgiving because I'd promised to invite the whole family. When he heard that I'd added Sam to the guest list, he was overjoyed.

My brother, Frank, arrived early. He's taller than me by more than half a foot, and has the same straight brown hair that he cuts short and mousses upward. At twenty-six, he's still in the buddy stage. He and his friends are into hanging out and drinking beer; and family holidays tend to leave them at a loss. The parade's for kids, and football doesn't start until the afternoon. Having left the invitation open-ended, I figured Frank would roll out of bed by eleven and be at my house around noon. He beat my estimate by fifteen minutes.

"Anybody home?" he yelled, letting himself in the front door.

"Uncle Frank!"

Davey was in the living room watching the Macy's parade on TV. He jumped up but Faith who'd been lying at his side was faster. She raced out into the hall, barking furiously.

If Frank had just held his ground he would have been all right. But I came out of the kitchen in time to see him step back as the Poodle puppy launched her affectionate attack. Her front paws bounced off his chest as he grabbed for the newel post and came up empty. The two of them went down in a heap.

"Call her off!" he cried, his voice muffled by forty pounds of hairy puppy. "I think she's killing me."

"Only if you can be licked to death." I looped both arms around Faith's neck and hauled her back. "Stand up quick. Now's your chance."

"This is getting to be as bad as going to Aunt Peg's."

"Bite your tongue. She's only one puppy. A bit overly exuberant, perhaps—"

"My turn!"

My brother had barely regained his feet when Davey launched the second offensive of the day. Luckily Frank handled this one better. Arms wrapped tightly around Frank's legs, Davey eyed the bag in his uncle's hands.

"What did you bring me?"

"Chocolate eclairs from St. Moritz. Enough for everybody. That is, if the hound from hell didn't just crush them."

"Can I have mine now?"

"Not a chance." I slipped in and snagged the bag of goodies. "That's dessert. I hope you brought plenty. I've added another guest."

As Davey and Faith went back to the TV, Frank pulled off his coat and hung it up, then followed me out to the kitchen. "Anyone I know?"

"Sam Driver," I said casually. "He's a friend."

"I see."

"Don't you dare, Frank."

"Don't what?"

I'd seen that butter-wouldn't-melt-in-my-mouth look before. He'd used it to great effect on our parents when we were younger, and I couldn't count the number of times I'd taken the rap for his misdeeds. "Don't you dare embarrass me."

"Me?" He opened the fridge and zeroed in on a hunk of Swiss cheese. "I'll be the least of your worries. You must be serious about this guy if you're letting him brave the Turnbull dragons."

With unerring instinct, Frank had gone straight for what worried me most. "Maybe marriage has softened Aunt Rose," I ventured.

"Not likely! But hey, it's your funeral."

I certainly hoped not. Just to get back at my brother, I asked about his job. Frank's resume—if he had one—would read like a textbook example of how not to plan a career. Unemployed more often than not, he was currently selling men's wear at a department store in the mall. He hated it and I knew it.

That's the problem with being siblings. You may grow up, but you never get past the petty squabbles of your childhood.

After that, Frank took Davey and a football outside and taught him how to throw as much of a long bomb as our small backyard could manage. I finished stuffing the turkey and got it in the oven. Then we all took Faith for a long walk around the neighborhood. By two o'clock, when everyone else began to arrive, Faith and Davey were pleasantly tired, most of the preparations were complete, and the house smelled deliciously of roast turkey.

Aunt Rose and Peter brought a pan of homemade cornbread. Aunt Peg arrived with a sweet potato and marsh-mallow casserole—representing the sugar food group, I supposed. Sam pulled in last and brought flowers; a pot of live tulips. In November, no less. The man was a marvel.

Most of the rest of the family was settled in the living room when Sam got there. Frank was serving drinks, but he took time out from his duties to come into the kitchen and size Sam up. The two of them circled each other like a pair of male dogs staking out virgin territory.

I was tempted to remind them it was *my* turf, and that both of them were there at my sufferance, but I was too busy stirring the cranberries and dribbling in sugar to dive into the middle of that testosterone fest. Instead I let them work things out for themselves. Even wolves get along once they've established dominance.

"So you're Mel's new boyfriend," said Frank. Well, that set the tone.

"I suppose I am." Sam opened the refrigerator and helped himself to a beer. So that Frank could see how comfortable he was in my kitchen, no doubt.

"You two known each other long?"

"Not yet, but we're working on it."

"Mel doesn't invite many . . . friends . . . to family gatherings."

Sam popped the top on his beer and had a sip. Over the top of the can, he gave me a look. "I guess I should be flattered."

"Not necessarily." Frank was enjoying himself now. "Did she tell you much about the family?"

"She did everything but make me sign a waiver of liability. I hear Peg and Rose don't get along." Sam had been introduced on the way in.

"Never have."

"I'll tell you what. Any trouble starts, I'll go for Peg and you take the scrawny one."

Frank grinned. "What about Peter?"

"He'll have to fend for himself."

"Deal."

They shook on it, finished putting the rest of the drinks on the tray, and headed into the living room, already halfway to being friends.

When the cranberry sauce was ready, I turned off the heat and moved the pot to a back burner. I got out a platter of chopped veggies and dip that I'd prepared earlier and carried it into the living room. To my amazement, everything seemed to be going smoothly. Peter, who was teaching his first semester of political science at Connecticut College, was holding court.

Though he and Aunt Rose had been married only a few months, they already had that comfortable look of long married couples about them. Peter was in his mid-fifties, a few years older than Rose. His ginger brown hair had receded back from his temples and was thinning seriously on top. The buttons of his cardigan sweater gapped over the beginnings of a new paunch. Perhaps Aunt Rose was feeding him better than the seminary had, although after thirty years in the convent, I couldn't imagine where she might have learned to cook.

She, too, had changed in the short amount of time since I'd seen her last. Though her face was still thin and angular, her expression had softened. Rose was a woman who had taken her duties as an emissary of God very seriously. Now she was on her own time, and appeared to be enjoying the change.

Her graying hair, kept short for so many years to combat the wages of vanity and to fit beneath a cowl, had now grown long enough to curl around her ears. She was wearing pale peach lipstick and just a hint of blush. A slim gold wedding band was her only jewelry.

Rose and Peter were holding hands and I found the sight unexpectedly touching. It was a simple gesture, almost old-fashioned in a way; a silent communication of affection and support.

"It sounds as though you've been keeping yourself busy," Aunt Peg said when Peter had finished. She turned to her sister-in-law. "What about you, Rose? Now that you've put prayer and good works behind you, what do you do all day?"

Peg had disapproved when Rose left the convent. That was nothing new. Peg disapproved of nearly everything Rose did; and the two of them had been at each other's throats for years.

"I wouldn't exactly say I've put them behind me," Rose said complacently. I saw Peter give her fingers a squeeze. "Actually I've been doing volunteer work at a shelter in New London. As I'm sure you know, the secular world has no shortage of worthwhile projects that need attending to."

"And of course you'd be just the one to set them straight on how things should be done."

"I do my best." Aunt Rose actually smiled this time.

I could see Aunt Peg's frustration level rising. What good did it do to toss barbs at someone who refused to rise to the bait? Before she could try another insult, I stood between them and offered the vegetable platter.

"Here, Aunt Peg. Have a carrot."

"I'm not hungry, dear."

"Have one anyway."

"My, we have gotten pushy, haven't we?" She looked past my shoulder to the couch where Rose was sitting. "I guess we know which side of the family that comes from."

"There's nothing wrong with knowing what you want," Rose said firmly. "I'd say that's a sign of intelligence, wouldn't you?" She directed the question to Sam, who looked as though he'd just been lobbed a flaming howitzer.

He recovered quickly, though. "I'd say the surest sign of intelligence is knowing when not to step into the middle of an argument."

"Good answer." Peter applauded.

"Good answer!" Davey echoed. I don't think he had a clue what we were talking about. "Is it time to eat yet?"

Bless that boy for asking.

"Just about," I said, escaping to the kitchen to finish the preparations.

Sam found me there, shaking my head and muttering as I took the turkey out of the oven. He came up behind me and slipped his arms around my waist. "Don't worry," he said. "Things will settle down."

"Settle down? Those two aren't even warmed up yet!"

He chuckled softly into the back of my neck. "You see? Now we have something to look forward to."

Maybe it was the good food that mellowed them. Or the wine I kept pouring willy-nilly into their glasses. But for some reason the rest of the day didn't go nearly as badly as I'd feared. Clearly Peter had a calming influence on his new wife. And with Frank, Sam, and me tag-teaming Aunt Peg, there simply wasn't an opportunity for her to get into much trouble.

There was an awkward moment when Rose looked askance at the sweet potato and marshmallow casserole. And then another when Peg tried to do Peter out of the last eclair by glancing at his waistline and inquiring if he was sure he thought he ought to have seconds. But overall, I thought it went well. At least nobody came to blows.

Aunt Rose and Peter had the longest drive home. They left first, followed shortly by Aunt Peg who had her Poodles at home to attend to. Sam had the same excuse, but he didn't seem in a hurry to go anywhere.

While I finished cleaning up, Frank and Sam sat Davey down on the couch between them and introduced him to the manly joys of watching football. By the time I got out of the kitchen, my son was ogling cheerleaders and trying out a victory dance. I drew the line at audience participation when he spiked his rubber football and knocked over a lamp. Then I settled down beside them—four was a pleasantly tight fit on my couch—and watched the second half.

I've had holidays that have gone worse.

Frank left when the game ended. I'd hoped Sam might stay later, but it turned out he couldn't. To my surprise, he had a plane to catch. His sister in Atlanta had invited him to come visit for the holiday weekend. He'd accepted, then delayed his departure by a day when I'd tendered my invitation.

I tried to feel guilty that he'd missed Thanksgiving with his family, but the emotion just wouldn't take hold. Real, deep-down happiness took its place. For the first time in a long time, I felt truly cared for.

"So," he said as I walked him outside to his car. "Did I pass the test?"

The night air was cold and I hadn't bothered with a coat. I didn't mind a bit when he wrapped his arms around me. I snuggled closer for warmth, and other things.

"What test?" I asked innocently.

He didn't answer that question. Instead he dipped his head down and we kissed. Long moments passed before he pulled his lips the tiniest bit away.

"You're running out of excuses, Melanie."

"Thank God."

It was too dark to see, but I thought he was smiling.

❧❋ ❀ *Twenty-three* ❀ ❋❧

The Springfield cluster of dog shows is held at the Eastern State Exposition Grounds in West Springfield, Massachusetts. It's a wonderful location for the purpose because it's easy to get to, the buildings are large and well-lit and there is plenty of room for parking. Every year, the number of dog clubs making use of the site seems to grow; and the November cluster has become one of the largest on the East Coast.

The shows over Thanksgiving weekend run Friday through Monday. Aunt Peg was planning on showing her bitch all four days; Faith was entered on Saturday and Sunday. Two shows were plenty for a puppy her age, and besides, Davey and I needed to be back at school after the weekend.

Most of the breed competition was scheduled to be held in the largest building on the site. Eighteen rings filled the middle of the huge hall. The grooming area formed a wide band around the rings, and dozens of concession stands hugged the walls. Faith wasn't showing until the next day, but when we arrived on Friday I pulled up to the unloading zone and brought in all my stuff. At a cluster this size, everybody stakes out their territory early and there is much vying for the best spots.

Aunt Peg and I would be taking our Poodles back to the hotel with us at night; but many of the other exhibitors simplified their lives by leaving their dogs in the building. The dogs ate and slept in their crates, and exercised in paper floored pens that were set up in the aisles after the show ended each day. The building was locked at eleven o'clock each night and reopened at seven in the morning. Show dogs travel a lot and are used to such restrictions. For them, it was all just part of the routine.

It was mid-morning when Davey, Faith, and I arrived and the first day's dog show was already in progress. It took me nearly twenty minutes to find Aunt Peg's set-up, mostly because she'd chosen a spot that was nowhere near the Poodle ring. In that time my tour of the building had taken me by Crystal's concession stand, where she hadn't returned my wave, and past numerous food booths where my ever-hungry child had exclaimed hopefully over everything from foot-long hot dogs to candied apples.

"What are you doing way over here?" I set my grooming table down on the ground with a thump I hoped was loud enough to convey my displeasure.

"Spying," Aunt Peg confided in a low tone. She gestured toward the next aisle over and I saw the stacked crates and green monogrammed towels of Shamrock Kennels.

Exhibitors may set up anywhere within the grooming area they wish. Since it's most practical to be near your ring, however, the dogs tend to cluster together by breed or group. As I placed my table in the space Aunt Peg had saved, I could see that we were in the thick of sporting dog territory. Not only were Rick and Angie next door on one side, but Harry Flynn was only an aisle away in the other. Unfortunately the Poodle ring wasn't even within view.

"What have you seen so far?"

"Nothing."

Just about what I'd expected. I looked around the setup. With the four-day stay in mind, Aunt Peg had built herself a home away from home. The crates, tack box, and grooming tables went to every show. But for Springfield, she'd also added chairs, buckets for spot cleaning, and her big, free-standing blow dryer so that Peaches's bracelets and tail could be freshly washed and dried each morning. An orange extension cord snaked off through the crates, hooking us up for electricity.

I hopped Faith up on her table and told her to stay, then cleaned a stack of new *Dog Scenes* off a folding chair and got Davey settled with a juice box and a book. When I got back from parking the car, he was still happily occupied. Thank goodness for Richard Scarry and lowly worm.

Aunt Peg had left Peaches on her table and was standing at the end of the aisle, staring off toward the rings. As I came up behind her, I could see that Ascob Cocker Spaniels were being judged in ring five. Angie and Charlie were standing ringside awaiting their turn, but that wasn't the direction Peg was looking.

"What's going on?" I asked.

"Bearded Collies."

The dogs were medium sized and covered with long, flowing hair. Ring eight was filled with them. I scanned the faces of the exhibitors and felt none the wiser. "So what?"

"Look who's judging."

I did, but it didn't help. The man was of average height, but strongly built. His features were coarse and a thick head of silver hair was matched by bushy eyebrows and an equally full mustache. His hand on a dog was confident, but gentle. Most were wagging their tails by the time he was done.

"Who is he?"

Aunt Peg glanced over to the Shamrock set-up before answering. "Roger Peterson."

It took a moment for the name to register. Then I joined her in staring. "Jenny and Angie's *father?*"

Peg nodded. She was holding the catalogue in her hands. "According to the roster, Lavinia's here too. She's judging a full slate of toy breeds over in ring one."

I glanced toward the Cocker ring. Angie and Charlie were still waiting outside the gate; specials had yet to be called. From her vantage point, I doubted if she could see her father, but she'd angled the Cocker so that they were facing the other way.

"Do you think Angie knows?"

"She must. Actually considering how many shows a year the Petersons judge, it's probably less surprising that they're here than that we haven't run into them sooner."

"Do you think Angie will talk to them?"

"Not during the show, certainly. There are gray areas of involvement between judge and exhibitor that the AKC frowns upon. Not that Angie will be showing any dogs under her parents—she couldn't do that. But still, if they're going to talk, I'm sure it will be afterward."

I turned to see what Angie was doing. The Best of Variety class was in the ring. Only two specials were in contention: Charlie and a red Cocker with Harry Flynn, presumably the one he'd beaten Charlie with the week before in Boston. This time, however, Angie and Charlie sailed right through. The judge took almost no time in making her decision and awarding the purple and gold rosette to Florence Byrd's dog.

Peg headed back to her tables to finish grooming. Since Faith wasn't showing until the next day, I waited and watched as the photographer was called and the win pictures taken. Angie, of course, was all smiles. The judge held the ribbon, looking proper and dignified and very satisfied with her choice. Charlie's plush coat gleamed. When the photographer threw a squeaky toy to get his attention, he cocked his head to one side becomingly.

Only one thing marred the happy tableau. When the picture had been taken, Angie gathered up dog and ribbon and stepped aside to let the next winner take her place. She headed for the gate, then paused. Standing on her toes, she looked across at ring eight where her father was judging.

Was she hoping he'd seen her win? If so, she had to be disappointed. Roger Peterson never turned around; never even looked up. Angie cradled Charlie against her chest, and left the ring, her expression bleak.

Davey and I went off to get lunch while Aunt Peg progressed from brushing to putting in Peaches's top-knot. The food sellers were at the other end of the building and on the way there, we took a detour past ring one. Yorkshire Terriers were being judged and a schedule posted by the gate identified the judge as Lavinia Peterson. I slowed down to take a look.

Like Jenny, Mrs. Peterson was petite. From things I'd heard, I imagined she was in her mid-fifties, but she looked at least a decade younger. Her hair was blond—a shade too brassy to be natural—and gathered back in a smooth chignon. She wore a boxy suit made of nubby fabric, support hose, and sturdy shoes that looked as though they'd been chosen with comfort in mind. Her hand on a dog, like her husband's, was steady and efficient.

"Come on," said Davey, tugging on my arm. "I'm *starving*. You can see dogs anytime."

I allowed myself to be pulled away and we spent the next twenty minutes waiting in line at the food concession. Luckily Davey didn't faint from hunger before our turn came. He scarfed down a hamburger in no time flat and polished off most of the french fries while I was nibbling at a chicken sandwich. Dog show food is nothing to write home about.

On the way back, pictures were being taken in ring one. Mrs. Peterson was chatting with Crawford Langley, who had a Yorkie posed on the table in front of them. A plaque, also on the table, identified the dog as having won Best of Winners. I glanced up at the schedule. The judge was on lunch break now. Her next assignment didn't begin until one fifteen.

Pictures finished. Mrs. Peterson headed for the judge's table in the corner of the ring. She gathered up her things and Davey and I were waiting at the gate when she came out.

"Excuse me," I said.

She stopped and stiffened, as if bracing herself for an encounter with a disgruntled exhibitor. Up close, I saw she had Jenny's eyes, rich brown flecked with gold.

"Yes?"

I held out my hand. "My name is Melanie Travis. I was a friend of Jenny's. I just wanted to tell you how sorry I was about what happened."

She looked me up and down carefully, then took my hand and shook it briefly. "Thank you," she said before turning away.

"I also wanted to mention, in case you didn't know . . . I'm sure you know, but in case you didn't . . ."

Lavinia Peterson listened to my fumbling with a hard stare.

"Angie is here."

"I'm aware of that."

"I think she's hoping you'll watch her show her dogs."

"That won't be possible. I have my own job to do. Now if you'll excuse me, I'm late for lunch."

Her steward had waited while we'd spoken and the two of them walked away together. I stared after them. With family like that, it was no wonder Angie and Jenny couldn't wait to get away.

Davey and I went back to the set-up. Aunt Peg was ready to take Peaches up to the Standard Poodle ring. I slipped Faith into one of the empty crates, picked up hair spray, a big comb, and scissors to take with us, and ran interference for them on the way over.

After all those hours of preparation, Peaches only placed third in the Open class. For all her hard work, Aunt Peg got a little strip of colored ribbon and a thank-you-for-coming. Worse still, Peaches was beaten by a brown bitch with a long back and a straight hindquarter shown by a handler from Ohio. I was hopping mad, but Aunt Peg who has been around longer than just about anybody, only shrugged.

"But the bitch is ugly," I whispered furiously. "I don't see how she could have beaten you."

Aunt Peg gazed back into the ring where Winners Bitch was being judged. "She has a pretty head. And Dermott's known for liking browns."

"But Peaches is a better Poodle!"

"That's your opinion. Obviously not the judge's. Don't worry, this is only the first day. We'll have three more chances to do something."

That made me think of the next day's judging, and of Faith who was sitting back at the set-up in a crate. She hadn't been exercised for several hours. I left Davey with Aunt Peg at ringside, went back and got my puppy and took her outside for a run. She hopped and played and spun exuberantly on the end of her lead.

Ten minutes later, when I brought her back into the building, Faith still refused to settle down. The noise and crowding and confusion didn't upset her, but it did seem to make her forget every bit of training she'd ever had. I couldn't imagine how I'd ever be able to get her to behave in the ring the next day.

There was a small open space in the grooming area near our set-up and I took Faith there for a few minutes practice. It quickly became evident how badly she needed it. When I walked her into her stand, she fidgeted. When I set her front legs, she moved her rear. When I reached out to fix her back legs, she scooted out from under my arm.

I tried coaxing. I tried being stern. Nothing seemed to help. I began to lose my temper, which is about the worst thing that can happen when you're trying to train a puppy. I was about to give up and put her back in her crate when a familiar voice said, "Here. Try this."

Rick must have returned to the Shamrock set-up while I was busy with Faith. He came over to where we were standing and held out a piece of dried liver. "There's too much going on in here. Her attention's all over the place. Let's start with getting her to look at you."

What he said made sense. But since the last time I'd seen Rick Maguire, I'd talked to a lot of people and done a great deal of thinking. At the moment, my thoughts in his direction were far from kindly. At the very least his treatment of his wife had compelled her to concoct a desperate plan to escape. At worst, I might have been standing next to a murderer. I might not have been able to prove much of what I knew about Rick, but that didn't mean I had to be civil to him.

When I didn't take the liver, Rick shifted his hand, dangling the treat under Faith's nose. Almost immediately it had the desired effect. The puppy stopped thinking about everything that was going on around her and focused on Rick's fingers. He started to take Faith's leash but I snatched it back out of reach.

"Leave her alone."

"Sure, if that's what you want." He held out his hand once more. "But try the liver yourself. It'll help."

"I don't want your help," I said firmly. Unfortunately my exit was spoiled by Faith who, having scented the bait in Rick's hand, was determined to remain where she was.

"Is something wrong?"

"Yes, something's wrong!"

I don't lose my temper very often. But when it goes, it's gone. Six weeks worth of anger and frustration came to the surface. Six weeks of watching Rick and Angie going on about their lives as if Jenny had never even existed. Six weeks of talking to people who didn't seem concerned about the injustice of Jenny's death, but rather worried about how it might effect their dogs' careers.

I looked around. We were surrounded on all sides by spectators and exhibitors. That, added to my anger, made me brave.

"I know what you did to Jenny."

"What are you talking about?"

"She was planning on leaving you. You'd stopped her once before, Rick. Is that what happened this time too?"

Anger narrowed his gaze. He glanced around, checking to make sure we weren't being overheard. "You must be out of your mind."

I crossed my arms over my chest. "My mind is perfectly clear. You're the one who's in trouble."

A long moment passed. Rick was obviously wondering how much I knew. "I'll admit sometimes Jenny made me mad," he said finally. "But believe me, if I had ever hurt her, it would have been done quickly, out of passion. And I'd have done it with my bare hands."

Faith didn't like his tone; she began to growl. The rumble was low and menacing, deep in her throat. I looped my fingers through her collar.

Rick glared down at her, then up at me. "Don't make

accusations you know nothing about. Talk like that will get you in trouble."

"Are you threatening me?"

"No." His voice was hard. "I'm telling you like it is."

⊱❖ *Twenty-four* ❖⊰

"I did something really stupid," I said. The Poodle judging was over and Aunt Peg and Davey had finally reappeared. My son grabbed Faith's leash and they began to play. I held a whispered conference with Aunt Peg. "I told Rick what I knew about him and Jenny."

"And?"

"He admitted they'd been having some problems, but denied everything else."

"Of course he denied it. I wish I'd been here. Why didn't you wait for me?"

As if accusing someone of murder was something you planned to do in advance. "It just happened. I was working with Faith and Rick came over. He tried to give me some handling tips, and I blew up. I know it was a mistake, but the whole situation just makes me so angry. Jenny's gone, and nobody even seems to care."

"I'll bet Rick cared when you called him a murderer."

"He did. And he also said something else that was interesting. He said if he had ever hurt Jenny, it would have happened quickly, out of passion."

Aunt Peg looked up. She'd put Peaches up on her table and was spraying the mane coat with a conditioner that would dissolve the hair spray. "That makes sense."

"It does, doesn't it?"

Both of us frowned at that, but neither had any more input. Aunt Peg got back to work, and Davey and I put on our coats and took the puppy with us outside for a look at the big rigs. When we came back in, the group judging had started. Roger Peterson had already finished doing Hounds. The Non-Sporting group was in, and Sporting was next. Angie and Rick were at their set-up, getting Charlie ready. On the other side, Harry Flynn was working just as hard on his Springer Spaniel. Each group was pointedly ignoring the other.

I slipped Faith into her crate and took Davey up to the group ring. Aunt Peg was there somewhere cheering for the Poodles; but the crowds were so thick I couldn't find her. There was an opening on the rail just behind the steward's table. I moved in close to the ring and picked Davey up so he'd be able to see.

The Tibetan Terrier had just won the Non-Sporting group, with the Standard Poodle placing fourth. As the sporting dogs came filing into the ring and lined up in size order I realized that several of the day's judges had taken advantage of the empty steward's chairs to sit and watch. Roger Peterson was among them.

A young sandy-haired judge was sitting next to him. The younger man gestured toward Charlie and said, "That's the dog to beat in this group. I had him myself in Annapolis last summer and he's every bit as good as he's supposed to be."

Roger Peterson merely grunted.

"You must have judged him yourself," said the man

pushed, probably hoping to make a good impression on his esteemed colleague.

"No," Peterson said shortly. "I haven't."

"But—" The man stopped, his face coloring as he made the connection between them. Neither Angie nor Jenny was eligible to handle a dog in their parents' ring, and there was no way the Petersons could have judged Charlie. "Listen, I'm sorry . . ."

"Don't mention it."

The officiating judge sent the line of dogs around the ring. From the beginning, Charlie was a stand-out. The individual examinations began and I shifted my attention back to the two men in front of me.

The younger judge was squirming in his seat, probably trying to figure out how to make up for his earlier faux pas. Roger Peterson was watching the dogs. As far as I could tell, he wasn't paying any more attention to his daughter than to anyone else.

When Charlie's turn came on the table, the young judge leaned over and whispered, "She does a very nice job with that dog."

"Good enough." Having been prodded, Peterson studied his daughter's technique. "Jenny was better."

Angie swept Charlie down off the table. At the judge's direction, she gaited the Cocker in a straight line down and back the length of the big ring.

The younger man tried again. "They make a good-looking team, don't they?"

Peterson considered the pair for a moment, then finally nodded. "Angie's been working at it. Must have been. With Jenny, all that talent just came naturally. Angie always had to work for everything she got."

As he spoke, the group judge started down the line, selecting the dogs that would make her first cut. It soon became obvious that if Angie was going to win the blue ribbon, she was going to have to work for that, too. The judge liked Charlie, but she was also interested in Harry Flynn's Springer.

As she singled those two out for special attention, the spectators at the ringside chose up sides and enthusiastically applauded their favorites. It wasn't easy to clap with Davey in my arms, but I managed. The judges sitting inside the ring, remained carefully neutral.

From my vantage point, I had a good view of the crowds lining the ring. Dirk's height made him easy to pick out. He was standing behind Florence Byrd's chair. She was staring intently into the ring, while Rick knelt beside her and whispered something in her ear. When the judge motioned the Springer to the head of the line, all three faces fell.

The judge placed Charlie second behind him, then stepped back for a last look. There was absolute silence in the hall. The judge lifted her hand—to send them around, I thought—then used it to wave Angie and Charlie into first place. The applause that accompanied the win was loud and sustained.

Angie looked stunned as she brought the Cocker over to stand near the first-place marker. Immediately her gaze slipped over to where her father was sitting. Peterson was facing forward and I couldn't see his response. But after a moment he excused himself, stood up, and left the ring.

Davey still in my arms, I pushed through the crowds and followed. Father and daughter met up in the crush outside the gate.

"Congratulations," Peterson said formally.

"Thank you." Angie was glowing. "That's the sixth group I've gotten with him. Wasn't it great?" She sounded like a little girl, hoping desperately for daddy's approval.

"Very nice," Peterson said, but he wasn't smiling. He reached out to finger the Cocker's coat. "Watch his top-line. If the Springer'd gotten you, that would have been why."

Peterson dropped his hand and walked away. Angie was surrounded by well-wishers, but I knew she had to be hurting. Less than a minute. That was all the time that jerk had had to spare for his daughter. Feeling for her, I hugged Davey to me fiercely.

"Hey!" he cried, struggling. "You're squishing me!"

"Sorry, sport." I loosened my grip and let him slide to the ground. "Let's go see if we can find Aunt Peg, okay?"

It was late and the crowds were beginning to thin out. We located Aunt Peg on the far side of the ring, arguing with Crawford over the merits of a Briard in the ring. Together, we watched through Best in Show. Charlie was a strong contender, but the top award was won by the Doberman. Nobody at ringside seemed surprised.

We went back to the set-up to pick up our Poodles and head back to the hotel. All around the grooming area, exercise pens were blossoming in the aisles. The air smelled heavily of warm kibble and frozen Bil-Jac. The show was over for the day, but the professional handlers still had hours of work to do. It wasn't an easy way to make a living.

As a reward for Davey, we ate dinner at McDonald's. McNuggets and milkshakes all around. With the Poodles in the cars, we didn't linger. Our motel was only a mile from the show grounds, but in that stretch of road, Aunt Peg managed to pick out a small pink building with a neon sign that read, "Doughnuts Divine." Driving ahead of me in her own car, she honked and gestured. Planning ahead for breakfast, no doubt.

We all went to bed when we got to the motel. It was just as well I was tired, because I fell right to sleep which meant that the first chance I had to get nervous about showing Faith was the next morning. Early the next morning. The motel must have mixed our wake-up call with someone else's because they roused us before six. Standard Poodles weren't scheduled until afternoon.

We showered and dressed, then gave the dogs a luxurious half-hour walk. On the way to the show, there was plenty of time to stop for coffee and doughnuts. When we reached the show grounds, Aunt Peg and Davey took the Poodles and went on ahead. Since they'd left me to juggle the big pink box, plus a flimsy cardboard tray containing my coffee, Aunt Peg's tea and Davey's milk, I followed more slowly.

Even though it was early, things were already humming in the grooming area. Davey and Aunt Peg had taken the Poodles up to the rings for a practice spin on the mats, so all of our tables were free. I set out breakfast, digging around in the bottom of the tack box for a roll of paper towels to use as napkins.

"You wouldn't happen to have a spare, would you?"

I straightened and looked around. The Shamrock setup was open, but empty. I turned the other way. Harry Flynn gestured toward the pink box. "Looks like there might be a dozen or so in there. One would sure go great with my coffee."

He wasn't one of my favorite people, but thanks to the fact that Aunt Peg had done the ordering, we did have plenty of doughnuts to spare. I opened the box and had a look. "Is glazed, okay?"

"Fine by me."

I fished it out, wrapped it in a paper towel and handed it over. As I crossed the aisle into his set-up I saw that his coffee was in a big cardboard mug with the words "Doughnuts Divine" lettered on the side.

"Didn't stop off myself," he said following the direction of my gaze. "The girls are outside exing the dogs. One of them must have picked it up for me." He lifted the mug and took a swallow. "Fresh and hot, just the way I like it. Can't think why they didn't have the sense to get some doughnuts too, but I thank you for this one."

"You're welcome," I said, as he took a big bite and washed it down with another swig of coffee. Flynn seemed to be in what for him was an expansive mood. I decided to visit for a bit. "That's a nice Springer you've got."

He nodded. "Nicer than he's getting credit for at the minute. The Cocker's had everything his own way for too long, if you ask me. Next year, he'll be out of the way. That's when Bandit will really take off. Still, I'd like to think I've got a shot or two this weekend."

"I thought you were going to win yesterday's group."

"Yeah." Flynn chuckled under his breath. It wasn't a happy sound. "So did I, for about a minute. I guess that's how long it took the judge to remember that Florence Byrd was the one who got her on the panel at two all-breeds next spring."

I wondered if that was true or not. Flynn sounded so cynical, it was hard to take anything he said at face value.

According to Aunt Peg, he'd also been the driving force behind a rumor that one of Jenny's dogs was dyed. Every breed has its share of persistent malcontents. I decided I didn't want to spend any more time in the company of this one.

"Nice talking to you," I lied. Ingrained manners are a bitch. As I skirted around the crates and went back to our set-up, Flynn was stuffing the last piece of doughnut into his mouth.

Aunt Peg and Davey returned, and we all stood at attention while the loudspeaker played a tinny rendition of the Star Spangled Banner. At eight o'clock precisely, the show began.

With plenty of time to kill, Aunt Peg decided to go watch the obedience competition. She offered to take Davey with her, and I settled in a chair with the latest issue of *Dog Scene.* I saw a picture of Rick winning with a Brittany; and several pages farther on, one of Angie beaming over a group win with Charlie.

I was reading the gossip page when Harry Flynn passed by on his way back from the ring. It was the thump that made me look up. Walking by the end of the aisle, he'd stumbled into one of our big crates. Flynn was leading his dog rather than carrying it. He righted himself slowly and didn't look at all steady on his feet.

"Are you okay?" I asked.

Flynn didn't answer. He staggered into his set-up and put the Beagle in a crate. Concerned, I followed. "Harry, what's wrong?"

"Don't feel so good."

Beads of sweat appeared on his forehead. His fingers tangled in the leash he'd just taken off the Beagle as if he couldn't figure out how to free them. When I reached to take it from him, his skin felt cold and clammy. Suddenly he sagged back against the grooming table, clutching at his stomach.

"What's the matter?" I said. "What can I do?"

"Get . . ." He pushed the words out with effort. ". . . help."

"Of course. Who?"

His knees crumpled beneath him. I grabbed for his arm, but Flynn felt like a dead weight. As I tried to help, the handler sagged to the floor. "Doctor," he whispered. The word sounded harsh and painful.

Then I was running, out of the grooming area, past the rings, over to the blue draped podium where the officials were sitting. "I need a doctor!"

Three faces looked up from their paperwork. A man on the end smiled. "We have a vet."

"No, I need a doctor! It's an emergency!"

"I guess we could make an announcement . . ."

"There's a man in the grooming area who's very ill. He needs help quickly!"

The official frowned. He looked at the other two as if wishing they could take a meeting. "Maybe we should call the local paramedics."

"Yes, please do that. Hurry!" I pointed out where we were. One of the officials went to the phone. Another came with me. We ran together back to the set-up, dodging around crates and busy exhibitors.

Harry Flynn was right where I'd left him and he didn't look good. He was still on the floor, and he'd drawn his knees up to his chest. His mouth was half open; so were his eyes.

The official stopped running so suddenly I plowed right into the back of him. He turned around and firmly pushed me away. Still I was close enough to see as he stooped down and laid his fingers along the top of Harry's throat, feeling for a pulse.

"Is he . . . ?"

"Barely."

We stayed with him until the paramedics came. By that time Harry's assistants had returned. Both were young women, one American, one Japanese. They clutched each other and looked close to tears. The grim looks on the face of the medical team as they strapped an oxygen mask over Harry's face and lifted him onto the stretcher didn't help matters any.

The ambulance left the grounds with lights on and siren blaring.

∽❀ *Twenty-five* ❀∽

After that the show went on as usual. Most exhibitors aren't rubberneckers. There's a lot of time and money invested in their participation in a dog show, and it would take more than an ambulance to distract them from their business. In this case, the paramedics had done their job so quickly and efficiently, most people seemed unaware that anything unusual had occurred.

One of Harry's assistants had gone with him in the ambulance. The other, the Japanese girl, had stayed behind to tend to the dogs. She was brushing a Scottie and introduced herself as Yuko. I asked if there was anything I could do.

"Bring Harry back?" she asked hopefully, her English limited.

"Not yet. We'll hear something later. I'm sure they're taking good care of him at the hospital."

She nodded unhappily and went back to her dog.

Davey came skipping back to the grooming area, with Aunt Peg following more sedately behind. "Guess what we saw?" my son demanded.

I lifted him up and swung him onto a crate top. "What?"

"An ambulance. With sirens and flashing lights and everything!"

"Oh," I said. "Right."

Aunt Peg's gaze narrowed. "Is something wrong?"

"Harry Flynn collapsed." I told her what had happened.

"Any idea what caused it?"

"No, but he looked really bad. I hope we'll hear something soon."

When news came, it wasn't good. By early afternoon, Harry Flynn was dead. I wished someone would mention a heart attack, but no one did. Poisoning was suspected. The medical examiner was going to do an autopsy.

It was the police who delivered the news; a tall, spare black man named Detective Brucker. He brought a handful of uniformed officers with him. They cordoned off Harry's set-up and began asking questions of everyone in the area.

We'd just gotten back from the ring after the judging of Standard Poodles. Faith had shown nicely and beaten two other puppies. Aunt Peg's bitch, Peaches, had taken the points and gone Best Opposite. We were feeling pretty pleased with ourselves until we got back to the grooming area and found the police waiting.

When Detective Brucker found out that I was the last person who'd spoken to Harry, he put me at the top of his list of people to see. Peg and I banded the Poodles' hair out of their way and put them in their crates, then she took Davey for a walk. The detective and I put a pair of chairs in the aisle between the two set-ups.

We started with the preliminaries, and it quickly became obvious that the information I possessed was woefully lacking. I hadn't known Harry well; and aside from giving him a doughnut, I hadn't been paying any attention to him or how he'd spent his morning.

"You want to talk to his assistants about that," I told Detective Brucker.

"We will. But first I'd like to nail down your involvement."

My involvement?

"You arrived at the building at what time?"

I thought back. "A little before eight."

"And you came inside and offered Mr. Flynn a doughnut?"

"Actually he asked for one, to go with his coffee. He saw the box I was carrying and we had plenty of extras."

"What happened to the rest of the doughnuts?"

"Mostly we ate them. I think there might be one or two left." I indicated the box, which had been shoved into a tote bag underneath a table.

Brucker motioned to one of the uniformed officers. The box and its contents were bagged and removed.

"We would be who?"

"Myself," I said. "My son, Davey, and my aunt, Margaret Turnbull."

There was a pause while he took down the names. "What kind of doughnut did Mr. Flynn have?"

"Glazed."

"And were there other glazed doughnuts in the box?"

"Several. That's why I gave him one."

"And Mr. Flynn was also drinking coffee at this time?"

"Yes."

"Did you give him that, too?"

There was something in the deceptively casual way the detective slipped the question in. Surely I wasn't a suspect?

"No," I said, holding my voice neutral. "I didn't."

"Do you know where he got it from?"

"Harry said he thought one of his assistants must have stopped on the way to the show and picked it up for him."

"We spoke with one of his assistants at the hospital." Brucker consulted his notes. "A Rhonda Levine. She says that neither she nor the other young woman saw Mr. Flynn drinking or eating anything."

"They were outside with the dogs at the time—"

"And that although she did see an empty coffee cup on one of the tables, she had no knowledge how it might have gotten there."

I glanced over to the cordoned-off set-up. "Where's the coffee cup now?"

"Ms. Levine was cleaning up and threw it out."

There were two large garbage cans in the vicinity. I was glad I wasn't the one who would have to sift through them. "You believe Harry was poisoned," I said.

"It's a strong possibility."

"By what?"

"We don't know that yet. I understand the dog shows run through Monday. If we have any further questions, will you be available?"

"My son and I are going home tomorrow night."

That occasioned the need for another note. Brucker looked up. "Do you know of anyone who might have wished to harm Harry Flynn?"

"There were probably lots of people. From what I could tell, he wasn't a very likable man."

"Any names in particular you'd like to give me?"

I thought for a long minute, then glanced over to the Shamrock set-up. For the moment it was empty. Both Rick and Angie were probably up at the rings. "Yes," I said finally. "Jenny Maguire."

He wrote the name down. "What was her relationship to Mr. Flynn?"

"Up until six weeks ago, she was a competitor of his."

"What happened six weeks ago?"

"She died," I said, choosing my words slowly and for effect. "Of arsenic poisoning."

That got his attention and he asked a lot of questions, mostly about the circumstances of Jenny's death and who in Ridgefield had been handling the case. He didn't ask me who I thought had done it, and I didn't volunteer the information. It wasn't that I was trying to shield Rick, only that I couldn't figure out how this latest development fit into the case I'd been building against him in my mind. What would Rick have had to gain from Harry's death?

It was a question I broached to Aunt Peg after Detective Brucker had finished interviewing everyone in the area and moved on to talk to the club officials. His team had dusted Harry's set-up for fingerprints, sifted through the few belongings there, and were now removing the two big garbage cans from the building. Davey was munching on a hot dog and zooming his matchbox cars in and out of one of the large crates. Though we'd missed lunch earlier, neither Peg nor I had any appetite. We got the Poodles back out of their crates and were breaking down topknots and brushing out hair spray.

"With Harry out of the way," she said, "Charlie wins that much more easily. That's got to look good for Shamrock."

"Good enough to be worth killing over?" I asked skeptically. "According to Florence Byrd, Charlie's going home in a couple of weeks anyway. If Rick wanted to kill Flynn for that reason, he should have done it months ago."

"Months ago, Charlie was beating Harry's dogs handily."

"Because Jenny was showing him," I said, and Aunt Peg nodded. "The poison must have been in the coffee. Harry thought one of his assistants had left it for him. That's why he drank it. So the murderer has to be someone who was here early this morning."

"That doesn't rule out anybody. All the handlers get here as soon as the building opens to tend to their dogs and get ready for the day."

"Rick and Angie were here when we got here. I didn't see them but their set-up was unpacked."

"So was Crystal Mars," said Aunt Peg. "When Davey and I were walking the Poodles, she was rehanging the banner above her booth."

"It sounds like everyone was out and around this morning."

"That's not unusual for a show this size. But I'll tell you what was unusual, now that I stop to think about it. I saw Dirk here this morning too."

"What's unusual about that?"

"It's the first time I've seen him at a show when he hasn't been with Mrs. Byrd. If she wasn't here, why was he? And if she was here, why? It's the handlers who need to get a headstart on the day. The owners usually don't appear until judging time."

I reached for my schedule and had a look. "Ascob Cockers went in at noon. I wonder if Charlie won."

"He did," Aunt Peg confirmed. "I saw Angie carrying the ribbon when she brought him back. I mentioned that Harry had been taken ill and she said she'd been wondering where he was. Then she laughed a bit and said she hoped he didn't improve by group time."

"I guess she got her wish."

"Did the detective question her and Rick?"

"He must have." I smoothed out the long hair on Faith's ear, wrapped it in a colored plastic sheet, tucked it under and banded it in place. "I told Brucker about what happened to Jenny, and I saw him go over to the Shamrock set-up. Rick was getting ready to show a Bichon and Brucker followed him up to ringside."

Faith stood up on her table and began to bark.

"Cut out that racket!" Florence Byrd said sternly. "Haven't you ever seen an old lady with a cane before?"

I quieted Faith as Mrs. Byrd made her way slowly to our set-up. Dirk was nowhere in sight. Aunt Peg opened up a chair she'd stashed between two crates and Mrs. Byrd sat herself down.

"Well, this is a fine mess," she said. "Harry Flynn dead, and police everywhere. What is the world coming to? In my day, dog shows never used to be like this."

Unless I was mistaken about the amount of winning her dog had been doing recently, this still was her day. If she'd come to complain, I could think of better ways to spend the time. "We were just talking about you," I said boldly.

"Really?"

"And Dirk," said Aunt Peg, following my lead.

"We were wondering what time you got to the show this morning."

"Just in time to see Charlie win," Florence said firmly. "By then I gather all this business with Flynn was over and done with. I always thought of him as a particularly nasty man. Still, no one deserves to die like that."

"Dirk was here earlier," Aunt Peg mentioned. "I saw him leaving the building before the start of judging."

"Dirk had business to attend to. I don't pry into my employees' affairs. It's none of my business and it's none of yours either."

"No," I allowed. "But it's something the police might be interested in."

"The fact that my driver was in the building this morning? I doubt it. There must have been hundreds of people here."

"But not hundreds of people with a connection to Jenny."

"What are you trying to say, young lady?"

Aunt Peg moved over to stand beside me. "I imagine what she's trying to say is that two people are dead, most likely by the same hand. And the sooner this whole thing gets itself cleared up, the better."

"The same hand?" Mrs. Byrd's gnarled fingers clasped the top of her cane tightly. "Does that mean arsenic was involved?"

"The police don't know yet. They're going to be doing an autopsy to find out."

"Then it would behoove you not to jump to conclusions, wouldn't it?"

Lord, she was making me angry. "I'd rather jump to conclusions, than stand around with my head buried in the sand. You've been showing dogs a long time. I imagine you remember the days when people put arsenic in their dogs' food to improve their coats."

"I most certainly do. Fowler's solution, that's what people used. You could get it from the druggist. A remarkably stupid practice, if you ask me. Quality care will achieve the same results in the end."

"Not everyone has your resources," said Aunt Peg. "And there will always be people looking to find a short-cut."

Mrs. Byrd didn't appear to be listening. She was staring into the next aisle at Harry Flynn's set-up. Her face was creased by a perplexed frown.

"Was there something we could do for you?" asked Aunt Peg.

"I was just wondering," she said. "I understand the Springer won his breed this morning. They were judged early, when Flynn was still on his feet."

I supposed that was one way of putting it. "What were you wondering about?"

Mrs. Byrd braced the cane on the floor and pushed herself to her feet. "Are they showing the dog in the group or not? That's what I came over to see. But there's nothing going on over there at all."

"The set-up has been cordoned off."

"I can see that with my own eyes, can't I? But where are the dogs?"

Aunt Peg and I shared a puzzled glance. "Rhonda and Yuko must have taken them somewhere," I said. "Maybe they've gone home."

"Good for them." Her thin lips drew into a terse smile. "A little sorting out of the competition never hurts a bit."

Unless you're the one who got sorted out, I thought grimly. Mrs. Byrd reached out with her cane. In the narrow aisle, it thudded off the side of a crate and I quickly cupped a hand around Faith's muzzle before she could bark again.

I wondered what business Dirk could possibly have had in the building early that morning. Florence Byrd had told us she'd waited nearly a half century to win the Quaker Oats Award. Now she was this close. How determined had she been to finally get the job done?

☜❀ *Twenty-six* ❀☞

After Mrs. Byrd left, I took Davey to the bathroom and for a browse around the many concessions stands. With the application of a little imagination, it's amazing how many dog toys can double as presents for a child. All right, bribes really. But so far, Davey'd handled the weekend of shows without major complaint. By way of a reward, he ended up with a new ball and a stuffed octopus, both of which he promised to share with Faith. Right.

When we got back to the set-up, Angie was getting Charlie ready for the group. Like Mrs. Byrd, she kept casting surreptitious glances over toward Flynn's set-up on the other side of us. Then again, maybe she wasn't wondering about the competition. Now that word was out about what had happened to Harry, it seemed like half the show had found a reason to wander by and have a look.

Aunt Peg was sitting in the seat she'd gotten out for Mrs. Byrd. An open issue of *Dog Scene* lay across her lap. As I drew near, I realized she was talking to Angie about a Standard Poodle in one of the ads. I leaned over and had a look. Neither dog nor handler looked familiar.

"I've heard good things about Trent Parness," Angie was saying.

I boosted myself up and had a seat on the grooming table. "Who's Trent Parness?"

"A handler in Colorado," Aunt Peg told me. "Potentially a handler for Charity. Her owners are determined to have someone local."

"It's hard when you sell puppies so far away," Angie sympathized. "And it's amazing the way this business has grown. Twenty-five years ago when I started going to shows, everything was so much smaller—"

"Let me see," Davey demanded. He marched over and snatched the magazine off of Aunt Peg's lap.

"Davey!"

He ignored my protest and frowned. "It's only a dog."

"Of course it's a dog," Angie said, laughing. "It's a dog magazine. What did you expect?"

"Cars?" my son asked hopefully.

"Not likely." I hopped down and went to look for the bag where he'd stashed his matchbox models.

"Try page fourteen," Angie recommended.

"What's there?" Aunt Peg asked as Davey flipped through the pages. His counting skills weren't perfect and it took him three tries to find the right page.

"Charlie."

"Yea!" cried Davey. "A car! Can I cut it out?"

"Not until everyone's had a chance to read the magazine," I said, taking it from him for safe keeping. The ad was one I'd noticed earlier. "Nice picture."

Angie was visibly proud. "I got some extra copies from

Pat. I'm going to frame one. Rick said I could hang it on the wall in the office."

"Speaking of Rick," said Aunt Peg. "Why is he running?"

We all turned and had a look. Rick was definitely running our way. "Angie! What the hell's going on? They've called the Sporting group twice!"

"I thought Hounds were next." She dropped the brush she was holding, slithered out of her apron and grabbed a wool plaid blazer off the back of a chair.

"They changed the order. Didn't you hear the announcement?" Rick swept the Cocker off the table and was already heading back the way he'd come.

"Keep your pants on," Angie muttered. She was running a dog comb through her hair as she hurried along behind. "We'll make it."

They did, but only just. By the time Charlie got into the ring, the rest of the sporting dogs had already been around the ring and the first one was on the table being examined. Mrs. Byrd, sitting ringside, looked murderous. Dirk, hovering in his accustomed place behind her, appeared equally grim. I quickly scanned the line of dogs. Harry Flynn's Springer was nowhere in sight.

Fortunately for Angie, the judge didn't take punctuality into consideration. Without the Springer to push him for the win, Charlie coasted to first place easily. I looked to see if Roger Peterson was sitting inside the ring as he had the day before. He wasn't, but his wife was. I wondered if she'd enjoyed watching her daughter win.

"Mommy?" Davey tugged at my sleeve. "Can I go play?"

"With who?"

"Sarah."

I looked the direction he was pointing. With most of the judging finished for the day and all the action concentrated in the group ring, much of the large hall was empty. Crystal's daughter had brought out a soccer ball. She was dribbling it up and down the mats in one of the unused rings.

The idea had a certain appeal. After a day and a half of being confined to my side, Davey was sorely in need of physical activity, especially with someone nearer his own age. On the other hand, he was simply too young to be on his own in the big building. Still, it was worth investigating.

"Come on," I said, taking his hand. "Let's go see."

"Hi Mrs. Travis." Sarah smiled and waved as we approached. She shot her ball into an imaginary goal beneath the steward's table, lifted her hands and yelled, "Score!"

Davey broke away and ran on ahead. He fished out the ball and kicked it back to her.

"How about taking on a teammate?" I asked her.

"Sure." Sarah caught the ball with her foot and sent it flying back.

"Do you think you're responsible enough to keep an eye on him for a little while?"

Sarah cocked her head to one side and planted her hands on her hips. Brown bangs slanted across her eyes. Her expression was a mixture of childish exasperation and adult resolve. "I'm ten years old, and I'm very responsible. Mom even lets me run the shop at home sometimes."

"Then I guess you're big enough to look out for Davey. Don't lose him, okay?"

"Fat chance." Sarah giggled, watching as my son dribbled away down one of the mats. "He's got my ball!"

The Hound group was halfway done by the time I got back. Aunt Peg had saved a spot for me up near the railing and I squeezed in between her and an older man smoking a thin black cigarette. There was a "No Smoking" sign on the wall right across from us but all that nicotine must have impaired his vision because he didn't seem to notice. By the time the groups were finished, I was feeling distinctly light-headed.

"I'm going to go find Davey," I said.

"You can't leave now," cried Aunt Peg. "It's Best in Show!"

The Rolling Stones could have been belting out *Satisfaction* and she still couldn't have convinced me to spend one more minute standing next to that smoker. I elbowed my way to the back of the crowd jammed at ringside and had a quick scan of the surrounding area. Davey and Sarah were nowhere in sight. They'd probably grown tired of kicking the ball around and gone back to Crystal's booth.

Her concession space was on the other side of the big building. With Best in Show going on, the rest of the cavernous space was nearly empty. It was late and the casual shoppers and spectators had long since left. All the booths I passed were closed up tight for the night. Even the lighting seemed dimmer.

Which is why when I first saw Roger Peterson standing behind the All Natural Dog Munchies booth hugging Crystal Mars, I had to blink twice to be sure. Then I stopped dead. As hugs went, it wasn't a big deal; more platonic than sexual, and over in a matter of seconds. But the surprising thing was that it had happened at all.

Peterson stepped back and put his hand into his breast pocket. A small white envelope showed up clearly in the half light. Crystal glanced at it, but didn't take it. Peterson put it down on the counter and left.

He cut across through the rings and didn't notice me standing off to one side. Nor did Crystal, until I drew near. By then, she'd picked up the envelope and tucked it away.

I gave her a friendly wave and gazed around the area. "I came for Davey. He's supposed to be with Sarah."

"Yeah, they're fine. She's reading him a story." Crystal gestured toward the booth next door and I saw them sitting together on a pile of sheepskin dog beds, leaning over a book.

Crystal stepped out from behind her own counter to intercept me. She had to be wondering how much I'd seen.

"That was Roger Peterson, wasn't it?"

She nodded shortly, her expression daring me to make something of it; and in that moment, I knew. I looked back to where my son and her daughter sat; Sarah, with her shiny dark hair and mischievous eyes.

"Don't say it," Crystal muttered in a low tone. "Don't say a word."

I didn't have to, because suddenly I saw the truth of what had been sitting right in front of me. *I'm ten years old*, Sarah had told me proudly. Ten years earlier, Jenny had been on her own for a year. When she'd left home, her father had been having an affair with Crystal Mars.

It wasn't that Jenny hadn't blamed Crystal for what she had done. She'd forgiven her. Because Crystal was the mother of Jenny's half-sister. "That's why Jenny drove all the way over to Stratford to buy dog food."

Crystal nodded. The defiance was gone, spent as quickly as it had come. Now her eyes looked tired, defeated. "She wanted to see Sarah. It's not like I was going to keep her away. Neither of them had much family they could lean on, did they?"

I stepped in closer and found myself whispering. "What about Angie?"

"That one." Crystal sniffed contemptuously. "She won't even talk to me. As far as she's concerned, Sarah doesn't even exist."

"Does Sarah know about her father?"

"No. I'll probably tell her when she's older. But for now, going to shows where she might run into Roger, the whole thing could be incredibly awkward. He's never denied paternity, I'll say that much for him. But I was the one who wanted Sarah, and I've taken responsibility for that. It was my decision and I'm dealing with it."

I pretty much knew how she felt. And Sarah was a great kid. I certainly wasn't going to condemn Crystal for any of the choices she'd made.

I looked at our children, their two heads, one fair, one dark, bent over the big picture book. Then I glanced at Crystal and saw she was doing the same.

"Ziggy's her dog now," she said softly. "It just seems right."

I thought so too.

When Davey and I got back to the group ring, the Doberman had just won his second Best in Show in as many days, and Aunt Peg had been invited out to dinner. She was finagling extra invitations for her tagalong relatives when we arrived.

"Thank you, but no," I said firmly as Davey smothered a large yawn with his hands. It was already after eight. At this hour, a quick take-out dinner would be about the most he could manage. We agreed that I would take the Poodles back to the motel with me, and Aunt Peg's friends would drop her off there later.

At our set-up, I slipped collars and leashes on our charges, both of whom were delighted to be released from their crates. Faith was more rambunctious, but Peaches was bigger. Davey got the puppy and I took the older bitch. I also picked up the *Dog Scene* and tucked it under my arm. Reading material for later when, with Aunt Peg out and Davey asleep, there wouldn't be much to do.

As we left the building Faith was pulling at the end of her lead, with Davey trotting along behind to keep up. That meant Peaches wanted to go fast, too. If Angie's voice hadn't been raised, I probably never would have noticed the two figures standing in the shadows outside the door.

"I can't believe it!" Angie cried angrily. "You had no right—"

"Shhh." Lavinia Peterson reached out and laid a hand on her daughter's shoulder. Angrily Angie shrugged her off. "It was for your own good . . ."

There was more, but Mrs. Peterson was speaking softly and thanks to the pace Davey and Faith were setting, I was already out of range. I was tempted to circle back and listen some more, but with Best in Show over, cars were starting up all around us and I didn't dare let Davey out of my sight.

We found the Volvo, hopped the Poodles in, and I drove back past the door where I'd seen Angie and her mother arguing. Both were now gone, and Davey was in the back seat clamoring to be fed. Now I knew why Nancy Drew had been such a successful sleuth. She didn't have children. Or Poodles either, for that matter.

The excitement seemed to be over, so we headed back to the motel. On the way, I gave Davey his choice and he cast his vote for a Big Mac. At least he's consistent. We had our food bagged and brought it outside to eat in the car. Having been a dog owner for a full two months now, I knew enough to buy a couple of extra hamburgers, hold the fixings.

Aunt Peg would have said I was teaching Peaches to beg—an art Faith had long since perfected—but she was off in some fancy restaurant, probably sipping wine and talking dogs. I was the one holding down the fort and I figured what she didn't know couldn't possibly hurt me too much.

Dinner revived Davey's flagging energy. On the way back to the motel we drove past Doughnuts Divine and he jumped up and down in his seat. "Dessert! Dessert!" he yelled. The Poodles weren't sure what all the fuss was about but they threw in a few barks for good measure.

"Not tonight," I said. After what had happened that morning, doughnuts were about the last thing I wanted. Not to mention the fact that Harry's coffee had been in a Doughnuts Divine cup. . . .

The tires squealed on dry pavement as I yanked the wheel hard to the right. One wheel caught the driveway, the other bumped up over the curb as we made the turn into the parking lot.

"Yea!" cried Davey, as the Poodles righted themselves in the back seat.

"Two doughnuts. And that's all."

"Two each?" Davey opened the door and scrambled out.

"Oh, all right." By that time of the day, my ability to argue was on low ebb. I gathered up the *Dog Scene* magazine and followed my son inside.

A large glassed-in showcase was filled with more than a dozen different kinds of doughnuts. There were two small booths and a sit-down counter over to the right. Aside from a teenage girl in a pink smock standing behind the cash register, we had the place to ourselves. The girl, whose name tag identified her as Sandy, had out a compact and a tube of cherry red lipstick, which she was smoothing over her full lips. As we let ourselves in, she shoved both under the counter.

Davey went straight to the wall of doughnuts. His eyes were round as saucers. Choosing his two—not only the kind, but the actual doughnuts themselves—would occupy him for at least the next ten minutes.

"What can I get you?" Sandy asked.

"Four doughnuts."

She took out a white grease paper bag and shook it open.

"You weren't working this morning, were you?"

"Nah. I'm on four to midnight."

That made sense. Still, it had been worth a shot. "Do you know who was on duty this morning, say around seven?"

"Sure, that's Jeff. He's in back."

"He's working now?"

Her head bobbed. "Tuition's pretty steep. Jeff does double shifts whenever he can manage around his classes. He's real studious, you know what I mean?"

I gathered that meant he was too busy with his books

to appreciate the cherry red lips. "Do you think he might have a minute to step out and talk to me?"

"Probably." She stepped back and stuck her head in the kitchen door. "Hey Jeff! There's a lady out here who wants to see you." She waited a moment, then said back to me, "He'll be right out."

She pushed the door and followed it through. When it swung back, it brought in a white-smocked teenage boy wearing a peaked paper hat over close-cropped hair. He was tall and skinny and a faint line of acne scars shadowed his jaw. "Sandy said you wanted to see me?"

I spread the *Dog Scene* down on the counter. I'd creased the ad featuring a picture of Rick showing the Brittany and the magazine fell open to that page. "Did this man come in here this morning and buy a cup of coffee? Maybe between seven and seven-thirty?"

Jeff bent down for a closer look. "I don't think so. But business is pretty good then, you know? Sometimes we get real busy and I'm just on automatic pilot. I'm too busy serving doughnuts to spend any time looking at faces. Does this have something to do with that guy who died?"

"It might."

"The police came over to school and talked to me this afternoon. They didn't have any pictures, though, and there wasn't much I could tell them. I must have sold a hundred cups of coffee this morning."

I flipped the magazine shut. "Thanks anyway. Davey, are you ready?"

"I want one jelly and one honey glazed." He pointed with a firm finger. "That one."

Jeff picked up the bag. "Sandy said you wanted four doughnuts, right?"

"Right. I just need to have a look. . . ." All right, so if

Davey took his time deciding, let's just say I knew where he got it from. "Maybe a raspberry."

Jeff leaned back against the end of the counter and waited. Davey fished his jelly doughnut out of the bag and began to eat. A spray of powdered sugar decorated the tip of his nose. "Want to see a really cool car?" he asked Jeff.

"Sure."

Davey pulled the *Dog Scene* across the counter top. "Page fourteen," he said with authority.

"Raspberry," I decided as the pages flipped behind me. "And a chocolate cruller."

"Got it," said Jeff. He quickly bagged my choices. "You know, she was here."

"She who?"

"That girl." His finger poked at the ad with the really cool car. Champion Shadowlands Super-Charged.

And Angie.

"When?"

"She came in here this morning. Just like you asked."

Twenty-seven

"Wait a minute!" I cried as he rang up our purchase. My voice sounded unnaturally loud. "Are you saying that Angie was here this morning?"

"Is this Angie?" He poked at the picture again.

I nodded.

"She was here. Like I said, most people blend together. But I noticed her because she bought two coffees and had trouble getting out the door carrying them."

Two coffees?

Maybe she'd been buying one for Rick.

Then again, maybe not.

I opened my wallet and tossed a couple of singles down on the counter. "Come on, Davey. Let's go."

"Don't you want your magazine?"

We were halfway to the door and had to come back for it. In the car, the Poodles were all over us. Davey let them help polish off his jelly doughnut and I didn't say a word.

I was too busy thinking. *Angie?*

She was Jenny's sister. I'd seen how upset she was at

the funeral. I'd watched how hard she'd worked since to fill her sister's shoes.

And how well she'd succeeded.

Her words came floating back to me. *Jenny never gave me a chance. . . .*

"Mommy, why are we just sitting here?"

I fished out the key and fit it into the ignition, still tumbling things end over end in my mind. Angie had always seemed so young and immature. She was the follower, not the leader. And Jenny and Angie had been family; close enough that when Angie left home, she'd run to her older sibling.

But not close enough to know about Jenny's own plans to run away . . .

I drove the mile to the motel at well under the speed limit. The way my thoughts were swirling, I was an accident just waiting to happen. Aunt Peg wasn't back yet, no surprise there. I got Davey into his pajamas, fed and walked the Poodles. And considered the notion that Angie might have been the murderer.

For years, she'd stood in Jenny's shadow. But now with her sister gone, Angie had come into her own. For the first time, her ambition had been allowed free rein. She'd brushed aside Rick's objections when he hadn't wanted her to show Charlie. And she'd been working on Florence Byrd to extend the dog's career. Now that sympathy was wearing thin, Harry Flynn had been pushing her hard for wins. Had she brushed him aside, too?

I shook my head irritably. It all seemed incredible. I'd wanted to find all the pieces to the puzzle; but now that I had them, they were forming a picture I didn't necessarily believe. To quote Aunt Peg, the girl was a child. I had to talk to Angie. Face to face. I needed to hear what she had to say about all this.

I put Davey in bed and read him *Peter Pan* from start to finish. By the time Hook had been vanquished, he was snoring softly into his pillow. I picked up the phone, dialed the front desk and got myself connected to Angie's room. Rick picked up.

"She's back at the show exing the dogs for the night," he told me. Mindful of our conversation the day before, his voice was distinctly cool. "I'll tell her you called." He started to hang up.

"Rick, do you drink coffee?"

There was a long pause as he considered what had to sound like an odd question. "Of course I drink coffee," he said finally.

"Did Angie—?"

The phone clicked in my ear.

I was debating what to do next when Peaches stood up on the bed and whined. Faith cocked her ears. A moment later, I heard the scratch of Aunt Peg's key in the lock. She pushed the door open and stepped carefully over the threshold. She was grinning like she'd just won the lottery and her eyes had a distinctly tipsy glaze. I leapt up and caught the Poodles before their boisterous greeting could knock her over.

"Dinner was grand," she announced, throwing her coat on the bed.

"You look it."

Peg peered at her reflection in the mirror over the dresser. "I most certainly do not."

I'd been planning to tell her what I'd learned and ask her advice. But from the looks of Aunt Peg, she wasn't in any shape to absorb details. Nothing if not flexible, I went on to plan B. "I have to go out for a little while. Can you keep an eye on Davey?"

"You're going out *now*? Where on earth to?"

"Back to the show. Angie's there and I want to talk to her."

"Oh. Of course." Aunt Peg nodded as if my partial explanation made perfect sense. She's usually very quick on the uptake so I took her easy acquiescence to mean that her evening had been very pleasant indeed.

When I pulled the door shut behind me, she was singing "The Impossible Dream" and dancing around the room with Peaches for a partner. I wondered how much she'd remember in the morning.

At ten-thirty at night, the Eastern States Exposition Grounds were a good deal darker and quieter than I'd expected. A parking lot off to one side was filled with motor homes and although a few lights were visible, most people seemed to have already bedded down for the night. I pulled the Volvo up beside the building and let myself in a heavy metal door with a light shining overhead.

A uniformed guard walked by, carrying a steaming cup of hot soup. "You've got half an hour," he said curtly. "Then I'm closing up."

"Right." I nodded and kept on going. Depending on what Angie had to say, I might be in and out in ten minutes.

Still, it was nice to know there was some sort of security force in the building. Half of me realized I might be about to confront a murderer. The other half thought of all the time I'd spent in her company lately and flatly refused to accept the possibility. Nor was I able to take

Angie seriously as an adversary. She was slightly taller than me and probably weighed a few pounds more, but I doubted that either of us would be able to inflict any significant physical damage upon the other.

On the other hand, I certainly wouldn't be drinking or eating anything in her presence.

I made my way quickly through the grooming area, skirting crates and ex pens, and dodging across the haphazardly formed aisles. The building was only half lit and nearly empty. After the bustle and crowds of daytime, the quiet seemed almost unnatural. Somewhere a rap song was playing in a boom box; and I could see a few people on the other side of the rings finishing up their chores. But over where we had set up, everyone had already packed up and gone home.

For a moment I thought I'd missed Angie. Then as I veered around a grooming table and started up the Shamrock aisle, I saw a black Cocker Spaniel sniffing around the paper floor of its exercise pen. Angie was bending over to fasten the gate.

"Hey," she said, straightening as I approached. "What are you doing here? Did you forget something?"

"No. I was hoping we could talk."

"Sure. I've got time." She watched as the Cocker lifted his leg, then hoisted him up out of the pen and covered the wet spot with fresh white paper from a big roll. "I've got two more to do. What's up?"

I waited until she'd put that dog back in its crate and gotten the next one into the pen. I'd thought she might stop moving then, but she didn't. Angie fidgeted around the set-up, rearranging, tidying, basically doing everything but giving me her full attention. There was a grooming table in the aisle behind me, with a big, waist-high hair dryer standing beside it. I shoved the heavy nozzle out of the way and braced back against the edge of the table. This might take longer than I thought.

"The clerk at Doughnuts Divine told me you were in this morning and bought two cups of coffee."

Her back stiffened slightly; or maybe it was a trick of the half light. Angie didn't say a word.

"Harry Flynn was poisoned by someone who slipped something into a cup of coffee that came from there." I didn't know that for sure, but it seemed likely. Besides, unless Angie was the killer, she wouldn't know either.

"So?" She still wasn't looking at me, but her tone conveyed her irritation.

"Harry Flynn was poisoned Angie, just like Jenny. The police will be looking into the connections there. They may have started already."

She spun around, scowling. "Why are you telling me this?"

"Because you're the only person I can think of who stood to profit from both their deaths."

"Jenny was my sister. She was my best friend!" Her voice was high and keening. It was almost enough to convince me she was in pain. Almost.

It was like shifting the focus on a camera ever so slightly and seeing a whole new picture emerge. When I'd believed Angie to be innocent, she looked innocent. But now her protests didn't ring as true as they once had. I settled in on top of the grooming table and crossed my arms over my chest.

"If you and Jenny were so close, why didn't she tell you she was leaving?"

"What are you talking about?"

"Jenny was getting out. She was going to leave Rick and everything else behind. In another week, she would have been gone."

"No!" Angie shook her head violently.

"Yes. She'd been planning her escape for weeks. You can ask Florence Byrd if you don't believe me. She knew all about it."

The silence was so thick it was almost palpable. Angie put the Bichon away, used the poop scoop to do some cleaning and got out another Cocker.

"If only you'd been a little more patient," I said finally.

"I don't know what you're talking about." Her tone was equal parts anger and incredulity.

"I think you do. I think you figured you'd been the assistant long enough. You wanted your turn and you were going to get it."

"That's a lie—"

"And then once you had Jenny's clients and Jenny's dogs, you still weren't winning as much as you wanted and you realized Harry Flynn was in your way."

Angie snorted loudly. "Harry didn't worry me."

"Then why did you kill him?"

She stared at me round-eyed. "You're crazy, you know that?"

Rick had said much the same thing. Now here I was accusing someone else whose first response had been righteous indignation at my stupidity. But while Rick had managed to come to his own defense, I had yet to hear Angie do the same.

"Somebody left a cup of coffee at Harry's set-up this morning. Somebody who probably knew his habits.

Somebody who'd been in dogs long enough to know where to get arsenic and how to dose it. Florence Byrd told me just last Sunday she was furious when Charlie was beaten by Flynn's Cocker in the variety. I think that's when you knew that just getting Jenny out of your way wasn't enough, that Harry was going to have to go, too."

It was an impressive speech, I thought. Some guesswork on my part, but heavily laced with fact. Angie should have crumpled like a stale biscuit.

Instead, she shook her head. "I didn't buy that coffee for myself."

"No?"

"I bought it for Dirk."

Talk about throwing a spanner into the works. *Dirk?* "Why?"

"He asked me to. We both left the motel this morning at the same time. He offered me a ride over and I told him I wanted to stop for breakfast. He said he was in a hurry, but could I pick up some coffee for him."

Well shoot. "And did you give it to him?"

"Yeah, sure." Angie scooped up the Cocker and put it away. She cleaned up the dirty paper and laid out fresh for the morning. "Two cups, just like he asked for."

"Two cups?"

Angie shrugged. "He's a big guy. I guess it takes a lot of caffeine to get him started in the morning."

Dirk? I tossed him around in my mind, trying to work him into my theories. It was like trying to force a working dog into a toy-sized crate. Bits and pieces fit, but not the whole thing.

Angie was back fishing around in the tack box. Probably looking for keys so that she could lock up for the night.

"Did you tell the police about that?" I asked.

"No." Her voice was muffled as she dug deeper into the large bottom compartment. "They didn't ask."

Then she straightened and turned to face me and I saw what she'd been looking for.

A gun.

It was black and shiny and looked big in her hand. It was also pointing straight at me. So much for not being able to inflict significant physical damage.

"Angie, what are you doing?"

"Rick bought this for protection," she said calmly. "I told him he was nuts, but I guess he wasn't."

"Protection? Who do you need protection from? Dirk?"

She gave me a pitying look as if I was being entirely too slow and after a moment, I realized I was. All that business about Dirk had been a distraction, a detour she'd thrown my way while she figured out what to do next. Like a sap, I'd been too busy being ambivalent to take her as seriously as I should have.

"You think you know so much," Angie said. "You don't know anything. I don't need protection from Dirk. He's the one who was supposed to be looking out for me. And Jenny, too. That's a laugh, isn't it?"

She didn't sound as though she found anything about the situation to be even vaguely humorous. The gun in her hand never wavered. I wondered if it was loaded. I wondered if she knew how to use it. At this short range, it probably didn't even matter. Then I thought about what she'd just said.

"What do you mean Dirk was supposed to be looking out for you?"

"It turns out he's been giving reports to my mother for

years. She's been paying him to keep an eye on us all this time, and we never even knew it. As if that big oaf could ever be trusted to get things right!"

"So that's what you were fighting about with your mother earlier."

Angie shot me a glare. "I guess Dirk isn't the only spy around here."

"Is that why he was in the building early this morning?"

"Yeah, it's ironic, isn't it? He was here to see my mother before judging started."

"And he saw you leave that cup of coffee at Harry Flynn's set-up."

"I guess I should have been paying more attention," said Angie. It was the first time I'd heard her admit she'd done anything wrong.

"Did he tell the police?"

"No, and he won't either. My parents are taking care of that. Roger and Lavinia Peterson. They can put a good face on anything, didn't you know that?"

Her tone was bitter. I wondered if she actually believed what she was saying. The Petersons were a power in the dog show world, but Angie would have to be insane to think they could cover up a murder. Then again, she probably was. Otherwise, I wouldn't be standing there with a gun pointed at my middle.

"What about Jenny's death?" I asked incredulously. "Are your parents willing to overlook that, too?"

"They blame Rick for what happened to her. That part was easy. They never liked him much anyway."

Easy. How could she possibly feel that anything about murdering her own sister had been *easy*? I'd thought that when I had some answers, I'd begin to understand. But I didn't. None of this made any sense to me at all.

"You liked Rick, didn't you?" I asked. "More than a brother-in-law. More than just a friend."

"You don't know anything!"

"You're right." I braced back and hiked myself up onto the grooming table. Sitting gave me a small feeling of security, like it meant I was going to be there for a while. "Why don't you tell me about it."

"Why should I?"

"Maybe it will make you feel better."

"You mean, like a confession? I don't think so."

"Jenny was your *sister*."

"As if I could have missed that fact," Angie snapped. "As if I could have ever, for one moment, have gotten out from behind her shadow. Jenny was always the favorite, the one things came easily to. Good grades, good dogs—anything she ever wanted, all she had to do was snap her fingers and it was hers."

"You were jealous."

"Not of who she was. Just of what she got. Jenny was always the center of attention. Everybody thought she was so wonderful. I was smart, too. I was good with the dogs. But nobody ever noticed because Jenny . . . was . . . *always* . . . *there*."

Angie spaced her words for emphasis, to make sure that I got the point. I nodded, not taking my eyes off her. If I'd had a gun in my hand, I'd have been sweating. But the opposite was true of Angie. She seemed calmer now, more sure that she was in control. That was good. It meant I might be able to keep her talking, which was certainly preferable to any other alternative I could come up with.

"So you figured out a way to make Jenny disappear."

"No."

"Yes."

"No!" Angie said violently. "It wasn't supposed to happen like that. I never meant for her to die."

I wondered if that were true, or if it was something she'd convinced herself of afterward in order to soothe her conscience. "You poisoned her with arsenic."

"I only meant to make her sick. Jenny never took a day off, not ever. I wanted a chance to show what *I* could do, but she was always there in my way. She wasn't supposed to die, honest. I thought I could control it."

"Just like your parents controlled the dosage they gave the show dogs when you were little."

"Right." Angie nodded. "I started putting it in her morning coffee. I thought that would be enough, but it wasn't."

So she'd upped the dose. Jenny had collapsed and died after dinner. And Angie had calmly gone on about life, immediately setting her sights on the fame and fortune that had eluded her up until that point.

I still hadn't seen any sign of remorse. Now I was beginning to doubt that I ever would. No wonder Angie had been able to fool me—to fool everybody—for so long. From her warped point of view, getting rid of Jenny had been the right thing, the only thing, to do. Even if it meant getting rid of her for good.

Casually, I let my gaze drift around the area. It seemed like eons had passed since she'd pulled out the gun; but in reality I supposed it was only minutes. The security guard wasn't in sight. Nor had anyone come over to our end of the grooming area to do a late night check of their dogs.

"What about Harry Flynn?" I asked.

"Everybody hated him."

As if that made it all right. "Harry was beginning to beat you with his Springer. Was that why you killed him?"

"Of course not." Angie looked at me as though I was dense. "He knew."

For a moment I had no idea what she meant. Then I realized she was talking about Jenny's death. Harry must have known about Angie's part in it. But that didn't make sense; surely she wouldn't have been stupid enough to tell him.

"How did he find out?"

Angie sighed heavily. "I got the arsenic from him. Fowler's solution. You used to be able to buy it at the drugstore. But not anymore. Now there are laws. I was stuck until I thought of Harry."

"Where did he get it?"

"How should I know? I guess he still had his connections from way back. He said it wasn't a problem."

"Did he know what you planned to do with it?"

"I told him it was for a dog."

I shook my head, disbelieving. "Harry Flynn competed against you—tooth and nail, from what I've seen. Why would he have agreed to help you?"

"Back then, I wasn't the one he was competing against. I was only the little sister that nobody ever noticed." The bitterness was back in her tone. "If he had any suspicions, so what? Anything that put Jenny out of commission for a while could only work to his benefit."

She was right about that. Of course, later, the same would have been true about Angie. Harry Flynn had been an opportunist. So why hadn't he told what he knew?

"Are you kidding?" Angie said when I asked. "I would have taken him down with me and he knew it. I'd have told the police that he coerced me into doing something terrible, something I never should have done. And who do you think they would have believed? Jenny's grieving baby sister, or a man who's held a public grudge against the Maguires for years?"

I remembered the story Aunt Peg had told me about Harry trying to get one of Jenny's dogs disqualified. Everyone had been aware of the animosity between him and Jenny Maguire. Angie was right. Harry would have had a hard time making his story stick.

"If he wasn't going to tell, why did you kill him?"

"I didn't have any choice. He overheard me talking to Mrs. Byrd at Fitchburg. About how I wanted Charlie to go on showing next year. Harry called a couple of days later. He said next year was his turn, and if I tried to get in his way, I was going to be sorry."

"So you poisoned him too."

"I had to. Don't you see? He was going to ruin me. What happened to Jenny was an accident. But Harry was going to make it look as though I were to blame. I couldn't let him do that."

Angie stared at me, her expression hardening. "And I can't let you do it either. I've waited my whole life to be where I am now. You're not going to take that away from me. The police don't have any connections in the dog world. Once you're gone, they'll never be able to put it all together."

"I'm not going anywhere." I tried to sound firm, but I could hear my voice wavering.

"Yes, you are." Angie took a step forward. She gestured with her gun hand and I realized I was meant to stand. "For starters, we're going to leave the building together."

Right. That was about the last thing that was going to happen. Outside, I'd have no defense. At least in here, there was a chance. Eventually, the guard was bound to come by to tell us he was closing things up.

I slid another look around. There was nobody within earshot. Even the boom box on the other side of the building had been silenced. The place had been relatively empty before. Now it was deserted.

"Come on," Angie said impatiently. "Let's go."

I grasped the edge of the grooming table and hopped down. Slowly. "Do you know how to use that thing?"

"Sure," said Angie. Now that we were both standing, with a deadly weapon filling the space between us, her voice didn't sound any steadier than mine. "Point, and shoot. Don't worry, I won't miss."

I wasn't worried about that at all. On one side, the narrow aisle was blocked by the ex pen. On the other was the big hair dryer I'd pushed out of my way earlier.

"Go on," Angie said between gritted teeth when I hesitated. "Just get through. I'll be right behind you."

Quickly I weighed my options. The exercise pen was no help; but the hair dryer had possibilities. The heavy engine piece stood upright on a three-legged base. Attached to it was a fourteen-inch steel nozzle. The machine was meant to free your hands for other uses; the thick nozzle swiveled, swung, and moved up and down.

"This way." I nudged the grooming table to one side with my hip and stepped carefully over the four-legged base. Like a sheep, Angie fell in behind me. The hair dryer was so much a part of each set-up that I knew she hadn't given it a thought. Always the little sister, always the follower, never the one in charge.

I hoped she hadn't changed too much in the last six weeks.

I took two more steps, then glanced back over my shoulder. Angie's eyes were downcast; she had to watch where she was going so her feet didn't get tangled up in the stand. I wished the nozzle was on the right side—Angie's gun side—but I'd take what I could get.

I lifted both hands and gave the metal tube a hard shove. It swung around in a short arc and crashed into her shoulder with a satisfying thud.

Angie screeched and staggered sideways. If the grooming table hadn't been in her way, she would have fallen. As she lost her balance, one foot caught in the dryer's base. Her leg twisted beneath her and her injured arm flew up in the air. I grabbed her other wrist and slammed it hard against the edge of the table.

Her fingers opened and the gun fell from her grasp. It hit the concrete floor, bounced once, then fired.

The boom echoed through the building. Immediately dogs all around us began to bark. I was so busy trying to figure out where the gun had been pointing when it went off that I didn't see Angie's fist coming until just before it connected with my jaw.

Pain exploded in my head. Everything went black, then bright white. Through eyes swimming with tears, I saw Angie scrambling on the floor for the gun. I reached around for the dryer, lifted it off its base and swung the nozzle once more. It caught her on the back of the head and she crumpled.

The table gave way as Angie fell beneath it. I had just enough energy left to kick the gun. It skittered away out of reach. The hair dryer weighed a ton and I let it fall too.

I thought I heard people yelling. I knew I heard dogs barking. I'll close my eyes for just a second, I thought.

God, I had a headache.

❧❋ *Twenty-eight* ❋❧

For the second time that day, the police were called to the show grounds. It took hours for them to get things sorted out; after fetching Rick and Dirk and the Petersons from the motel and sitting everybody down for questioning. In the meantime, Angie woke up, hissing and screeching like an angry cat. I hadn't done any permanent damage, only given her a nasty headache. As far as that went, I figured we were even.

Angie immediately protested her innocence and for a while, I thought she might be able to make the claim stick. Dirk was stonewalling; the Petersons, calling for a lawyer. But when Rick finally saw the direction the questions were heading and jumped to the right conclusion—that Angie had killed his wife—all hell broke loose. He got his fingers wrapped around her throat before Detective Brucker leapt in to restrain him. After that, the jig was pretty much up.

It was close to three A.M. when I finally dragged myself back to the hotel room and I'd been asleep a good deal less time than I needed when I awoke to Davey bouncing on my stomach. That morning, Aunt Peg had a similarly bleary-eyed look about her. I drew a bath for Davey that he swore he didn't need and filled her in on the details while he soaked.

"I should have known," she said irritably.

"Why?"

"The dogs. She never was that good with them. You can always tell a person's true character by the way they handle their dogs."

My puppy was snoozing in my lap. I scratched her muzzle and wondered what sorts of psychological insights Aunt Peg was mining about me. Then Faith reached out and licked my palm with her long pink tongue, thumping her tail contentedly, and I figured I was doing okay.

Davey, Faith, and I packed up and went home that morning. I needed a break from dog shows; and aside from waving Faith's entry under my nose once or twice, Aunt Peg didn't protest much. I found out later that Peaches had gotten her second major; and that Charlie, with a pick-up handler on the end of the lead, had won both the remaining groups. Apparently Florence Byrd had been right—fame or notoriety, it all worked the same in the end. With only a handful of shows remaining in the year, the wins from Springfield weekend were enough to assure that the Quaker Oats Award was hers.

Amazingly, it turned out that the Cocker was lucky to have even been in contention. The bullet fired from Angie's gun had gone in through the grilled door of his crate and blasted out through the wooden ceiling. Charlie, presumably lying down when the commotion started, had been asleep below the line of fire. Still, Angie had come within a hair's breadth of blowing away her meal ticket and the irony was lost on none of us. Mrs. Byrd took the Cocker home for good at the end of the weekend.

During my lunch break on Tuesday, I wrote her a note of congratulations and dropped it in the mail. I wondered if Florence Byrd had known about Dirk's other source of employment, and decided she probably had. She didn't seem like the type of woman who would relinquish any control if she could help it.

After lunch, I worked with my third graders. Timmy hadn't done his homework and after I got the others started working on maps of South America, I sat down beside him and asked him why.

His big brown eyes were guileless. "I didn't want to."

"Homework isn't always something you want to do. It's something you need to do."

"Yeah, I guess." He drew in a deep breath and I watched his narrow chest fill with air. "There are lots of things I need to do. Do you ever feel like you're being pushed all different ways at once?"

I nodded slowly, feeling for him. "What do you do when that happens?"

"I hide." He sounded almost proud.

"Where?"

"In a book, sometimes. And sometimes I just tune everything out. I don't even have to go anywhere at all."

Coping mechanisms. We all had them. What a shame Timmy had to develop his so early. "Sometimes I hide, too," I told him.

"But you're a grown-up!"

"Even grown-ups get confused sometimes. But hiding doesn't help, does it?"

"Not really."

Not really. I guessed I'd found that out too. I wondered if Sam was back yet. I wondered if he'd call when he got in.

I reached out and slipped my hand over Timmy's. "Sometimes you have to confront the things that are bothering you. You have to say to yourself, 'I'm doing okay. I'm a really good kid and I'm doing the best I can.' That's the most anybody can ever ask of you."

"What if my best isn't good enough?"

"It *is* good enough. What isn't good enough is not trying." I picked up the half completed homework assignment.

"You want me to finish it?"

"I do."

Timmy looked over to where the other children were working. "What about my map?"

"That, too."

"I won't have time."

"Yes, you will." I got a piece of construction paper and lined up a set of markers. "I'll help."

"Is that allowed?"

"Just for today. Tomorrow you won't need me. Tomorrow you're going to finish your own homework."

Timmy cracked a smile. "Don't forget, Chile's at the bottom and Venezuela's at the top."

"I'll try to get it right."

The homework and the map both got done and went in on time. A small victory, but a victory nonetheless. As the class lined up and left the room to go to Art, Timmy was trading jokes with another boy from his desk group. I sighed as I watched them go. Regardless of what I'd said, there are times when your best doesn't feel nearly good enough.

Sam announced his return by inviting himself over that evening. He showed up with pizza and a movie, which made him an instant hit with Davey. I bent the rules and let my son eat in the living room in front of the television.

No fool she, Faith elected to keep him company. She'd only been with us a matter of weeks, but the Poodle puppy was such an integral part of the family, I couldn't imagine how we'd done without her. Davey and Faith curled up on the couch together, limbs comfortably intertwined, pizza box within easy reach. I hoped the puppy would let him eat at least a piece or two.

While the movie played, Sam and I sat in the kitchen and compared notes on our respective weekends. His sister was fine. His brother-in-law was up for a promotion. The nephews were hellions. They'd eaten leftover turkey for three days straight. In other words, a perfectly normal family visit.

"It was good to get away," said Sam. "It's even better being back."

I told him what had happened at Springfield. Actually I elaborated on the sketchy details I'd given upon his arrival when he noticed the purple bruise extending along my jaw line.

"I never would have guessed it was Angie," he said.

"Me neither. But then I guess we're all pretty good at hiding that part of ourselves we don't want anyone else to know."

"Not me." Sam spread his hands. "I'm an open book."

"Really? What about that blonde I found at your house last summer? Susan, wasn't it? The one in the tight dress who was supposedly giving you information?"

"She was."

"Yeah," I said, grinning. "Right."

His hand came across the table, fingers skimming lightly over the inside of my wrist. "My investigative technique is very thorough."

"I'll bet."

His other hand cradled the back of my neck. His palm was at the pulse point in my throat. Both of us could feel the pounding. "When I know what I want, I don't ever give up." He smiled lazily. "What time does Davey go to bed?"

"Soon." I looked at the clock above the sink. "Very soon."

"Good."

"And after that?"

Sam's chair scraped on the floor as he drew it closer. So close that I could feel the heat emanating from his body. His lips came up next to my ear as he whispered, "Keep your options open."

"I'll do that." I felt ready for anything.

With luck, I might even get it.

If you enjoyed Laurien Berenson's
UNDERDOG
then turn the page for an exciting sneak peek
of Melanie Travis's debut in
A PEDIGREE TO DIE FOR,
now on sale wherever
paperback mysteries are sold!

☙❊ *One* ❊☙

There's a lot to be said for dying in the midst of something you love. But fond as Uncle Max was of his Poodles, I doubt that he'd ever envisioned himself being found dead on the cold, hard kennel floor, his curled fingers grasping at the open door of an empty pen.

For their part, the Poodles didn't seem to think much of the idea either. All seven of the big black dogs were scratching at their doors and whining when Aunt Peg came out the next morning looking for Max, who was inexplicably missing from her bed when she woke up. The moment she saw him, she knew what had happened. The Turnbull men weren't known for their strong hearts; the doctor had warned Max more than once to slow down. But in the end, all the things they'd done together—giving up smoking, taking up walking, watching their cholesterol—hadn't made the slightest bit of difference.

Not one to panic when composure served better, Aunt Peg had closed her husband's eyes, then covered him with a blanket before picking up the phone and calling for an ambulance.

I learned all this from my brother Frank, whose name she'd supplied when asked by the police if there was someone they could call. One look at Aunt Peg and they must have realized that the sedatives the paramedics had so thoughtfully left behind were going to go to waste. That's when they started making comforting noises about next of kin.

We've never been the type of family to advertise our emotions. Aunt Peg would no sooner keen and wail than join the chorus line of the Rockettes. Nevertheless Frank had arrived prepared to offer whatever support was needed. That none was needed soon became apparent when Aunt Peg declared that his hovering was making her nervous and sent him home.

Now, three days later, Frank was kneeling beside me in the front pew of Saint Mary's Church in Greenwich. He looked every bit as uncomfortable as I felt when the rest of the funeral party trooped up to the altar to receive communion. It was painfully obvious that we were the only two to remain behind.

Thanks to my Aunt Rose, Max's sister and a member of the order of the Sisters of Divine Mercy, the church was full. As the priest began dispensing hosts from the golden chalice, I pushed aside the missals that littered the pew, sat back, and resigned myself to a long wait. Two by two, the sisters glided by, their rubber-soled shoes noiseless on the church floor. Many, I noted absently, were of the old school, which meant that they still wore the dark habits and crisp white wimples I remembered so vividly from my youth.

The soft rustle of cloth, the muted clacking of polished rosary beads that swung from the sisters' waists, both were sounds from the past. For a moment, I found myself transported back to the narrow halls of the convent school where I'd been raised. It wasn't a trip I enjoyed. Some Catholics refer to their faith as something that has lapsed. I tend to think of mine as expired.

Until that afternoon, it had been years since I'd been inside a church. Five years, to be exact, since an icy patch of road had sent my parents' car careening down a steep embankment and into a river, leaving me—newly married and newly pregnant—also newly orphaned. Bob, my husband then, ex now, maintained at the time that anyone who had reached the age of twenty-five was simply too old to qualify for orphan status.

"I know what I feel!" I wanted to shout at him. In later years, I wouldn't have been so reticent. Later we shouted about a lot of things.

Still, I had Bob to thank for my son, and in my mind, that more than evened the score. Davey was home now with a sitter, no doubt spurning the glorious May weather to watch Oprah Winfrey on TV. There'd be plenty of time later for him to learn about funerals—and about people who die long before you're ready to say goodbye.

A throat cleared scratchily, and I looked up to find Aunt Peg standing above me. One of the first to go to the altar, she was now ready to return to the pew. Quickly I stood up to let her by.

Behind her came Aunt Rose, Sister Anne Marie to the other nuns. Her head was bowed, her eyes half-closed. Her fingers were braced together at the tips, forming a slim arrow that pointed upward toward the heavens. In contrast to Aunt Peg's grim-lipped frown, her expression had a soft, unmolded quality. She was talking to her God, I realized. Uncomfortable, I looked away.

The line at the communion rail dwindled, then finally ended. The sisters glided back to their pews. At the altar, the priest mumbled the remaining words of the mass before offering a blessing to the assemblage.

I was turning to retrieve my purse from the bench when the sisters began to sing. Their voices rose, filling the large church with the harmonious cadence of a well-rehearsed choir. I straightened, then paused to listen. The hymn was Latin, its words vaguely familiar. But it was the music itself that reached out to me; the voices joined as one sent a tingle racing up the length of my spine. The sound was pure and sweet and uplifting. For a moment, I could almost believe that the sisters *were*, as I'd been taught years before, in the business of sending souls to heaven.

I waited until the song ended before leaving the pew. Uncle Max, who'd always had a dramatic flair, would have loved the pageantry of it all. As a child, in the years before the family drifted apart, I'd found him fascinating. Everything about Uncle Max was just slightly outsize; he had no use for the ordinary, and little tolerance for anyone who did. He enjoyed beauty and style, and surrounded himself with plenty, like the kennel full of Standard Poodles that he bred and exhibited. The funeral mass, with all its pomp and ceremony, would have suited him just fine.

I rode to the cemetery in the first limousine with Frank and Aunt Peg. Aunt Rose was curiously absent. Perhaps she felt the chauffeur-driven Lincoln was too ostentatious for her station in the world. Or perhaps the impression I'd gotten over the years that she and Aunt Peg didn't get along was true.

Aunt Peg was silent during the drive, and Frank and I followed suit. Somehow I didn't feel I had the right to intrude. The dark brim of a fedora was pulled low over her eyes; the set of her shoulders was stiff. Whatever emotions she was feeling, she kept them to herself.

The graveside ceremony was brief. In keeping with family tradition, there were no histrionics, only a quiet prayer beside the coffin. As we turned to leave, I heard a quiet sigh.

"Goodbye, Max," Aunt Peg whispered. Her lower lip trembled briefly, then stilled.

Walking back toward the line of parked cars, I reached out impulsively and took her hand in mind. "If there's anything at all I can do . . ."

Little did I know.

Please turn the page for
an exciting sneak peek of
Laurien Berenson's

DOG EAT DOG

Now on sale wherever
mysteries are sold!

⌒❖ *One* ❖⌒

Phone calls in the middle of the night never mean good news. Something's wrong, or somebody needs help. Otherwise they wouldn't be waking you up. The way I see it, any call you have to regain consciousness for is one you don't want to get.

I'm a mother, so when the phone began to ring on that cold March night, I was instantly awake. The fact that my son, Davey, is only five, and that I'd tucked him safely into bed right down the hall several hours earlier, didn't dull the maternal reflexes one bit. I was already reaching for the receiver before the end of the first ring.

To do that, I had to maneuver around Sam Driver, whose long, lean body lay between me and the phone on the night table. He opened one eye as I slithered across his chest and smiled appreciatively. Neither one of us had been asleep. We were just dozing contentedly; warm, satisfied, and utterly pleased with ourselves, enjoying a last few minutes of cozy harmony before Sam had to get up and go home.

I trailed a kiss across his chest and reached for the receiver. Before the phone was halfway to my ear, I could hear the insistent thump and twang of a lively country music tune. Immediately I felt better. It was a wrong number; it had to be.

"Hello?"

"Hey Mel, guess who?"

I had no intention of guessing, nor did I have to. I hadn't heard the voice in years, but I recognized it right away. It belonged to Bob Travis, my ex-husband.

I glanced at Sam. He lifted a brow. I levered my weight up off him, yanked the cord until it stretched to the other side of the bed, then sat up and clutched the blanket to my breasts.

"Melanie? You there?"

Could I say no? I wondered. Was there any possibility of getting away with that? Probably not.

"I'm here."

"It's been a while, huh?"

He was shouting into the phone, probably to make himself heard over the music blaring in the background. A woman, her voice tinny like it was coming from a juke box, wailed about losing her man. The Bob I remembered had been a rock and roll man. Country western? No way. But then a lot could have changed in four and a half years.

"A while," I agreed. There was a moment of silence and I let it hang.

If Bob had something to say, let him figure out how to start. I wasn't going to make it easy for him, any more than he'd made things easy for me when he'd packed up the car and run away from home one day when Davey was just ten months old. Bob had made his choices; among them, child support payments that had dried up in the first six months, and a presence in his son's life that was limited to a small framed picture on the kitchen shelf. As far as I was concerned, he was on his own.

I heard the soft pad of footsteps in the hallway and the door to the bedroom pushed open. It wasn't Davey, but rather our ten month old Standard Poodle puppy, Faith. She sleeps on Davey's bed, so I knew he was okay. If he'd been awake, she wouldn't have left him.

Faith trotted across the room and leapt up to land lightly on the bed. Sam loves dogs and has Poodles of his own. He patted the mattress beside him, where I'd been lying happily only moments before. The big black puppy turned twice, then laid down.

"Have you been missing me, darlin'?" said Bob. "I've been missing yew."

He had to be kidding. I wondered if he was drunk. And where had he gotten that accent? I'd heard he'd gone to Texas, but somehow I couldn't picture button-down Bob turning into a good old boy. Maybe after a few beers, the lyrics from the juke box had gotten stuck in his head and the only way he could think to get rid of them was by calling me up and passing them along.

Sam tugged at the blanket to get my attention. "Who is it?" he mouthed silently.

"Bob," I said.

Sam frowned.

"Right here, darlin'," the voice on the phone said cheerfully.

"Stop calling me that!" I said, irritated. This aspect of my relationship with Sam was new enough to still feel fragile. I'd hate for him to think that I made a habit of fielding late night calls from my ex-husband. "What's the matter with you? Are you sure you have the right number?"

"I could hardly be calling all the way to Connecticut by mistake, now could I?"

"I don't know, Bob. It's been a long time. I really don't know anything about you anymore."

"Well darlin', that's about to change. In fact, that's the reason for my call."

Behind him, the music subsided. "Hey Bob!" yelled a voice. "You standin' us another round?"

"Hell yes!" Bob roared and a lusty cheer went up.

Now I knew he was drunk. The Bob I'd known hadn't been much of a drinker, and certainly not one to buy a round for the house. Perversely, that made me feel better. With any luck, this call was nothing more than an alcohol induced trip down memory lane. In the morning he'd wake up and remember that we hated each other, and everything would be fine.

"Bob," I said gently. "I think maybe you've had enough to drink."

"Nah," he disagreed. "The party's just getting started. We're celebrating."

"Lucky you." It was time to wind this call down. Actually way past time, if the look on Sam's face was anything to go by. "I won't keep you from it—"

"Melanie, wait!"

I was already inching back across the bed toward the night stand. Faith's tail thumped up and down on the blanket as I passed. "What?"

"You didn't even give me a chance to tell you my good news. I struck oil!"

I'm a teacher. I work with eight year olds, so I'm used to dealing with tall tales. This one, however, seemed a mite taller than most. My guess was that Bob was going to have one hell of a hangover in the morning.

"You couldn't have struck oil, Bob. You're an accountant."

"Well sure, but I own a well."

He owned a well. My brain received the message, but flatly refused to process it.

"Not a whole well. Actually a share of one." Bob was talking faster now, as if he was afraid I might hang up before he'd gotten out everything he wanted to say. The Texas twang was becoming less and less pronounced. "A friend of mine was buying up old mineral leases and drilling wildcat wells. Just speculating, you know? He didn't have any money, but he needed someone to do the books. So we made a deal."

He paused as if he expected me to say something. No chance of that. All the words I could think of were stuck in my throat.

"I never expected anything to come of it. I just thought I was doing a friend a favor. Then this morning Ray comes flying into town to tell me he'd brought one in. Can you beat that?"

No, I thought, I certainly couldn't.

"What's the matter?" asked Sam, looking at the expression on my face. He leaned closer, cocking an ear toward the receiver.

"It seems Bob owns an oil well."

"A share in a well," my ex corrected. I heard him take a swig of beer. It must have sharpened his perception. "Hey," he demanded, after he'd swallowed. "Who's that you're talking to?"

If there was any easy answer to that question, I certainly didn't know what it was. Nor did I owe Bob any explanations. "Nobody," I said firmly.

That went over well. Sam glared and pulled back.

Bob dropped the phone. At least that's what it sounded like. There was a loud thunk and a sudden increase in the decibel level of the music. Now a man was wailing about love gone wrong. "Hang on, darlin'!" Bob yelled.

Sure. Like I had nothing better to do.

When he didn't return in a few seconds, I put the receiver down on the blanket. Unless Bob had used a credit card, I figured the long distance operator would probably disconnect us soon anyway.

"I didn't mean that the way it sounded," I said to Sam.

"I hope not." He pushed back the covers, easing Faith gently aside, and got up.

I knew he had to go, but that didn't stop me from wanting

to reach out and pull him back. Instead, I drew my legs up under the covers and wrapped my arms around them. On the bed beside me, the phone was silent.

"It was none of his business, that's all I was trying to say."

"I guess you made your point." Sam glanced at the receiver. "Where'd he go?"

I shrugged as if it wasn't important, which it wasn't. Bob was my past. I thought of him sometimes as a stage I'd gone through, like Farrah Fawcett hair or disco. If it wasn't for Davey, I'd have said we had no reason to ever speak to each other again.

Up until now, Bob had played almost no part in his son's life. That had been his choice. Mine was that he keep it that way.

Faith reached out with one large black paw and batted the receiver gently. It rolled over several times and lodged beneath a pillow. Good place for it.

Though the bedroom was dark, the moon outside was nearly full. Sam crossed the room, passing through a shaft of silvery light. He walked with the easy grace of a man who was comfortable with his body. And no wonder. A bit over six feet tall, he was trim and tightly muscled. Downy golden hairs covered his chest and legs, matching the thick, often unruly thatch on his head.

At thirty-four, he was in his prime. Three years younger, I found myself cultivating crow's feet and battling the effects of gravity. Biology's a bitch.

I watched as Sam slipped on his jeans and a long sleeved thermal tee. The weathered denim shirt he buttoned over it was the same color as his eyes. My eyes are hazel, a middle of the road shade. So's my hair. It's brown and hangs straight to my shoulders. But when Sam turned and looked at me in the moonlight, I felt beautiful.

"I wish you didn't have to go," I said.

"So do I."

He came back and sat on the edge of the bed. The mattress dipped beneath his weight. Both of us left the rest unsaid. He had dogs at home that needed to be taken care of. And I had Davey.

It wasn't that Sam and my son weren't friends. But Davey had never known his father, and I was wary of his forming too deep an attachment to Sam. Maybe I was wary of doing the same thing myself. Davey had never woken up to find a man sitting at the breakfast table. I wasn't sure either one of us was ready to start.

Sam reached over and brushed his lips across mine. I reached out my hands and ran them up over his shoulders. The blanket slipped down, pooling around my knees. The cool air made my nerve endings tingle.

"Hey Mel!" the receiver squawked suddenly. Faith cocked her ears and nudged it with her nose. "You still there?"

Sam drew back. Slowly I did the same.

"Aren't you going to pick that up?" he asked.

"I guess." I sighed and lifted the phone to my ear. Talk about a mood breaker. "Now what?"

"Sorry about that," said Bob. The twang was back. "Billie Sue just spilled a few beers. Wasn't her fault. If Jocko hadn't goosed her, she'd have been okay. I guess I've had my bath for the night."

"Bob—"

"Now listen darlin'. There's a reason why I called."

I figured there might be.

Then he told me what it was and I felt my whole world tilt, ever so slightly, on its axis. I wanted to rant and rave and tell him no. I wanted to slam down the phone and pretend that the call had never happened. I wanted to run into Davey's room, gather him in my arms and hold him tight against whatever was to come.

Instead, I scarcely moved at all. I simply listened until Bob had finished speaking, then hung up the receiver, placing it gently back in the cradle without saying another word. Around me, all was dark. I could feel the warmth of Faith's body pressed along my leg, and the slight rise and fall of her even breathing. I wondered if I sat very still I could convince myself that it had all been nothing more than a bad dream.

"What?" Sam demanded.

Funny, I'd almost forgotten he was there.

"He's coming."

"Where?"

"Here," I said quietly. "Bob's coming to Connecticut to get to know his son."

❧✳ *Two* ✳❧

The next morning I overslept. If it hadn't been for Faith, who wandered in at seven-thirty and licked my face until she got a response, Davey and I might never have made it to school.

I ran downstairs first thing and let the puppy outside. Poodles are extremely smart and once they learn something, like housebreaking, they hate to make a mistake even if—especially if—it's not their fault. Faith is a Standard Poodle, the largest of the three varieties. She stands twenty-four inches at the withers, has a beautiful head and expression, long legs, a high tail-set, and a dense coat of long black hair. I've just started taking her to dog shows and according to my Aunt Peg, when Faith matures, she should do very well.

If anyone should know, it's Margaret Turnbull. She's Faith's breeder, and owner of the Cedar Crest Poodles, one of the top Standard Poodle kennels on the east coast. She and her husband had been involved in breeding and showing for nearly thirty years, until his death the summer before. Now Aunt Peg was carrying on alone.

She's an imposing woman, with keen intelligence and a boundless supply of common sense. She's almost sixty, but that hasn't slowed her down a bit. At half her age, I sometimes have trouble keeping up, especially when Poodles are involved.

I opened the back door and Faith bounded down the steps. There were still six inches of snow on the ground from a storm the week before. Freezing temperatures overnight had covered it with a thin film of ice. I watched long enough to make sure that the puppy could handle the footing, then turned on the coffee maker and got out a box of instant oatmeal for Davey's breakfast.

"Mom!" Davey called from upstairs. "Where are my clothes?"

At five, my son has yet to master the art of choosing an outfit. Left to his discretion, he invariably ends up dressed in the same color from head to toe. Last time it was red. He looked like a misplaced Christmas elf. I work at Hunting Ridge Elementary, where Davey goes to school, so I have to watch things like that. It's hard to inspire confidence in other parents when your own child looks to be sorely in need of adult guidance.

"Be right there!"

The coffee was starting to drip; Faith was waiting at the back door to come in. If only I'd had a third or fourth hand, I'd have switched on the TV and tried to find the weather. March in southern Connecticut always leaves you guessing. I opened the door for Faith and threw down a bowl of dry kibble, then grabbed a cup of scalding coffee and ran back upstairs. I could only hope the day's forecast wasn't critical.

Davey and I made it to school by the second bell, but just barely. The last of the big yellow buses was parked at the curb when we pulled into the already full side lot and designated our own unmarked parking space.

The ride to school had taken less than ten minutes, but in that time Davey had managed to shed both his hat and his mittens. I had his backpack on the front seat next to me or he probably would have unpacked that, too. Organization isn't a strong suit with him. He gets that from his father.

It was only a stray thought, but it stopped me where I sat. A chill washed over my head and neck. For a moment I thought it was an omen; then I realized Davey had opened the Volvo's back door.

He got out and jammed his hat on his head. "I thought we were late."

"We are."

Still I didn't move, except to smile as I gazed at my impatient child. My son. In the space of an instant, his birth had transformed everything I thought I knew about love.

Davey's cheeks were pink with cold, his breath coming in small puffs of steam. He'd gotten the green knit cap on crooked, covering one ear but leaving the other bare. Sandy hair stuck out from beneath the rim. He had mink-brown eyes much like his father's. They were heavy lidded and rimmed with long dark lashes. Someday he'd be a heartbreaker, I had little doubt of that. He already held my heart in his hands.

For five years, I'd been the focus of Davey's world and he of mine. I'd always thought I wanted Davey to have the opportunity to get to know his father; but now that it seemed he would, suddenly I was apprehensive about the prospect. When Bob reappeared, everything would change. I wasn't sure I was ready for that.

"Come on," Davey said insistently. He wasn't allowed to cross the parking lot alone. "Hurry up!"

"I'm coming." I gathered up my things from the seat, got out and locked the car behind me.

"Race you to the door!"

"Davey, wait! Take my hand!"

Fat chance. We hit the school running and went inside to start the day.

My formal title is Learning Disabilities Resource Room Teacher. What that actually means is I'm in charge of special education. I work with all the elementary school grades at Hunting Ridge, taking aside in small groups any children who are in need of extra help.

My job is varied, hectic, and often rewarding. On a usual day, I can barely cram everything I need to do into the time allotted. Tuesday was no exception. I had a small mountain of paper work still sitting on my desk when the last bell rang, and a Pupil Placement Team meeting scheduled for after school.

Davey was going home on the bus with Joey Brickman, a friend from down the street. I'd arranged for him to stay through dinner, as that evening was the monthly meeting of the Belle Haven Kennel Club. I was too new to dogs to be a member, but Aunt Peg had invited me to attend the meeting as her guest.

Peg Turnbull can be hard to say no to under the best of circumstances. When she thinks she's doing something for your own good, she's apt to roll over opposition like a Humvee in low gear. I had only the vaguest notion of what went on at a kennel club, and no idea at all why anyone would want to join one, but it seemed I was going to find out. Aunt Peg was picking me up at six.

When I got home, Faith was waiting at the door. I threw my gear in the hall, snapped on the puppy's leash and took her for a long walk around the neighborhood. Flower Estates is a small sub-division in north Stamford: compact houses on tiny plots of land, built in the fifties and meant to appeal to the young parents who were busy producing the generation of children that would come to be known as baby boomers.

Those families are long gone now. Luckily for us, Flower Estates remains. With its outdated design and air of weathered practicality, the neighborhood is a haven of relatively affordable housing on Connecticut's gold coast.

We'd completed our walk and I was in the kitchen mixing Faith's dinner when the puppy ran from the room, raced through the hall and skidded to a stop by the front door, barking wildly. That's one benefit of getting a dog: guests never arrived unannounced. Aunt Peg was already letting herself in by the time I got to the hall. Standing five foot eleven and swathed in scarves and gloves and boots, she bore more than a passing resemblance to Nanook of the North.

"Cut out that racket!" she said to Faith. "It's me, your grandmother."

Dog-talk for breeder. Immediately the puppy stopped barking and wagged her tail. As Aunt Peg doffed gloves and hat and unwound her scarf, Faith danced on her hind legs, offering to help. What a pair.

"You're early," I said. "I'm just feeding Faith."

"Six," Aunt Peg said firmly. "I'm right on time."

My watch said ten to, but it wasn't worth debating.

Aunt Peg followed me back to the kitchen. "Where's Davey?"

"At a friend's house for the evening. I told Joey's mom I'd be by around nine. We'll be back by then, won't we?"

"If we're lucky." Aunt Peg watched with a critical eye as I added a dollop of cottage cheese and some canned meat to Faith's kibble, then set the dish on the floor. "Sometimes these meetings go on until all hours. It depends how much arguing everyone wants to do."

"About what?"

"Anything and everything. The members of the Belle Haven Kennel Club are a diverse group, nearly all with different breeds and strong opinions about what's best for each of them."

I considered that. Faith was the first dog I'd ever had. In many ways, I was still feeling my way around Poodles. I knew even less about what went on in the other breeds.

"Actually," I told her, "you never did explain exactly what a kennel club is."

"It didn't occur to me. You know what the American Kennel Club is, of course."

I did. The A.K.C. was the largest registry of purebred dogs in America. From its offices in New York City and North Carolina, it registered puppies, issued pedigrees, and sponsored more than a thousand dog shows every year.

"Local clubs are a little different, both in their goals and their make-up. They serve a variety of functions, one of which is to give breeders in a particular area a chance to get together, socialize, and compare notes."

That seemed obvious enough. "What else?"

"A well-run club can act as a liaison between dog owners and the community. Club members take their dogs to visit nursing homes and hospitals. They put on programs in schools. They sponsor clinics, do breeder referral to help people who are shopping for puppies, and many now have rescue services, which take in unwanted pets and find them new homes."

"It sounds like a lot of work."

"It is. And that's only half the job."

Faith finished her food, and looked up. When Aunt Peg patted her leg, the puppy ambled over obligingly. Never one for subtlety, Peg ran her hands over Faith's body; checking, no doubt, to make sure that I was keeping her grandchild in good condition.

I picked up the empty stainless steel bowl and carried it to the sink. "What's the other half?"

"The kennel clubs put on the dog shows. One per year, for most clubs." Apparently satisfied, Aunt Peg straightened from her inspection and scratched Faith under the chin. "That's their most visible function, and certainly most profitable. If a club knows what it's doing, the show can support club activities for the rest of the year."

"Does Belle Haven know what it's doing?"

"Overall, I'd say yes. Like most dog clubs, we have a core group of dedicated members who do the lion's share of the work. Most of us have been in the dog game a long time. Which is not to say that we always get along. I'll say one thing for Belle Haven's meetings. They're seldom dull."

I opened the back door and let Faith out into the yard. When I let her back in a moment later, Aunt Peg's gaze went pointedly to the clock over the sink. "We wouldn't want them to start without us."

"The meeting starts at six-thirty. It takes twenty minutes to get there." Ten, with Peg driving, but I didn't bother to mention that. "We have plenty of time."

"So we'll be a bit early." She was already leading the way to the front hall. "That means we'll get the best seats. On the way, you can tell me all about what's new with you."

She meant with me and Sam. I knew that perfectly well. Aunt Peg had met Sam Driver before I had, decided he and I were meant for each other, then spent the next six months pushing us together at every opportunity. I'd retaliated by telling her next to nothing about how our relationship was progressing.

It's childish, I know. But sometimes you have to make use of whatever tools are at hand. Aunt Peg was ever resourceful, however. The week before I'd caught her pumping Davey for information.

Wait until she heard what I had to say now.

I got my good wool coat out of the closet. Gloves were stuffed inside the pockets. I figured I'd skip the scarf and hat. "Do you remember anything about Bob?"

"Bob who?"

It was as good a start as any.